CONTENTS

HALLOWEEN COSTUME
PART 1

"It's Halloween next week,"

said Jake.

"I'm going to dress like a robot.

What are you going to wear?"

Jake asked Ben and Lily.

"I have a Dracula costume.

It comes with huge teeth

with bloody paint," said Ben.

Lily said, "I'm going as

Little Red Riding Hood."

IT'S NOT ABOUT THE HUNTER!

Veronika Martenova Charles

Illustrated by David Parkins

TUNDRA BOOKS

Published in Canada by Tundra Books,
75 Sherbourne Street, Toronto, Ontario M5A 2P9

Published in the United States by Tundra Books of Northern New York,
P.O. Box 1030, Plattsburgh, New York 12901

Library of Congress Control Number: 2009938444

Library and Archives Canada Cataloguing in Publication

Charles, Veronika Martenova
    It's not about the hunter! / Veronika Martenova
Charles ; illustrated by David Parkins.

(Easy-to-read wonder tales)
ISBN 978-0-88776-948-1

    1. Fairy tales. 2. Children's stories, Canadian (English).
I. Parkins, David II. Title. III. Series: Charles, Veronika
Martenova. Easy-to-read wonder tales.

PS8555.H42242I8775 2010   jC813'.54   C2009-905859-6

We acknowledge the financial support of the Government of Canada through
the Book Publishing Industry Development Program (BPIDP) and that of the
Government of Ontario through the Ontario Media Development Corporation's
Ontario Book Initiative. We further acknowledge the support of the Canada Council
for the Arts and the Ontario Arts Council for our publishing program.

ONTARIO ARTS COUNCIL
CONSEIL DES ARTS DE L'ONTARIO

Printed and bound in Canada

1 2 3 4 5 6   15 14 13 12 11 10

"Bad idea," said Ben.

"Why?" asked Lily.

"You'll get eaten by the wolf,"

said Ben, "like in the story.

You'll need a hunter to save you."

"Huh? What hunter?"

asked Lily.

"That's not how the story goes.

Little Red Riding Hood

is saved by her magic red cape,"

she explained.

"You're thinking of Superman.

He wears a magic red cape,"

said Jake.

"But Superman's cape

doesn't have a hood.

That's different," said Lily.

"It's the hood that saves

Little Red Riding Hood."

"How?" asked Jake and Ben.

"Let me tell you how," said Lily.

LITTLE RED HOOD

(*Red Riding Hood* from France)

There was once a girl named Adele.

People called her Little Red Hood

because she always wore a red cape

that her grandma gave her.

"I made this with rays of sun,"

Grandmother told Adele.

"It will keep you safe."

One Sunday, Adele's mother said,

"Take this cake to your grandma.

See how she is and then come back.

Don't talk to strangers on the way!"

Adele promised, and off she went.

Grandmother's village was on

the other side of the woods.

The day was hot and the shade

under the trees was cool.

Adele sat down and fell asleep.

She dreamed someone was calling.

She awoke, and there,

standing close and watching her,

was a wolf.

At first Adele was frightened,

and she could hardly breathe.

But then the wolf smiled.

"Good afternoon, my dear,"

the wolf said.

"I hope you had a nice nap.

What are you doing here?"

"I'm on my way to Grandma's,"

Adele told him.

"I see," said the wolf.

"Where does your grandma live?"

he asked.

"She lives in the first house

in the village on the other side

of the woods," Adele told him.

"Well," said the wolf,

"I can tell you a much shorter way

to get there." But he told her

a way that was much longer.

Adele thanked him

and went the way he said.

Then the wolf ran

straight to Grandma's house.

He pushed the door open,

but there was no one was inside.

Grandma had risen early

to sell fruit at the market.

The wolf closed the curtains,

put on Grandma's clothes,

and lay down in her bed.

At last, Adele arrived at the door.

Knock, knock!

"Who's there?" asked the wolf.

"It's me, Grandma! Adele."

"Come in, the door is open,"

said the wolf.

"I'm in bed. I'm not feeling well."

Adele came in

and put the cake on the table.

Then, she sat down by the bed.

Adele looked at her Grandma.

"What very bright eyes you have!"

she said.

And the wolf said,

"All the better to see you with,

my dear."

Adele looked again.

"Oh, what hairy ears you have!"

"All the better to hear you with,

my dear," the wolf replied.

"Oh, my, Grandma!" cried Adele.

"What huge teeth you have!"

"All the better to eat you with,
my dear!" And with that, the wolf
opened his jaws to swallow her.
Adele ducked her head, and the wolf
only caught her red hood.

"Ow-ooo!" the wolf howled.

The hood was burning hot

like the blazing sun.

The wolf jumped out of bed in pain.

Just then, Grandmother returned

from the market.

She opened her big, empty sack

and caught the wolf inside.

Then she tied the sack

and threw it down the deep well

by the house.

And that was the end of him.

"Well!" Grandma said to Adele,

"It's good you wore your red cape."

She shared the cake with Adele,

and then she took her home.

And Adele promised never to talk

to a stranger again.

"I know a different story

about a big bad wolf who pretends

to be a grandmother,"

Jake told Ben and Lily.

"The girl in my story

doesn't get eaten, either....

She gets away

because she tricks the wolf."

"How does she do that?"

asked Ben.

"I'll tell you," said Jake.

FALSE GRANDMOTHER

(*Red Riding Hood* from Italy)

"Please take this bread and milk

to your grandmother.

I hear she's not feeling well."

said Mother to Anouk.

"I packed some ring-shaped cakes

for you to eat along the way."

Anouk set off.

She came to a river.

"River, will you let me pass?"

she asked.

"If you give me your

ring-shaped cakes to play with,

I will," the river answered.

Anouk tossed them into the water,

and the river let her pass.

Anouk came to the crossroads.

There she met a wolf.

"Where are you going?"

the wolf asked.

"I'm taking food to my grandma.

She is ill," said Anouk.

"How will you get into the house

if your grandma is sick in bed?"

asked the wolf.

"Oh, that's easy. I'll stand

on the stone, pull the string,

and the door will open."

"What road are you taking?

The Needles or the Pins Road?"

asked the wolf.

"The Needles Road," Anouk said.

Then I will take the Pins Road,

thought the wolf, and he ran to

Anouk's grandma's house.

When he got there,

he stood up and pulled the string

with his teeth.

The door opened, the wolf went in,

and gobbled up Anouk's grandma.

He put on Grandma's nightie,

got in bed, and waited for Anouk.

He was planning to eat her next.

Soon the door opened.

"Hello, Grandma," said Anouk.

"I brought you bread and milk.

What can I help you with?"

"I'm cold," said the wolf.

"Come here with me

and warm me up."

Anouk climbed onto the bed

beside her Grandmother.

She saw Grandma's hands.

"Oh, Grandmother, those long

fingers you have!"

"Good for holding you, my child."

"Oh, Grandmother,

those big ears you have!"

"Good to hear you with,

my child!"

"Oh, Grandmother,

that big mouth you have!"

"Good to *eat* you with,

my child!"

"Oh, Grandmother,

I have to go to the toilet!"

"All right, but don't be long,"

said the wolf. He tied a string

around Anouk's foot

and let her go.

Outside, Anouk untied the string,

wrapped it around a bucket,

and ran home.

"Are you finished yet?"

called out the wolf.

When Anouk didn't answer,

the wolf pulled on the string.

Only the bucket rolled inside.

The wolf jumped out of bed

and ran after Anouk.

Anouk ran fast,

and soon she reached the river.

"River, will you let me pass?"

she asked.

And the river answered,

"Of course, I'll let you pass.

You gave me your cakes."

The river parted its waters,

and Anouk ran to the other side.

When the wolf came to the river,

he jumped in to swim across

but was swept away by the waters.

From the riverbank,

Anouk thanked the river.

When she arrived home,

she told her mother everything.

★ ★ ★

"That reminds me of a story

I heard about a boy and a wolf,"

said Ben.

"But this wolf doesn't go to

a grandmother's house.

He comes to the boy's house

and pretends to be the boy's

grandmother.

"How does he get inside?"

asked Lily.

"I'll tell you the story," said Ben.

GRANDMOTHER WOLF

(*Red Riding Hood* from China)

"I must go to see your grandma,"

said Chen's mother.

"I will be back tomorrow.

Remember to lock the door,

and don't open it for anyone."

A wolf lived nearby,

and he saw the mother leave.

That evening he came to the house

and knocked on the door.

"Who's there?" asked Chen.

"My dear, this is your grandma,"
said the wolf.

"But Mother has gone to see you!"
said Chen.

"She has?" the wolf acted surprised.

"I did not see her on the way.

Let me in, now."

But Chen said, "Grandma,

why is your voice so low?"

"I have a cold, my child,"

replied the wolf.

"It's windy out here. Let me in."

Chen lit a candle so he could see.

He opened the door and instantly,

the wolf blew out the light.

"Why did you do that?" asked Chen.

"Now it's dark in here."

The wolf didn't answer,

but he climbed into the bed.

"Your grandma is so tired.

Come and rest with me."

Chen climbed into the bed,

and as he stretched

he touched the wolf's tail.

"Grandma, why does your foot

have a brush on it?" Chen asked.

"I wrapped some strings around it

to weave a basket for you,"

the wolf answered.

Chen touched the wolf's claws.

"Grandma, why are your nails

so sharp?" he asked.

"I fell on the road, and thorns

stuck in my hands," the wolf said.

Chen didn't believe it.

Those didn't feel like thorns —

they felt like animal claws!

He thought fast.

"You must be hungry, Grandma.

Let me bring you some peanuts.

They're just outside the door,"

said Chen.

"Bring some," the wolf agreed.

When Chen was outside,

he ran across the yard

to the kitchen and took a kettle

of boiling oil from the fire.

Then he climbed a tree with it.

Inside, the wolf waited and waited.

"What's taking you so long?"

he called.

When there was no answer,

the wolf jumped out of bed

and went to search for the boy.

He looked all around,

until he found Chen in the tree.

"What are you doing up there?

Come down right now

and bring me the nuts!"

"I will throw them down to you,"

Chen said. "Stand under the tree.

Now, close your eyes

and open your mouth!"

Chen told the wolf.

When the wolf opened his jaws,

Chen poured the boiling oil

down his throat, and the wolf died.

side the truck in the narrow alley left free between the parked cars.

Rather than step into one of the spaces between the cars, the man keeps forging ahead, forcing the two blue-overalled workmen to give way to him. This they do, as though acknowledging the aura of power the man has about him, marking him as someone to be deferred to, not to be crossed. One of them moves to one side, between the silver-grey Alfa and its neighbouring vehicle, a battle-scarred Fiat Uno. The other drops back, apparently waiting for the truck to pass so that he can fall in behind it and leave the way clear.

And this is where the strange thing happens. For as the male principal passes the first blue-overalled supernumerary, the latter turns around holding an object which must have been concealed in one of the many pockets of his costume. It appears to be a rolled-up newspaper, no doubt *L'Unità* or *Il Manifesto* or some such publication devoted to the aspirations and struggles of the proletariat, thus tying neatly into the director's jejune rethink. In an oddly elegant gesture, the workman waves the newspaper at the man in the overcoat, as though swatting a fly circling his head. At the same moment, although without any obvious sense of cause and effect, the latter tumbles forward as if he had tripped on the raised edge of one of the black paving slabs – always a hazard, even in this relatively well-to-do area of the city.

Luckily the other workman, now level with the rear of the still moving truck, is just in time to catch the falling man, thus preventing him from doing himself any serious injury. The gesture seems at first to indicate a compromise in the directorial line already established – the essential goodness of people everywhere, despite the ideological gulfs that appear to divide them – which half the audience fears and the other half secretly hopes will spill over into what the latter will applaud as human warmth and the former dismiss as feeble sentimentality.

As if to confirm this hypothesis, the first workman now tosses aside his newspaper, which hits the paving stones with a sharp metallic ring, and bends to grasp the victim's feet. Without a word, the two lift him clear of the ground, holding him suspended limply in mid-air by his shoulders and calves. By now the truck, in its inexorable progress, has passed them. With a single preliminary swing they heave the inert body up and over the tail-gate, where it disappears from view.

While the first workman retrieves the wrench which was wrapped in the newspaper, his colleague presses a green button protruding from a box mounted on the rear of the truck. With a loud roaring noise, the massive ram begins to descend. The top and sides are dirty and dull, but the curved blade has been polished by constant abrasion to an attractive silvery sheen. The ram moves steadily down into the body of the truck, the racket of its powerful machinery completely obliterating any sounds which might otherwise be audible.

At this point there is a welcome touch of comedy as the man's feet appear above the tail-gate of the garbage truck. Clad in highly polished brogues and red-and-black chequered socks below which a length of bare white leg is just visible, they proceed to execute a furious little dance, jerking this way and that like puppets at a Punch and Judy show – possibly a knowing allusion to the commedia dell'arte, which of course originated in this city.

The ram has meanwhile come to a halt in a series of shudders which shake the whole truck. One of the workmen runs over and activates another button on the raised console, reversing the mechanism for a moment while his colleague stuffs the upstart limbs down and out of sight. Then the ram continues its interrupted descent, this time completing its destined trajectory, scooping in all the rubbish which has been deposited there and crushing it into a compact mass, the individual components barely distinguishable one from another.

The blue-overalled workmen climb aboard the platform at the rear of the orange truck and wave to the driver, who immediately accelerates away, ignoring the overflowing skip standing outside the modern apartment block from which the man in the overcoat emerged earlier. The vehicle roars down the gently sloping street and disappears around the corner to the left. For a few moments its engine can be heard faintly in the distance, then all is still again.

4

If there had been anyone about in Via Greco on the morning in question, this is what they would have seen. And in fact several people were about: an old man shaving by the light from his window to save electricity, a single mother who had been up all night with her colicky baby, a child of ten taking in washing on a flat roof high above the street, a vagrant who slept in one of the parked cars by arrangement with the owner. But oddly enough none of them ever mentioned the extraordinary events they had just witnessed to the police or the newspapers, or even to their families, with the exception of Signora Pacca, the insomniac mother, who told the whole story in a low voice to her father that night over dinner. He smiled and nodded and muttered 'Really?' and 'Amazing!' from time to time. But Signor Pacca was stone deaf, and there was no one else in the room.

For the rest, no one breathed a word about what they had seen, although the affair soon became a matter of national notoriety. As if by unspoken agreement, they all acted as though they were opera-goers who, arriving fashionably late, had missed the overture.

La causa è amore

'Not Gesualdo!'

'Sabatino? Never!'

The man leaning against the counter smiled in a distant, almost supercilious way. He did not say anything.

'Mamma put you up to this, didn't she?' demanded the older of the sisters with a knowing look.

The man raised his eyebrows expressively.

'She has naturally mentioned her concern. Repeatedly and on numerous occasions, for that matter. But hers is not mine.'

'Then what is?' the younger sister returned swiftly.

Instead of replying, the man raised his hand to summon the barman.

'I think I could stand another coffee. How about you two? The pastries here are supposed to be the best in town.'

'I really couldn't.'

'I shouldn't, really . . .'

The man smiled again.

'Exactly what your lovers will say when a suitable opportunity presents itself, according to your mother.'

He turned to the barman.

'Two *sfogliatelle* for the ladies, and another coffee for me.'

The older sister fixed him with an intense glare. She was tall for a Neapolitan, but with the characteristic sallow skin, glowing dark eyes and very fine black hair, which she wore short. Her features were sharply delineated, especially the firm, decisive mouth and the long straight nose.

'I don't care whether this was your idea, Dottor Zembla, or mamma's,' she declared. 'In either case, it is a transparent attempt, as vain as it is despicable, to undermine the feelings which Gesualdo and I cherish for one another, feelings such as

6

persons of your generation are no longer capable of and whose strength and purity you cannot therefore be expected to understand. If I wished to be vulgar, I might suggest that it is precisely your inability to feel such emotions yourself which has generated the envy and rancour which lie behind this sordid attempt to discredit our poor lovers.'

Aurelio Zen shook his head.

'You are too ingenious, Signorina Orestina. My interest in this matter is entirely mercenary.'

'*Pronti, dottore!*' cried the barman, setting the coffee and the two scallop-shaped pastries on the marble counter.

'How does money come into it?' asked the younger woman, glancing down at the plate before her. Her appearance was softer and less formidable than her sister's, her hair longer and lighter, her flesh paler and plumper.

'Whose money?' Orestina enquired pointedly.

Zen sipped the scalding coffee, served in a cup preheated by boiling run-off from the espresso machine.

'Your mother's,' he said.

'Aha!'

'Let me explain to you her way of thinking . . .'

'We know that only too well,' returned the younger woman. 'She thinks that Sabatino and Gesualdo are thugs, criminals, gangsters, drug dealers, and Heaven knows what else!'

'Oh certainly, Signorina Filomena! That goes without saying. But where your mother and I differ is that she doesn't believe that they are really in love with you. Not only have you chosen to bestow your beauty, brains and breeding on these worthless individuals – I paraphrase your mother's rhetoric here – but, even worse, they are only diverting themselves with you, and will move on to new conquests as soon as they have got what they want.'

'That's a horrible thing to say!' cried Filomena, her green eyes watering. 'Sabatino is always very sweet and respectful to me and he really cares about my feelings. Mamma has no right to say that he doesn't love me. She's just jealous, that's all.'

'Gesualdo's only crime is that his parents were poor and lived in the wrong part of town,' her sister protested. 'It's simply

7

shameful of mamma to condemn him for that. He's the finest, truest, kindest, straightest man I've ever met, and worth any number of the snobby, snotty, spoilt brats she would like to marry us off to!'

Aurelio Zen drained his coffee and reached towards his pocket, then paused, frowning. He shook his fingers as though to relieve a cramp.

'My analysis of the situation exactly,' he replied. 'Which is why it's doubly unfortunate that you are unwilling to put their fidelity to the test. As it is, your mother and I may have to wait a long time to see which of us has won.'

'Won?' snapped Orestina. 'Won what?'

'Are you saying that you and mamma have made a bet on our future happiness?' demanded her sister. 'How dare you do such a thing? As though our lives were a horse race or a football match!'

Aurelio Zen shrugged.

'All I wanted to do was to prove your mother wrong. But since you won't cooperate . . .'

Filomena lunged forward impulsively and grabbed one of the *sfogliatelle*.

'And why should we cooperate?' she demanded. 'What's in it for us?'

'A trip to London, for a start.'

'*London?*'

'We'd need to make your sudden departure look natural, of course. What more normal than that two literature students in their final year at the university should go off to England to brush up the language?'

'I've always wanted to go to London,' murmured Orestina wistfully.

'Well, here's your chance,' Zen remarked with a broad smile. 'And if you turn it down, ladies, I shall be forced to conclude that, despite your fervent protestations, you're not really as sure of your boyfriends as you claim to be.'

'Sabatino would never be unfaithful to me!' said Filomena.

'I trust Gesualdo like my own self!' declared Orestina.

'I've found a very good package deal,' Zen went on. 'Air tickets, nice hotel in the centre, generous discounts at selected shops, clubs and discos. True, it means flying Alitalia, but a colleague of mine knows someone who works for the ground staff at the airport and he can get you upgraded.'

The younger woman brushed the pastry crumbs from her ample bosom.

'When would we be going?'

'Right away. That gives you a couple of weeks over there before you have to be back to sit your exams.'

'Out of the question,' said Orestina.

'I'll need to discuss it with Sabatino,' said Filomena.

Zen clapped his hand to his forehead.

'For God's sake! The whole point is that they're not to know that it's a test.'

'But I always tell Sabatino everything!' wailed the younger sister, starting to weep again.

'Look!' said Zen. 'If Sabatino and Gesualdo are the paragons you claim, what have you got to lose? You not only get the holiday of a lifetime in London, all expenses paid, but a chance to demonstrate once and for all that these young men, despite their other shortcomings, are indeed worthy of your devotion – and of your hand in marriage. In short, you get a chance to prove your mother wrong, and at her expense!'

There was a silence.

'How much?' asked Orestina.

Zen gave her an ingenuous smile.

'Pardon me?'

'You have just admitted that your interest in this is purely mercenary. So how much are we talking about?'

Zen twirled his left hand in the air.

'A hundred thousand? I forget exactly. The money isn't really important. I just suggested it to add a certain piquancy to the whole experience.'

Orestina nodded.

'I see. Well, let's see if we can't make this "experience" still more piquant for you, Dottor Zembla. I propose a side-bet for the same amount between the three of us. If you win, we will pay you fifty thousand each in addition to the hundred from

9

mamma. If you lose, Filomena and I split the pot, a hundred thousand lire each. What do you say?'

Aurelio Zen frowned and appeared to struggle for a moment. Then he thrust out his arm, grasped Orestina's delicate but surprisingly muscular hand, and shook it vigorously.

'What will you do with your winnings?' he demanded.

Filomena clapped her hands together, her face beaming with anticipated pleasure.

'I'll take Sabatino out for an evening on the town!' she cried enthusiastically. 'We'll go to a movie and then have dinner somewhere and dance the night away. I'll make it an evening we'll never forget, not even when we're your age, Don Alfonsetto!'

Zen turned to the older sister.

'And you, *signorina*?'

'I shall add it to my savings,' she replied coolly.

'You're good with money,' Zen commented. 'Like your father.'

'Leave our father out of this!' snapped Orestina.

She scooped up the remaining pastry, which her sister had been eyeing, wrapped it in a paper napkin and slid it into her bag.

'And now we must be going, or we'll be late for our classes.'

Aurelio Zen laid a hand on both their sleeves.

'Mind, don't tell your boyfriends! Otherwise the deal's off.'

'I don't *need* to tell Gesualdo,' Orestina replied scornfully.

'Exactly!' Filomena chimed in. 'Sabatino already knows whatever I'm going to say to him. We're so perfectly attuned. It's almost mystical, the rapport we have.'

Aurelio Zen stood looking at the two sisters, so different, so similar, so confident, so vulnerable. For a moment he felt a slight sense of regret, almost of guilt, at what he was doing. Then he shook his head, paid the bill, took them each by the arm and led them out into the bright wash of sunlight overlaying the town and the bay beyond.

Bella vita militar

By contrast with the balmy, expansive warmth of the street, the funicular station was dark and cavernous, the air cool, a faint draught edged with the smell of mould and oil. A pair of young rats chased one another playfully about between the rails. The cables were already in operation, slithering over the runners like silvery serpents. A few moments later the train appeared in the gloom below, inching up the hillside and slowing to a gentle, pneumatic halt alongside the steeply pitched platform.

Zen boarded the middle carriage, its floor stepped like a stairway, and opened his copy of *Il Mattino*. The headlines had a distinctly second-hand air, following up on stories which had made their début earlier in the week: the controversy over future plans for the site of the steel plant at Bagnoli, the initiative by the mayor to retain various measures hastily instituted to clean up the city in time to host the G7 conference, the disappearance of a former minister in the regional government who was under investigation for alleged association with organized crime.

The morning rush hour was long over and the train was almost empty, conveying mostly students and a few elderly women heading for the shopping streets around Via Toledo. In theory, Zen should have been at work over an hour and a half ago, but he did not appear at all concerned by this fact. Once again, his hand strayed to his pocket, as though he had mislaid something. It was now two weeks, three days and ten hours since he had smoked his last cigarette, but old habits die hard. The craving for nicotine had passed surprisingly quickly, but at certain ritualistic moments of the day – over a coffee, when reading the paper – he found himself reaching for the ghostly pack of *Nazionali* he could still hear calling out to him faintly.

Halfway down the hill, the train shunted on to a loop to pass its opposite number on the way up. On the sprayed concrete walling of the tunnel, Zen made out the slogan STRADE PULITE – 'Clean Streets' – crudely daubed in black paint. It sounded like an allusion to the 'Clean Hands' investigation into institutionalized corruption which had brought down the political class that had governed Italy since the war. But it was hard to see what 'Clean Streets' could mean, particularly on emerging from the funicular's lower terminus into the filthy, teeming, chaotic alleys of the Tavoliere district, where the morning market was in full swing.

Zen walked down to the grim bulk of the Castel Nuovo, crossed the wide boulevard which ran along the seafront and waited at the tram stop opposite. It was theoretically possible to take a bus from his home to the port, changing in Piazza Municipio, but given the vagaries of the city's public transport system Zen preferred to use the funicular and trams and walk the rest. Bus stops in Naples were purely notional markers which could be, and frequently were, moved without warning, and which in any case provided no guarantee that a given service would ever appear. But if a track existed, Zen reasoned, sooner or later something was bound to come along it.

And he was in no hurry. Quite the contrary! For the first time in his career, Aurelio Zen was his own boss, to the extent anyone ever could be in the police force. If he came in late and left early, or even failed to show up at all, the only way he could be found out was if one of his own staff snitched on him. And he had been at great pains to ensure that they had a vested interest in making sure that this never occurred.

One of the first effects of Zen's posting to Naples, predating his actual arrival, had been the hasty closure of various profitable and long-established business enterprises operating from the police station inside the port area, much to the distress of all involved. This painful decision had been reluctantly taken after an emergency meeting of the management and staff. This was the first time that anyone could remember an outsider being appointed to command the harbour detail. And not just any outsider, but a former operative of the illustrious Criminalpol, who worked directly out of the ministry in Rome!

For such a high-flyer to be transferred to a lowly, routine job in the South could mean only one thing, they all agreed. A clean-up had been ordered, and this Zen – his name didn't even sound Italian – had been selected to enforce it with ruthless efficiency. The only mystery was why their modest little scam had been singled out in this way when, as everyone knew, there was so much serious, big-time abuse going on. But perhaps that was precisely the point, someone suggested. The men at the ministry didn't dare touch the big names, to whom they were too closely linked and indebted, so they were making a show of doing something by sending one of their hatchet men to pick on low-level activities in which they took no direct interest.

Zen's first job had been to convince his new colleagues that this was not the case. It proved to be one of the toughest assignments he had ever faced. After holding out for over three weeks, during which time he had made no progress whatsoever, he finally decided to do something completely uncharacteristic, something so foreign to his nature that he debated the wisdom of the move right up to the last minute, and only then went ahead because there was no alternative. He decided to tell them the truth.

Since he could hardly convene the entire corps for this purpose, he deliberately selected the most hostile and truculent of the officers under his command, Giovan Battista Caputo. Caputo was a wiry, energetic man in his early thirties with a prow-shaped face, a hook nose, a flamboyant black moustache and a mouthful of sharp white teeth which were exposed up to the gums when he flashed one of his infrequent, vaguely menacing smiles. He looked like a composite of every gene pool which had ever flourished around the bay: Etruscan traders, Greek settlers, Roman playboys, Barbary pirates and Spanish imperialists. If he could win over Caputo, Zen reckoned, he would win the keys not only to his new command but to the city itself.

'You're all wondering what I'm doing here,' he declared when Caputo presented himself in his office.

'That's none of our business,' was the unyielding reply.

'I'm going to tell you anyway,' said Zen. 'Sit down.'

'I prefer to stand.'

13

'I don't give a damn what you prefer. I'm ordering you to sit down.'

Caputo obeyed stiffly.

'The answer to the question I just raised is very simple,' Zen went on. 'I requested a transfer.'

For all the effect of these words on Caputo, Zen might just as well not have spoken.

'You don't believe me,' Zen remarked.

'It's none of our business,' repeated Caputo stolidly.

'And it's easy to see why you don't,' continued Zen. 'Why should anyone request a transfer from the capital to a posting in a provincial city where he has no family, no friends and doesn't speak the dialect? And not even to the main Questura but to a dead-end job with the port detail?'

Caputo looked Zen in the eye for the first time, but still offered no comment. Zen took out his pack of *Nazionali* and offered one to his subordinate, who shook his head.

'The answer to this question is not so simple,' Zen said, exhaling a cloud of smoke. 'To use a classical allusion, I had to choose between Scylla and Charybdis. I had made enemies at the ministry, powerful enemies. I knew that they would not let me continue in my previous job, and I suspected that they might attempt to send me to a punishment posting. My only hope was to anticipate them by applying for such a move myself. I took a look at the positions vacant and chose this one. I'm the correct rank to command this detachment, and since it effectively constitutes a massive demotion from my former position with Criminalpol, my enemies could not intervene without revealing their hand. I had accepted defeat, but on my terms, not theirs.'

'Who are your enemies?' whispered Caputo, all attention now.

'Political.'

'On the right or the left?'

Zen smiled condescendingly.

'No one uses those words any more, Caputo. We're all in the centre nowadays. And my enemies are about as close to the centre as it's possible to be. In fact at the time of which I am speaking one of their number was the Minister of the Interior.'

Caputo's eyes widened.

'You mean . . .?'

'I do indeed.'

Caputo licked his lips nervously.

'Maybe I will have a cigarette after all,' he said.

Zen pushed the packet across the desk.

'That explains what I am doing here,' he said. 'It also explains my total lack of interest in any and all aspects of my job. This posting has been forced on me as the least of various evils on offer, but I do not feel the slightest degree of professional involvement or responsibility. I am sure that you and your colleagues are perfectly capable of carrying out your duties in a satisfactory manner, and my only wish is to leave you free to do so without interference or supervision. In short, just pretend I'm not here and carry on as you always have done. Do I make myself clear?'

Caputo flashed his shark's smile.

'Yes, sir.'

'The only thing that concerns me is that nothing occurs which might draw unwelcome attention to this detachment, and hence give my enemies an excuse to move me to the killing fields of Sicily or some God-forsaken hole up in the mountains. I'm sure I can count on your experience and discretion, Caputo, to ensure this does not happen. As far as everything else is concerned, I leave matters entirely in your hands. In fact the less I know about it, the better pleased I shall be.'

Caputo nodded briskly and stood up.

'Will there be anything else, sir?'

Zen was about to shake his head when a thought struck him.

'Actually, I'd like a *cappuccino scuro*. Not too hot, lots of foam, no chocolate.'

He lay back, glancing at the clock on the wall. Less than five minutes later there was a knock at the door and a uniformed patrolman entered bearing a tray laden with a glass of mineral water, a selection of freshly baked pastries and the *cappuccino*.

Every morning after that, an identical tray appeared a few minutes after Zen's arrival at the office. For a while, that was all. Then, about three weeks after his conversation with Caputo, he came in one day to find a large cardboard box in the corner of the

15

room. It proved to contain fifty cartons of *Nazionali*, 10,000 cigarettes in all. Zen removed three cartons and took them home,
and stacked the rest in the empty drawers of his filing cabinet.

After that, things improved by leaps and bounds. He was
greeted in respectful yet friendly fashion by everyone he met,
and his orders and requests were obeyed with alacrity, sometimes before he even realized that he had made them. He normally showed up at work each morning about eleven, unless he
had something better to do, leaving again shortly before lunch.
Today he was entertaining Valeria at home, so he planned to
make no more than a token appearance before stopping by the
market to shop for whatever took his fancy.

Cars and vans and lorries surged sluggishly along the parti-
tioned channel supposedly reserved for the trams, but in practice used by all and sundry as a relief route from the
traffic-clogged Via Cristoforo Colombo. Once in a while, the
city's *vigili* would swoop down and start handing out fines, but
such actions were sporadic and tokenistic, repressive blitzes by a
colonial power which knew that the struggle against the local
population was unwinnable but could not afford to concede this
openly.

In the dock area behind Zen, the white Tirrenia line steamer
which had arrived from Sardinia that morning was tied up on
one side of the passenger terminal. On the other lay a sleek grey
warship flying a flag he found familiar but which he couldn't
identify. Farther back, in one of the outer docks, a huge aircraft
carrier displayed the unmistakable emblem of the Stars and
Stripes.

A dull ringing from the embedded rails announced the arrival
of an elderly tram, swaying and nodding its way out of the tunnel burrowed under the Monte di Dio. Zen folded up his newspaper and waited patiently while it trundled through the
massed traffic towards him, its bell jingling plaintively. Ten minutes later, the tram deposited him in Piazza del Carmino, outside
one of the main entrances to the port area. Zen walked in
through the open gates, nodding perfunctorily to the armed
guard, who sketched a salute.

He crossed the concrete yard inside the gates and turned right towards the four-storey building which housed the detachment of the *Polizia dello Stato* responsible for law enforcement within the port area. Most of this enclave, as well as the neighbouring parts of the city centre, had been flattened by both Allied and German bombing during the war, but the police station had miraculously been spared. Thanks to its restrained proportions, sturdy design and traditional materials, it stood out as a model of old-world grace and charm amid the brutalities of the surrounding architecture.

The size of the building belied the modest number of personnel deployed there, having been constructed at a time when the port was much more active than it was now, after interminable labour disputes had diverted much trade south to Salerno. The ground and first floors were the only ones in official use, and the second used only as a dumping ground for forgotten files and broken furniture. As for the top storey, it appeared equally abandoned at this time of day, although once night had fallen it turned into one of the liveliest venues in the whole area, much frequented by sailors who for one reason or another did not have a pass permitting them to leave the port enclave. But Zen was careful to know nothing of this, nor about how the prostitutes who worked there got past the guards at the gate, and still less about the contraband goods and illegal substances which reputedly changed hands on the same premises.

He walked in through the open doorway, acknowledging the greetings of the three uniformed men lounging about in the hall, and climbed the stairs to his office on the first floor. The trio discreetly broke off their conversation until he had reached the landing, then resumed in a low tone. The murmur of their voices reached up through the cool, shadowy spaces of the stairwell like the distant drone of bees.

Tutti due fan ben la loro parte

He had been in the office barely a minute when there was a knock at his door.

'Come in!' called Zen, surprised and pleased that his *cappuccino* had arrived so quickly.

But it was Giovan Battista Caputo who appeared. His manner was unusually subdued.

'Sorry to disturb you, chief. Can I have a word?'

Zen waved his hand wearily.

'We had a spot of trouble last night,' Caputo announced, coming in and closing the door.

'Mmm?'

'We've got a couple of warships in at the moment. An American aircraft carrier and a Greek frigate. A group of sailors from the carrier spent the evening in that bar by the passenger terminal.'

Zen nodded. He had visited the place on a brief guided tour of the dock area with Caputo a couple of weeks earlier, the idea being to provide Zen with a bluffer's guide to his new job. The bar in question, he had been given to understand, was operated by the same consortium responsible for the various phantom enterprises which operated from the top floor of the police station, and served among other things as a perfectly legal front allowing prospective clients to be screened before being granted admission to this inner sanctum. It was a poky place which nevertheless managed to provide a splash of life and colour amid the grandiose austerities of the *stazione marittima*.

The most striking feature of the place was a large neon sign in the window, reading, in English: MIX DRINKS. According to Caputo's account of the incident the previous night, a group of American sailors had apparently taken this advice literally, downing a staggering variety and quantity of wines, beers, spirits and liqueurs before trooping off to explore the town. All went well until they ran into another party returning to the Greek frigate.

'One of the Americans comes from a Greek family,' Caputo explained, 'so he started trying to talk to them. Only it seems his Greek isn't all that good any more, or maybe he was too drunk. Anyway, whatever it was he said sounded insulting to the Greeks. A fight broke out, and the Americans got the best of it.'

'Mmm,' repeated Zen, inspecting his finger-nails.

'When the Greeks got back to their ship, the word went round about what had happened and a bunch of them go out looking for revenge. They come across a man in American uniform and start to push him around. Next thing they know he's pulled a knife and stabbed two of them. One of our men was coming back from the bar, where he'd been compiling a report on the earlier incident, and he immediately arrested the attacker.'

Zen yawned lengthily.

'Really, Caputo, I hardly think you need to bother me with this sort of thing.'

'I wouldn't have, sir, except for one thing. We informed the Americans that one of their crew was under arrest, and they sent a couple of officers over to identify him. And here's where it gets sticky. You see, it turns out this man we've arrested is not one of their men at all.'

A shrug from Zen.

'So?'

Caputo sighed.

'Look, chief, you made it very clear that you didn't want anything happening here which might compromise you and provide an opening for your enemies in Rome, right?'

'Mmm?'

'Well, this is shaping up to become just that, I'm afraid. One of the Greek sailors was badly injured, and he's still in critical condition. The Greek consul has lodged an official complaint, and the Americans aren't too happy that we allowed someone masquerading as one of their personnel into a supposedly secure area. I've already fielded three calls from the Questore this morning . . .'

'Damn! What did you tell him?'

'I said you were out of the office conducting further enquiries in person. But he didn't sound pleased. I think you'd better get back to him as soon as possible.'

'I don't even know the number.'

Caputo told him. Zen picked up the phone.

'Stay here,' he told Caputo, who was heading discreetly for the door. 'I may need back-up.'

Despite his alleged impatience to discuss the case, the police chief of the *provincia di Napoli* kept Zen waiting on the line for over ten minutes before deigning to speak to him. When he did, however, he left Zen in no doubt that Caputo had not exaggerated the gravity or urgency of the situation.

'I understand that you're new to the city,' the Questore remarked in a quiet, suave voice more effective than any hectoring. 'We naturally have to make allowances for that. I remember wondering at the time whether it was a wise appointment. Naples is a unique city, and one which in many ways is difficult if not impossible for an outsider to understand.'

Zen sat there gripping the receiver tightly and wishing that he had not given up smoking.

'But then I told myself that this was after all simply a matter of policing the port area, a relatively minor and routine operation. I assumed that a man of your apparent experience would be able to handle it, even allowing for your lack of local knowledge. But within a few months of your arrival here we now have all the ingredients of a major international incident in the making, a scenario which makes the city look like some Third World hell-hole where bands of drunken sailors and local thugs have it out with knives among the wharves. We've spent a lot of time and money trying to upgrade the image of Naples in the world, and our efforts were crowned with the G7 conference. Now your slackness and incompetence threatens to bring all that work to naught!'

'It's impossible for my men to be everywhere,' Zen protested feebly.

'This affray occurred less than fifteen metres from the main passenger terminal,' said the Questore. 'If you can't police that area properly, what *can* you do? Anyway, it's too late to worry about that now. The essential thing is to bring this investigation to a suitable conclusion in the shortest possible time, a conclusion which will satisfy and reassure all the interested parties – who, I need hardly remind you, include two of our principal NATO allies. What progress have you made?'

'What progress have we made?'

He eyed Caputo desperately.

'Well, the individual responsible . . .'

Caputo held up his arms, crossed at the wrist.

'. . . is in custody . . .'

Caputo ran one finger across his closed lips as though tugging at a zipper.

'. . . but has so far refused to talk.'

Caputo was now pacing up and down the floor, darting glances this way and that, one hand shading his eyes.

'My men are conducting a thorough search of the scene . . .' Zen went on.

Caputo made writing motions on the palm of his left hand.

'. . . and taking detailed statements from witnesses.'

'What leads are you working on?' demanded the Questore.

'What leads are we working on?'

'Must you repeat everything I say? Yes, leads! Theories, ideas, hypotheses. Something which might begin to explain this incident and which I can communicate to the Prefect for subsequent transmission to Rome.'

Caputo stood on the other side of the desk, his arm thrust forward, holding up three fingers.

'We are working on three main theories at the moment,' Zen replied evenly. 'The first is that the perpetrator . . .'

He glanced at Caputo, who was waddling bow-legged around the room with his hands clutched like claws beside his hips.

'. . . was a cowboy,' concluded Zen.

'A *what*?'

Caputo shook his head furiously. Zen covered the mouthpiece of the phone.

'An *American*!' hissed Caputo.

'. . . that he was an American,' Zen told the Questore.

'But the United States naval authorities have explicitly denied that he was one of their men!'

'Exactly!' retorted Zen. 'According to this theory, the suspect was an undercover CIA agent who had been entrusted with the mission of murdering one of the Greek sailors, the son of an influential Communist politician.'

He looked triumphantly at Caputo, who gave him an enthusiastic thumbs up.

'And the second theory?' pursued the Questore after a pause which suggested that he was taking notes.

'The second . . .'

Caputo had transformed himself into a smaller, slighter, quicker individual moving around the room with exaggerated naturalness, glancing furtively from side to side, his hands occasionally darting out to one side or the other as though of their own accord.

'. . . is that the man was a common pickpocket,' Zen went on, 'who had infiltrated himself into the port area disguised as an American sailor. He approached the Greek sailors, intending to make a touch, and when they started roughing him up under the mistaken impression that he actually was an American, he reverted to type and pulled a knife.'

'I don't like that one so much,' the Questore replied neutrally. 'Reflects badly on the city. What about the third theory?'

'The third?' replied Zen. 'Ah, you're going to *love* the third.'

He gazed helplessly at Caputo, who was prancing gaily about, his hands indicating the contours of a generous bosom and rearranging the folds of an invisible skirt.

'According to this theory, the man was in fact a woman,' Zen informed his superior.

'A woman?'

'A prostitute. We try to keep them out of the port area, of course, but . . .'

'Surely to God you can at least ascertain the sex of the individual in your custody?' demanded the Questore icily.

'His sex? Yes, of course.'

Caputo quickly sketched an enormous male organ in the air.

'He's a man. No question about that.'

'But you just told me that you were working on the theory that he was a prostitute!'

Zen hesitated a moment.

'Exactly, a transvestite prostitute.'

'But he was dressed as a *man*!'

'Outwardly, yes. But he was wearing female undergarments.'

The Questore was briefly silent.

'In other words . . .?'

'In other words, he was a man dressed as a woman dressed as a man.'

'But that's absurd!'

'Oh, there's a demand for that sort of thing,' Zen replied in a worldly tone. 'But unfortunately on this occasion he had mistaken his clientele. They started beating him up, and he drew his knife in self-defence. But be that as it may, all the indications are that this was merely a banal crime of mistaken identity. I'll have a full report on your desk within twelve hours . . .'

Seeing Caputo signalling frantically, Zen broke off. Caputo held up the first two fingers of his left hand and whirled the right round and round.

'. . . or twenty-four at the very most,' Zen concluded.

'I shall pass on what you have told me to the relevant parties,' said the Questore curtly. 'But I must remind you that if a satisfactory solution has not emerged within the period you mention, it is you and not I who will be held responsible. I am not prepared to cover for you on this case, and I regret that my department is too overstretched to permit me to dispatch one of our operatives to put your house in order for you. So I trust that you will give this matter your fullest and most urgent attention.'

'You may depend on it, sir.'

He hung up and turned to Giovan Battista Caputo.

'That's all right, then,' he remarked, stretching luxuriously. 'You've got till tomorrow to stitch something together.'

Caputo's face fell.

'What about you, chief? Don't you even want to interview the suspect?'

'Impossible, I'm afraid,' Zen replied, reaching for his coat. 'I have a prior engagement which I just can't get out of. Which reminds me, do you have any contacts at the opera? A friend of mine mentioned that she'd like to go, and I said I'd take her.

Then I phone the box office and they tell me the whole run's been sold out for a month.'

Caputo grunted sympathetically.

'I'll see what I can do.'

Amico Don Alfonso

'But are you sure it'll work?'

'When it comes to love, no one can be sure of anything.'

A short silence.

'Two weeks isn't much time.'

'The shorter, the better. Absence makes the heart grow fonder. If they were gone for a month, the lads might start to grow sentimental.'

A longer silence. It wasn't really silence, of course, not even this far up the Vomero, on one of the steep, stepped alleys inaccessible to the most daring or desperate of Neapolitan drivers. From the streets below, on the foothills sloping down to the bay, rose a muffled cacophony of car horns, all at slightly different pitches, a rhythmic urban symphony in some indecipherable time signature. Punctuating this medley, nearer at hand, came the gruff staccato barking of the shaggy, semi-feral dog kept chained up on the flat roof surrounding the cupola of Santa Maria del Petraio, presumably to ward off burglars. And, overlaying all, the cries of a gang of boys playing football on the steps below, a fast and demanding game whose main challenge was to prevent the ball going missing in one of the inaccessible walled gardens all around, or plunging precipitously down the entire length of the *salita*, 287 steps to the point where it crossed the broad curve of paved street looping up the hillside.

Most dramatic were the intermittent appearances of aircraft on their final approach to Capodichino, monstrously large, deafening and unpredictable apparitions, seemingly near enough to touch. And yet, despite everything, the terrace where they were sitting seemed an oasis of calm and stillness, a secluded refuge miraculously isolated from the stress and stridency of the city all around.

Calling it a terrace was a bit of an exaggeration, too. In reality it was merely a section of flat tarred roof extending around two sides of a partial one-storey extension added illegally twenty years earlier to allow the original building to be converted into two apartments. The extension housed the kitchen and bathroom, while the bedroom and sitting room were on the floor below. There was a small eating area adjoining the kitchen, but now the summer had arrived Aurelio Zen preferred to take his meals outside, at an old marble-topped table in the shade of the green-and-white striped canvas awning.

The silence which still persisted between him and his guest was not at all awkward, and neither showed any urgency to break it. It was a large, comfortable silence, as unconstrained and embracing as the hazy sunlight which coated every surface around them, or the blowsy air which shifted caressingly to and fro. In the extreme distance, the ghostly outline of the peninsula of Sorrento could just be made out, like an old print bleached out by the sun. The peak of Vesuvius loomed above the imposing perimeter wall of the San Martino monastery. To the right, Capri was almost completely obscured in the haze, a fading memory. In the strait between the island and the peninsula the dark rectangular block of a ship seemed to hover on the horizon, perhaps the ferry which Zen had seen that morning, now on its way to Sicily, or even farther south, to Malta and Tunisia.

'Anyway, I suppose we had to do *something*,' said the woman sitting beside Aurelio Zen, as though concluding a lengthy internal debate.

'Of course we did,' he agreed idly. 'Whatever the truth about that pair may be, they certainly aren't the sort you want your daughters associating with. Family background unknown, consorting with known criminals, frequenting some of the worst streets in the city, no visible means of support but plenty of money to throw around . . .'

'Not to mention handsome and charming,' added Valeria.

Zen nodded slowly.

'It's a deadly combination all right. One which both demands and justifies the measures we're taking.'

'Yes, but will it work?'

They had met by the purest chance at a party given by the

British Consulate. Zen had been invited through an official whom he had helped to uncover a scheme to smuggle illegal Asian immigrants into Britain on cargo ships plying between Naples and Liverpool. As for Valeria, she was there thanks to her friendship with the wife of some politico in the economic affairs department of the Campagnia regional government, who had made a polished, vapid, interminable speech of the kind which such functionaries can turn out at a moment's notice to suit any occasion from a conference marking the anniversary of the birth or death of X to the inauguration of a new building, bilateral agreement, cultural artefact, exhibition or plaque to, by, in or about Y.

The idea behind the gathering, as far as Zen could make out, was to sip industrial-grade sparkling wine, nibble at fiddly, self-destructing canapés and socialize at the top of your voice with people you already knew or who were eager to know you. This left Zen, a nobody who knew no one, at a distinct disadvantage. He was just wondering how soon he could decently leave when his contact appeared and led him across the room to be introduced to Signora Valeria Squillace.

The Englishman was a bluff, burly, jovial type who had recently been transferred to Naples in a fit of bureaucratic whimsy after many years in Finland, whose idiosyncratic language he had apparently mastered to the degree that foreigners ever can. His Italian, however, was still rudimentary, and Zen's English – to say nothing of his Finnish – practically non-existent. Their official dealings had been through an interpreter, but now they were on their own. To make matters worse, the room was crowded and noisy, while Signora Squillace was slightly deaf in one ear and too vain to wear a hearing aid.

As a result, Zen discovered once they were alone together that his new acquaintance was under the illusion that his name was Alfonso Zembla and that he was looking for a house to rent. For a while he kept waiting for a suitable opportunity to correct her, but eventually gave up. The matter was of no consequence. He had no interest in finding somewhere permanent to live in Naples, and no reason to suppose that he would ever see the woman again. She was in her forties, tall and well-proportioned, with hazel eyes, wavy black hair with the odd streak of silver, and an expressive mouth which seemed to be perpetually strug-gling to suppress an ironic smile.

But none of this was enough to persuade Zen to try and follow up on the encounter, nor had Valeria Squillace given the slight-est hint that she would welcome such an attempt. So it came as a complete surprise when he received a telephone call from her two days later at the hotel where he was staying at the time. She reminded him of their meeting, explained that she had got his number from their mutual acquaintance at the Consulate, apolo-gized for disturbing him at home and then got to the point.

'I understand you work for the police, Dottor Zembla. I have a personal problem which you might be able to help me with. In return, I would be prepared to offer you a limited lease at a very reasonable rent on a small property I own near San Martino.'

Zen was lying on the bed, nude except for his socks, watching a Japanese cartoon featuring children with enormous eyes engaging in hand-to-hand combat with evil adversaries whose eyes were undesirably small.

'What sort of problem?' he said guardedly, flipping over to the neighbouring channel, where an overweight egomaniac with insincere hair was direct selling a 64-piece set of silver-plated cutlery.

'It's something I'd rather not discuss on the telephone,' his caller replied coyly. 'Do you think it would be possible for us to meet briefly, say tomorrow?'

They made a date for the following afternoon in the bar of Zen's hotel. That morning at work he asked Giovan Battista Caputo if he knew anything about the Squillace family. Caputo screwed his face into a mask of mental effort.

'Name rings a bell,' he said. 'Let me make a few calls.'

He returned fifteen minutes later with a précis of his efforts. Manlio Squillace, the *capofamiglia*, had died of a heart attack two years earlier following his arrest on charges of 'financial irregu-larities'. He had been an eminent local entrepreneur who had made a fortune from speculative land transactions in the sixties and seventies, and was widely rumoured to have been associ-ated with organized crime. He was survived by his wife Valeria and two daughters, Orestina and Filomena.

28

It was the latter, Zen discovered that afternoon, who were the problem which Signora Squillace hadn't been prepared to discuss over the phone. They were in their early twenties, language students in their final year of university. With their looks and qualifications, to say nothing of the family connections, they could have had their pick of any number of nice boys from good homes and with excellent career prospects.

'Instead of which they want to throw themselves away on a couple of gangsters!' Valeria Squillace wailed over her *cappuccino* and brioche. 'At times I worry that it must be in the blood, something they got from their father. Not that he was a criminal himself, of course, but he had to associate with all sorts of people in his line of work, and some of it must have rubbed off on Orestina and Filomena. How else do you explain them taking up with those hoodlums?'

It didn't seem to Zen that an explanation was that far to seek, but he sensed that it wouldn't be helpful to say so. Instead he asked Signora Squillace how he could help her.

'The worst of it is that they don't seem to realize what they're getting themselves into,' she replied. 'Whenever I raise the matter with them, they simply accuse me of snobbery and prejudice. And of course I have no proof that those two are criminals, but I can sense it in my bones.'

She looked at Zen.

'If you were to look through the police records, Don Alfonso, perhaps you would be able to find something definite, some hard evidence I can use to open their eyes to the truth before it's too late.'

Intrigued and amused, Zen had agreed. The next day he sent in a routine request to the Questura for information relating to Troise, Gesualdo and Capuozzo, Sabatino. The results were unexpected, to say the least. First came a written reply, via fax, stating that no records existed in those names. Given that the police maintained a dossier on just about every man, woman and child in the country, even if only to list whether or not they had fulfilled their legal duty of voting in every local and national election, the complete absence of the men's names was itself a form of negative proof that something was amiss.

But it was the next development which seemed to confirm that Signora Squillace's suspicions had not been exaggerated. This took the form of a telephone call from an official at the élite *Direzione Investigativa AntiMafia*. He explained that Zen's request had been routinely copied to him since the two names were on a file of suspected gang members whom the DIA had under long-term surveillance, and wanted to know what had brought them to the attention of the port police. Zen invented a vague but plausible cover story and promised to relay any further information he might have to the DIA before taking any action himself.

At a second meeting, over lunch in a restaurant beneath the Castel dell'Ovo, he had reported his findings to Valeria Squillace. Oddly, she seemed almost reassured by this proof that her worst fears had been realized. The question was what to do now.

'Why not just forbid your daughters to see them?' Zen had suggested.

Valeria merely smiled sadly.

'You're out of touch, Don Alfonso. The girls simply wouldn't obey me. They're in love, or think they are. For the young these days, that's a licence to do anything. Besides, it might just make matters worse as far as the men are concerned. Gangsters never take no for an answer, even if they're not really that interested. It's a question of principle with them.'

Things had come a long way since that stiff-backed, exploratory rendezvous at La Cantinella. In retrospect, the turning-point had probably been Zen's agreeing to give up smoking. Valeria's late husband had been a sixty-a-day man, and the smell of cigarettes, she explained, still evoked disturbing memories. Much to his surprise, Zen had simply shrugged and said, 'All right.' It was just another example of how he had changed since moving to Naples. All his habits and attributes had come to seem provisional, decorative impedimenta related to choices he had once made for reasons now forgotten, no more a part of him than his clothes. He'd started smoking at a certain moment, now he would stop. Why not?

The decision had meant handing over the remaining 320 packets of the contraband *Nazionali* to old Signor Castrese across the street, but it had been worth it. Never before had Zen had a relationship like this with a woman: warm, intimate, friendly, informal, but completely non-sexual. This is what it would have been like having a sister, he thought as they lay sprawled side by side beneath the green awning, the table between them littered with the remains of the simple meal Zen bought on his way home – a selection of cold *antipasti*, half a crusty loaf and some *insalata Caprese*.

They still had their differences, though, notably over the success of the plan Zen came up with for separating Valeria's daughters from their unsuitable suitors.

'But will it work?' she repeated. 'That's the question.'

'Of course it will,' Zen replied lazily.

She shook her head.

'I don't feel right, playing with their emotions like this. They're such darlings. I remember when they were babies . . .'

'But now they can *have* babies. And it's your responsibility to make sure that that happens with the right person and in the right circumstances.'

'You're so logical, so *Northern*! Life isn't that simple.'

She glanced at her watch.

'I must go. The girls will be home in half an hour. I don't want to have to lie to them about where I've been.'

'The essential thing now is to make sure they don't try and back out. Take them shopping, let them choose suitable clothes and accessories, pick up a guidebook and maps of London.'

Valeria sighed.

'But what about the men? I still don't understand how you're going to get them to be unfaithful in such a short time.'

'Leave that to me. Just remember to leave me the key to the downstairs flat. Oh, and have you got those snapshots I asked for?'

Valeria Squillace handed over these items, and Zen led her down the stairs to the front door. The football players had dispersed and the steep basalt steps were deserted. From the sill of a barred window across the alley, Don Castrese's cat watched them warily.

'I'll set up a meeting between our four young lovers just before the girls leave,' Zen told Valeria. 'But it's most important they shouldn't meet until then. If Sabatino and Gesualdo find out what's happening and get to work on the girls, they could destroy the whole plan.'

Valeria nodded.

'I'll take them off to visit their aunt in Salerno. They've been promising to go for weeks, and this is the perfect opportunity.'

She turned to Zen.

'So I'll see you on Sunday night,' she said lightly.

'What about the neighbours? The porter is bound to see me coming and going, and it'll be all over the building in no time.'

Valeria waved dismissively.

'I've told him I'm expecting a cousin from Milan who's down here on business for a few weeks. That and a large tip from you should do the trick.'

Zen smiled and nodded.

'*A presto, allora.*'

'*Arrivederci*, Don Alfonso.'

Due delinquenti

At about the time Zen and Valeria parted in a quiet alley on the slopes of the Vomero, with only a cat for company, the two men who were the subject of their discussion entered a shop in Spaccanapoli amid the shriek of sirens and the raucous shouts of street vendors. The shop sold wine and beer and filling snacks: balls of cooked rice with a soft heart of melted mozzarella, folded pizzas stuffed with curd cheese and ham, potato croquettes laden with oil and melted cheese.

The elderly woman behind the counter was adding to the general din by yelling an order to the kitchen, where her husband and a teenage boy were hard at work in the ferocious heat of ovens the size of tombs. Then she saw the two men who had just come in and her face became studiously blank.

'Giosuè here?' asked the older and taller of the pair. He was dressed in designer slacks and a tight-fitting sweater which revealed his taut, muscled frame to advantage.

'Eh, oh!' the woman called to the back of the shop. 'And these *pizzette*?'

The other man reached over the counter and took one of the golden rice balls stacked on a plate. He was wearing jeans and a smartly pressed sports jacket over an open-necked shirt.

'Good,' he said appreciatively, biting into the *arancia*.

'What do you want?' the old woman asked.

'A double cone with pistachio and chocolate,' returned the first man in dialect as thick as her own. 'Oh, and a scoop of raspberry, what the hell.'

'We don't have ice-cream.'

The man looked shocked.

'You don't?'

He turned to his companion.

33

'They don't have ice-cream, they don't have Giosuè. So what the fuck *do* they have?'

The other swallowed a mouthful of rice before replying.

'They have problems,' he said, shaking his head.

The old woman made a face.

'Eh, problems! Of course we have problems, and so many!'

The first man flicked his forefinger at her face.

'Ah, but you have problems you don't even know about yet. Maybe you have ice-cream too, without knowing it.'

'Maybe they have Giosuè,' the other man put in.

At this point the woman's husband emerged from the kitchen, wiping his hands on a filthy towel. He was old too, just like his wife, and the neighbour's kid who was helping out was too young to be any help in a situation like this. Once upon a time he could have seen scum like this off the premises without any trouble, but not any longer. He knew it, and so did they.

'Gesualdo! Sabatino!' he cried with faked enthusiasm. 'How's it going?'

The taller one gave him a brief expressionless glance.

'You'll have to ask Giosuè,' he said. 'He's the one who knows how it's going.'

The old man shrugged apologetically.

'Eh! I haven't seen him for a long time.'

'How long?' demanded Gesualdo.

'Must be a week or more. He didn't say why. Just stopped coming in.'

'Maybe he lost his appetite,' said Sabatino, grabbing a *calzone*.

'Who knows?' replied the old man, still mechanically rubbing away with the towel. 'It can't be the food. There's nothing wrong with that, is there? You guys like it, right?'

Gesualdo surveyed the shop with a look of bored distaste.

'Sure we like it. We like it just fine. The problem is that nobody really gives a damn what we like or don't like. They just don't care. It's a shame, but there you go. What they care about is what someone else likes. And I can tell you right now that he isn't going to like it when we tell him Giosuè hasn't been around recently. Especially if it turns out he has. He *really* wouldn't like that. Not even a little bit.'

34

The old man nodded vigorously.

'It's true, I swear it! I haven't seen him, haven't heard anything. If I do, I'll let you know right away.'

'You do that,' said Gesualdo. 'Otherwise your insurance rates could soar sky-high. Right, Sabatì?'

'That's right,' agreed the other man through a mouthful of the stuffed pizza. 'See, we have two kinds of rates. Low risk and high risk, we call them in the trade. Up to now this establishment has always been regarded as a low risk, but if it turns out that you're selling ice-cream on the side, it might become necessary to reassess your classification.'

'Ice-cream is a very unstable substance,' Gesualdo observed solemnly. 'If it's not handled properly, the results can be disastrous. Remember what happened to Ernesto's workshop, just down the street here? The blaze was so intense they never did figure out how many Moroccans he had cooped up in there. Luckily for us, his insurance had just lapsed.'

He turned to his companion.

'Oh, Sabatì! Still feeding your face? We've got calls to make. Let's go!'

The men walked out into the crowded street, leaving the old man and his wife alone. They went about their work silently, avoiding each other's eyes.

Senza amor,
non senza amanti

'Stop here.'

The driver turned.

'You're not planning to have her in the cab, are you? That'll cost you plenty.'

Aurelio Zen eyed him coldly.

'I'll pay what's on the meter when we get back.'

'Eh no, *dottore*! What am I supposed to do while you're going at it? Stand around in the street and catch my death of cold? To say nothing of the fear of getting mugged. This is a dangerous area, you know.'

A thought struck him.

'Unless you want me to stay. Is that it, *duttò*? You want me to watch while you . . .'

Zen got out of the taxi, leaving the door open, and walked over to the open fire of broken-up fruit crates blazing at the street corner. One of the two prostitutes stationed there, a brunette with long slender legs, was feeding the flames from a pile of wood stacked nearby. The other, a busty blonde, watched Zen approach with a keen appraising look.

'Good evening, ladies,' he said.

The brunette straightened up and looked at him with an expression of amusement.

'What exquisite manners!' she enthused. 'And a very good evening to you, *cummendatò*.'

'What can we do for you?' demanded the other. 'It's a hundred for a one-off in the car, or a hundred and fifty per hour elsewhere, minimum two hours. And this week only we have a special package, you can have both of us at a twenty per cent discount.'

Zen flashed his identity card briefly.

'I'm with the police.'

The brunette fluttered her eyelashes.

'That's OK. We fuck anybody.'

'I've got a proposition I want to put to you,' Zen went on. 'Is there somewhere we can talk?'

'You want to *talk* about it?' the blonde exclaimed in a tone of mock alarm. 'I think we'll pass. This is just too kinky.'

Zen opened another fold of his wallet and extracted two bank-notes. He handed one to each of the prostitutes.

'Here's a little earnest money. If you don't like my proposal, you can keep this for your time and trouble. If you do, there's more where this came from.'

The brunette hoisted her skirt, revealing a further astonishing length of leg, and tucked the banknote under the strap of her suspender belt. She leaned over and murmured something in dialect to the blonde. After a rapid exchange, she turned back to Zen.

'There's a bar about four blocks from here. We can talk there.'

Zen pointed to the fire.

'What about your pitch? You want to arrange for someone to keep an eye on it for you?'

The blonde smiled.

'That won't be necessary.'

'Not after what happened to that newcomer who tried to mus-cle in while we were out of town one weekend,' the brunette explained as they walked over to the waiting cab. 'She still limps quite heavily, I understand.'

'And you know what?' the blonde put in. 'The bitch is making better money now than she ever did before. There's no account-ing for taste.'

'Or the lack of it.'

The bar was a large, anonymous place near the station, patron-ized at this hour by a few late travellers, a group of railwaymen, a municipal cleaning crew and a battered, bloated woman of indeterminate age who eyed Zen's companions with a piercing mixture of envy and malicious contempt.

Zen ordered a mint tea, the brunette an espresso, the blonde a hot chocolate. The only tables had been taken by the travellers and the hostile older woman, so they headed for a quiet corner above a glass display case where a few sad sandwiches lay curling up on metal trays under damp towels.

'We'd better introduce ourselves,' the brunette announced abruptly. 'I am Libera.'

'Iolanda,' murmured the blonde, peeking down at her extensive cleavage as though for confirmation.

Zen hesitated an instant.

'Alfonso Zembla,' he said.

'So let's hear your proposition, Signor Zembla.'

Zen removed the tea-bag from his cup.

'In a word, I want you to seduce two young friends of mine.'

Libera downed her coffee in two large gulps.

'They're young, you say?'

'In their twenties.'

'Good-looking?'

'Not bad.'

'Well off?'

'Loaded.'

Iolanda sighed languidly.

'So what's the catch? The girls should be falling over themselves to get at them.'

Extending the little finger of his right hand, Zen raised the cup to his lips.

'The catch is that they're already in love. And faithful. Models of devotion and constancy. Since they met their respective *fidanzate*, neither has so much as looked at another woman.'

The two prostitutes exchanged glances.

'And where do you come in?' asked Libera.

Zen turned his head and spat to one side.

'Those little prigs have been breaking my balls about this for months!' he exclaimed. 'They're just like these hypocritical politicians we have running around now, making out they're some new breed of men, clean, honest and incorruptible, unlike the old shits like us who've been running the country since they were crapping in their nappies. It makes me sick! Gesualdo and Sabatino claim they're not like other men, always checking out the room for something fresh and new. God forbid! Their love is the only one worthy of the name, the purest and most perfect emotion which the world has ever seen and which will endure eternally, etcetera, etcetera.'

'How sweet!' cried Iolanda, placing one hand on her breast.

'You may think so, *signorina*,' Zen retorted, 'but me and the rest of the lads have had just about as much as we can stand. So we've made a little plan. The two girls this pair are so mad about are out of town for a few weeks, and we aim to put all their fine talk to the test.'

Libera smiled thoughtfully.

'It's intriguing. Definitely more imaginative than our normal line of work.'

'But will it pay as much?' queried Iolanda. 'A girl's got to make a living, you know.'

Zen took a sip of tea and eyed them both.

'I can offer you five hundred thousand each down, and the same again if you succeed.'

'For two weeks' work?' the blonde exclaimed indignantly. 'We can make more than that in a few nights on the street!'

'Not if I bust you for prostitution, tax evasion, and corrupting a minor,' Zen retorted with a smile.

'What minor?'

He shrugged.

'I can easily find one. The city's full of corrupt minors.'

Iolanda pushed her hair back impatiently.

'I don't think it's very nice of you to threaten us.'

Zen laughed insincerely.

'Only joking! If you don't think you're up to the challenge, I can always find someone else. But you two are definitely the most stunning-looking women I've seen so far. If anyone can bring this off, you can.'

He produced the two snapshots which Valeria gave him earlier, showing each couple posed self-consciously against a view of a sunlit beach.

'Meanwhile, here's a look at the competition,' he said.

The two prostitutes scrutinized the photographs closely.

'God, that hair!' cried Iolanda.

'And those clothes!' added Libera.

'Those ghastly ear-rings!'

'That posture!'

'They definitely need a girlfriend to take them in hand . . .'

'To take them shopping, too.'

'But the guys are really cute!'

'What a waste!'

Libera looked at Zen.

'It's a deal,' she said.

'So the money's not a problem?'

Iolanda sniffed haughtily.

'It's not a question of money.'

'It's an act of charity,' explained Libera. 'To see two virile young men throw themselves away on a couple of homely *figlie 'e mammà* like that . . .'

'It'll be a pleasure to show them what a real woman is like!' said Iolanda.

'But how exactly are we to go about this?' asked Libera.

With a cautious glance all around, Zen lowered his voice and began to outline the details of his plan. Not that anyone was listening. In fact the bar had emptied considerably by now. The travellers had left to catch their trains, the railwaymen had returned to work, and the cleaning crew were on their way out too, apparently in response to a pager which one of them had clipped to the breast pocket of his overalls. Only the elderly whore remained slumped over her table, gazing morosely into her glass of wine.

The street cleaners climbed into their orange truck, which drove off along the main avenue for some distance before turning into a side-street riddled with deep potholes. The only illumination here, apart from the truck's headlights, came from the open fires of the prostitutes spaced at intervals along the pavement. And one of them, at least, appeared to be doing some business. A large saloon was parked at the kerb near her pitch, the engine still running. From the driver's window, a man beckoned to the thin, slight woman leaning against the wall at the corner. With an odd gesture, half-shrug and half-wave, she walked over to the car.

About fifty yards farther back another car stood beside the

kerb, its lights off and the engine silent. It might at first sight have appeared to be the scene of a similar encounter, but one which had progressed beyond the stage of negotiations. It would have taken a very keen observer to notice that the car had only one occupant, who was sitting bolt upright behind the wheel, looking straight ahead, with occasional glances in the rear-view mirror. As the garbage truck came into view he switched on the ignition and pumped the brake pedal three times. The headlights behind flicked momentarily to high beam.

Meanwhile the skinny prostitute and her prospective client had concluded the preliminaries. She got into the back seat of the car, a luxury import of some kind, which immediately pulled away from the kerb. The street was deserted and the truck had plenty of room to pass, but it unaccountably failed to pull over, ramming the rear of the car with a jarring shock and a loud metallic crunch.

The driver of the saloon got out, waving his arms and exclaiming angrily. A middle-aged man conventionally dressed in a suit and overcoat, he was clearly both shocked and hopping mad, as well he might be. Even a superficial inspection of the damage was enough to show that some extremely expensive bodywork was involved here. The crew of the truck also descended from their cab, three of them all together.

'What the fuck do you think you were doing?' the first man shouted angrily. 'Are you trying to pretend you didn't see me? If you assholes lose nothing but your jobs, you can count yourselves lucky!'

And so on, for some considerable time. When he finally paused for breath, one of the crew leaned forward confidentially.

'I understand how you feel, *dottore*. The fault was entirely ours, no question about it. On the other hand, it wouldn't do your reputation any good if it were known that you were hanging around an area like this at this time of night, right? So why don't we try and work out some mutually agreeable solution?'

The car driver started to splutter some suitably crushing reply, but broke off as the logic of the other man imposed itself. Everyone in Naples knew that single men in smart cars only came down here at night for one reason. His wife wouldn't be too happy, nor her influential family, to say nothing of his so-called 'allies' in the political arena. And as for the press, they'd have a field day, particularly if one of his former partners in pleasure should take it into her head to earn a hefty bonus by detailing some of the more esoteric requests with which, for a fat fee, she had reluctantly complied.

The garbage-disposal man glanced significantly at the woman waiting in the car, then gestured towards the back of the truck.

'Let's get out of earshot, *dottore*,' he whispered. 'I've got a proposal which I think will satisfy you, but it wouldn't do for us to be overheard.'

In the back seat of the car, the prostitute sat tapping her crossed legs in a bored fashion. The things some men get off on! She thought she'd heard it all, and for that matter *done* most of it, but this one had ideas she'd never even imagined. Still, he was prepared to pay, and this car – she stroked the leather seats – proved that he had the necessary. She would make more tonight than the whole rest of the week. Maybe she could even treat herself to a few days off, spend some time with the children.

She turned as the orange truck started up with a roar and drove away, disappearing round the corner. A moment later another car passed by and turned into the same street, some small domestic compact not to be mentioned in the same breath as the padded, perfumed limousine in which she sat waiting for her client to reappear, having sorted out this annoying accident, and drive them to the place he said he has nearby, with all the necessary equipment set up and ready to use.

Only he didn't reappear. And when she looked round again, the street appeared to be empty. Reluctantly, she climbed out of the car. There was no one in sight. For a moment she felt a sense of relief at the thought that she wasn't going to have to go through with it after all. Then she remembered the money, its loss all the more bitter since she had already spent it in anticipation.

But what about the car? No one, however rich, was going to go off leaving a machine like that behind, even with a badly damaged wing. Clearly her client must have gone off with the cleaning crew to phone for a tow-truck or something. Typical that he should just vanish like that without bothering to explain to her what was happening. She was only a whore, after all.

It was only then that she noticed the set of keys dangling from the steering column. He must have been so angry and shocked by the accident that he'd forgotten about them, just taken off, leaving her alone with about sixty million lire's worth of luxury import.

She opened the door, slipped in behind the wheel and started the motor, which hummed obediently into life. The woman sat there, thinking rapidly. The owner had almost certainly never seen her before, and if she didn't return to her pitch for a while he would never be able to trace her. As for the car, she could make that disappear equally effectively. They'd rip her off on its true value, of course, but even so she and the kids should be able to live on the proceeds for a year or so, maybe more. Fate had thrown this prize her way. She'd be an ungrateful fool not to accept it. It could only bring bad luck.

With a slight scraping sound from the rear wheels, the car moved away, its lights dwindling rapidly in the distance. A moment later the street was completely deserted. Indeed, the only sign that anyone had been there at all was a rectangle of orange paper lying in the gutter, as though discarded at random. STRADE PULITE read the big black headline. Underneath there was a logo of some sort, and the bold slogan 'A New Start for a New City'.

Un uom nascosto

If Aurelio Zen had reduced his working week to the minimal level necessary to sustain a professional existence, his weekends were totally sacrosanct. No more overtime for him, no more broken sleep or cancelled social arrangements.

The mistake had been going home. He had been bent and battered by previous setbacks, but his experience in Venice had broken him. To cap it all, the local politician at the centre of the case Zen had been investigating had not only got off scot-free, but shortly afterwards the regionalist party he led had been lifted from their provincial marginality to the heart of the government as part of a disparate group of untried, untested and therefore untainted personalities and movements united under the brash, breezy slogan 'Go for It, Italy!'

Nor had the one positive outcome been such as to enhance Zen's sense of professional responsibility. The American family for whom he had been moonlighting in Venice had initially baulked at paying out the reward they had promised, on the grounds that the murderers had not been brought to justice. But when Zen threatened to make public some of the information he had uncovered about their kinsman's war record, they had rapidly backed off and agreed to a kill fee amounting to a substantial proportion of the original sum.

Despite this, Zen had come to Naples in a mood of bitterness and defeat. At first he had dealt with this by pretending that he was not really there at all. He put in token appearances at the office, and spent the rest of his time in the hotel where he had made an advantageous arrangement for a single room Monday to Thursday nights inclusive. Each Friday he caught the train back to Rome, remaining there until Monday, when he caught an early-morning express back to Naples.

Not that the situation back home was exactly ideal, either. Most of his friends and acquaintances were linked with his previous job in the Criminalpol squad, and seeing them inevitably served to remind him of the effective demotion he had been forced into taking. Nor were the prospects any brighter romantically. Thanks to an opportunistic dalliance in Venice – misconceived and ill-fated, like everything else that had happened to him there – Tania Biacis was now out of the picture, seemingly for good.

So he was largely thrown back on the company of his mother, who viewed the whole country south of Rome as a bottomless pit of vice and degradation, with Naples as one of its deepest and most vicious abysses. That her son had been transferred there was cause for endless complaint and commiseration. When he revealed that he had requested the transfer himself, she concluded that he must have taken leave of his senses (a remark he let slip about his father not being dead provided further proof of this) and started treating him with a creepily solicitous reserve.

Then, imperceptibly, things began to change. The first sign was when he started returning to Rome less often and for shorter periods. But it was Valeria Squillace's offer of the house on Salita del Petraio which tipped the balance decisively. This property was eventually intended for the use of Orestina and Filomena when they completed their education and got married to young men the family approved of. Since there was no immediate prospect of this, and perhaps as a gentle hint to her daughters, Signora Squillace had kept her word and given Zen a short-term lease on the upper apartment, renewable quarterly, at a rate considerably less than he was paying at the hotel.

Even once he had moved in, it was a while before he regarded the place as anything more than a dormitory. But gradually that too began to change. He started rearranging the furniture to suit his needs, removed a couple of pictures that were getting on his nerves, and even smuggled a few items out of the flat in Rome to make his new home more attractive or convenient. His visits there became ever rarer and more grudging, an onerous duty which he soon came to resent having to perform every month. If it hadn't been for his mother, he eventually realized, he wouldn't have gone at all.

For, much to his amazement, he found himself liking Naples. Not as he had on his previous sojourn there, as an up-and-coming officer with every prospect of a brilliant career ahead of him, for whom Naples was one of a series of appointments to major provincial cities paving the road to Rome. Now he liked it for its own sake, not for what it could do for him but for what it was. He was enchanted by every aspect of the city which he had expected to drive him mad. He loved the noise, the crowds, the traffic, the chaos, the pushiness and resilience of the people, their innate sense of tolerance, negotiation and endurance. Above all he prized his anonymity in the midst of a city which neither knew nor cared where he was from, what he did, or even who he was.

Since Zen had never got around to correcting his new landlady's impression that his name was Alfonso Zembla, this was the name inscribed on the rental contract, and which eventually appeared on the bell-push outside the front door. Partly to avoid confusion, partly on a whim, he had decided to adopt it. He knew no one in Naples and no one knew him. Why not accept the pseudonym which fate had handed him? It would serve to mark the radical break between his old and new lives, and also between his professional persona and his private life, and to keep the latter private. At work he would remain Aurelio Zen, a dedicated slacker. In every other aspect of his life, he would become Alfonso Zembla, whose personality and attributes remained, for the moment, fascinatingly vague.

When the phone rang that morning, Zen was sitting out on the terrace sipping coffee, enjoying the sun and planning his weekend. At ten the carpenter, a nephew of Don Castrese, was coming to give an estimate of cost and time – above all time – needed to extend the shelves in the living room. After that, he'd go to the local restaurant he usually patronized, and then, if he felt up to it, wander around the side-streets around Via Duomo in search of a bedside lamp to replace the bronze horror he had deposited at the back of a cupboard. After so much frenetic activity, a slow start to Sunday seemed in order, punctuated by a visit to the café at the top of the steps which did such wonderful pastries. Then a stroll in the gardens of the nearby Monastery of San Martino, followed by a leisurely lunch somewhere at one of the good places down by the water before proceeding to the rendezvous where Orestina and Filomena Squillace were to break the news of their imminent departure to their undesirable lovers.

So it was with both incredulity and dismay that he answered the phone and heard Giovan Battista Caputo telling him that his presence was 'urgently required' at work. The deadline which he had given the Questura, and then completely forgotten, was about to expire, and according to his deputy the case was no further advanced than it had been then.

'The bastard just sits there grinning at us! We've tried everything – sweet-talking him, knocking him about – but nothing works.'

This, evidently, was as far as Caputo's interrogational skills extended. The carrot and the stick having both failed to produce any result, he was at a loss.

'But it's Saturday!' Zen protested. 'You don't mean to tell me the Questore's working today?'

'Not in person,' Caputo replied. 'But Piscopo is. She's his deputy, and a regular martinet. She's already phoned twice to find out what progress we're making.'

'Christ, what's happening to this country? Work isn't everything. I've got my own life to lead, you know.'

'Eh, eh! Me too, chief, believe me. But this case has raised a lot of dust, and until we either wrap it up or figure out a way to pass it on to someone else . . .'

He left an expressive silence. Zen sighed deeply.

'Very well. I'll be there as soon as I can.'

He depressed the rest on his phone and called Pasquale, the taxi driver of the night before, who had given him a card on receipt of a 10,000-lire tip.

'Any time you need a car, *dottore*, just call my mobile direct and as long as I'm free we can forget about all this nonsense,' he said, gesturing contemptuously at the meter and the logo of the taxi company.

Zen was not surprised to hear that Pasquale *was* free, having got the distinct impression that he went out of his way to remain in this state to service the no doubt lengthy list of 'special clients' on which Zen was now enrolled. He promised to be at the top of the Salita del Petraio in five minutes.

He was, too, or at least in fifteen, which amounts to the same thing in Naples.

'So how do you square all this private enterprise with the company?' Zen enquired as they swept down the double bends of the boulevard towards the coast.

'I don't bother them, *dottore*, they don't bother me. And the consumer benefits! Take the meter, for instance. If you call through the company, I need to show mileage on the meter consistent with the trip booked. Now the meter is a Northern invention, no doubt admirably suited to the conditions of life in that culture. *Ma cca' stamme a Napule, duttò!* The meter can only measure straight lines, which in Naples is never the shortest distance between two points.'

'It simply measures the length of a trip,' Zen objected philosophically. 'How can a given trip be any shorter with the meter turned off?'

'Because nothing is given here, *duttò*, it's fought over. Take this journey. There are a hundred and twenty-eight ways of getting from the Vomero to the port, not counting those which are seriously illegal. Now then, if I have the meter on, which one am I going to choose?'

Zen shrugged.

'I don't really know the city yet.'

'I *know* you don't!' Pasquale retorted triumphantly. 'So you'd get taken the most direct, least intelligent, slowest route, down to the sea and then along the shore. You know how long that would take at this time of day? Half an hour minimum! But why should I care? As long as the meter's running, I'm earning money.'

Still talking non-stop, he drove casually through a red light and turned sharp left down an almost vertical alley paved with cobblestones.

'But once we've agreed a price, it's in my interest to get you to your destination as soon as possible. So instead of sitting in a traffic jam while the meter ticks, I'm using every trick in the book, racking my brains for short cuts and alternative solutions – in short, exploiting every last drop of my professional skill and experience, and all for you, *duttò!*'

The cab shot out into a wider street. Pasquale wound down his window. In the distance, Zen could just hear the freakish ululations of an ambulance siren. Pasquale appeared to sniff the air briefly, then turned right down a narrow street.

'Plus the firm's switchboard is always busy,' he continued as though without a pause. 'It can take you ten, twenty minutes to get through sometimes. The boss won't put anyone but his own nieces and cousins on that work, and there just aren't enough of them when things get busy. Fortunately I happen to know someone with an interest in the mobile phone business who fixed me up with the equipment and hook-up, all at rates you wouldn't believe! I'd have been a fool not to take advantage.'

He negotiated another red light at the intersection of two traffic-clogged streets near the former royal palace. The sound of the siren was louder now.

'Speaking of which, *duttò*, I can get you the same great deal if you're interested. You're in the police, right? I heard you telling those two whores so last night.'

Zen glanced up at the man's wary, intelligent eyes reflected in the rear-view mirror. The cab slowed to a crawl as the ambulance appeared in the traffic behind, its siren and lights forcing the cars to give way. The moment it passed, Pasquale accelerated savagely, darting into the slipstream of the speeding emergency vehicle.

'I'm not really a policeman,' Zen replied. 'I just told those girls that to impress them.'

'Whatever. You'll still find it invaluable, both professionally and personally.'

'Is this really a good idea?' Zen asked as they thundered along, almost touching the rear bumper of the constantly swerving ambulance.

'A good idea? At just a hundred and twenty for the instrument, brand new, Korean manufacture, with a five-year guarantee, plus access fees that are the lowest in the . . .'

Zen started to say something, then broke off, horrified to discover that Pasquale was not looking at the road ahead, where the ambulance had just slammed on its brakes, but at his passenger.

'Believe me, *duttò*, it's not just a convenience but a necessity,' the cabby exclaimed. 'A regular life-saver!'

Parla un linguaggio che non sappiamo

This was the first time that Aurelio Zen had set foot in his nominal place of work at the weekend, when it seemed even more cavernous and deserted than usual, reduced to a purely symbolic status, a mere sign of the State's vacuous omnipresence. It didn't help that Zen felt himself to be an imposter of a particularly phoney and convoluted variety, someone reduced to impersonating himself. It was therefore a relief to see Giovan Battista Caputo swaggering along the corridor with his chilling grin, raptor's eyes and quick, decisive movements.

'The Questura just called again. I told them you'd gone to Rome for an urgent consultation with someone at the ministry and weren't expected back until tonight.'

Zen nodded and pushed open the door to his oppressively large and empty office.

'And the prisoner?'

'He finally opened his mouth.'

'Ah!'

'But only to say that he doesn't speak Italian.'

'So what *does* he speak?'

'English, so he claims.'

Zen sighed massively as he hung up his coat and hat.

'Get him up here,' he told Caputo. 'Also all his belongings, clothes, everything he had on him. And bring me the arresting officer's report.'

'It's there on your desk, chief.'

While he waited for Caputo to bring the prisoner up from the cells, Zen skimmed through the report. It was as impressively precise and detailed as a railway timetable, with every event timed to the nearest minute, every distance measured to the last fraction of a metre – and probably just about as reliable. The only features of interest were the fact that the Greek sailors had selected their victim because he was the first American they had come across who was about their fighting size, and that the man had been attacked while heading *away* from the dock area, apparently towards the main gate. The guard had been unable to say when he had arrived. With the aircraft carrier in port, American sailors had been coming and going all evening, and he had simply waved them through.

Zen looked up as Caputo led in the prisoner. Although on the short side, he was anything but puny in appearance. His limbs were muscular, his belly firm and his chest robust. His copper-coloured skin was covered with black hair everywhere except for his head, which was impressively bald. He was wearing handcuffs, underpants, a vest and nothing else. Caputo pushed him unceremoniously into a chair facing Zen and dumped a black plastic sack on the desk. Zen gazed at the prisoner, who was apparently studying the plasterwork with great attention.

'I'm told you don't understand Italian,' he said, watching the man's eyes.

There was a long silence.

'*Spik only Ingleesh,*' the prisoner replied at length, still giving his full attention to a patch of wall just to the right of one of the room's three windows.

Zen heaved another enormous sigh. Like all Italians, he had been protected from any bruising contact with spoken English thanks to a law – passed originally by the Fascists but, like so many of their laws, never subsequently rescinded – which required all films and other material shown publicly to be dubbed into Italian. On the other hand, he had the advantage of having spent much time at the home of Ellen, his clandestine American girlfriend for some years.

'Oh, yes, I'm the great pretender,' he said, 'adrift in a world of my own. I seem to be what I'm not, you see. Too real is this feeling of make-believe . . .'

'*Only spik Ingleesh.*'

Caputo stood looking on wide-eyed at this novel interrogation, obviously impressed by his superior's unsuspected linguistic skills. Zen leapt to his feet and came around the desk, towering over the prisoner.

'I wonder, wonder who, who wrote the book of love?' he demanded. 'Who wrote the book of love?'

'*Only Ingleesh.*'

'Who was that man? I'd like to shake his hand. He made my babay fall in love with me.'

It was amazing how much he could remember from those rowdy, drunken parties which Ellen used to give at the beginning of July for her expatriate friends. A shame he couldn't let rip here. His pleasing light baritone voice had been much admired at the time. How Americans loved to laugh!

'*Ingleesh only spik.*'

Zen turned sulkily on his heel like an artiste disappointed with his reception.

'Take him away!' he told Caputo.

As the prisoner was led to the door, Zen ripped open the sack of personal belongings and let the contents fall out on the desk. The clothes consisted of a pair of black shoes, a light blue shirt and the US naval uniform. There was also a leather wallet, a scattering of coins, a set of keys, the knife – a vicious item with a long retractable blade sharpened to a razor edge – and a light rectangular slab of grey plastic moulded into slots and grooves, rather like an outsize cassette tape, with a strip of metal contacts mounted on a card inside a recess.

'I take it all this has been dusted?' he called after Caputo, who turned in the doorway.

'Apart from the suspect's own, we found a number of extraneous prints. We're running the files for them now, but we won't hear before next week.'

Zen nodded vaguely, but he was looking not at Caputo but at the prisoner. His head was turned back towards the desk in the room he was just leaving, and his glowing black eyes were fixed on one item with an intensity which seemed capable of melting the plastic.

While Caputo returned the man to his cell, Zen examined the clothing piece by piece. The uniform was strongly made and neatly cut. To his eyes it looked very much like the real thing, apart from the absence of any labels or other identifying marks. The shirt and shoes, on the other hand, were both of Italian manufacture. The soles of the latter were stamped GUCCI.

'Fake,' commented Caputo, coming back in. 'Look at the position of the logo and check the sloppy stitching at the heel. You can buy them in Piazza Garibaldi for thirty thousand a pair. I can get you twenty,' he added automatically.

Zen held up the grey plastic cassette.

'Were any of the extraneous prints on this?' he asked.

Caputo walked over and picked up the sheaf of pages forming the report Zen had skimmed earlier. He turned a few pages.

'There's a partial thumb on one side, and a nice forefinger and obscured second digit on the other.'

Using the edge of the cassette, Zen rapped out the rhythm of one of the songs he had quoted earlier on the desktop.

'All right, Caputo, I need you to do three things. One, take this uniform over to our American allies. I'm pretty sure it's fake too, but we need to make sure.'

He held up the cassette.

'Two, try and find out how we can go about comparing the extraneous prints with those of the crew of that aircraft carrier. Their prints must all be on file somewhere for identification purposes. Make it clear we don't suspect anyone, and it's purely for purposes of elimination.'

'And the third?' asked Caputo, frowning at the prospect of these onerous duties which were going to cut into his weekend.

Zen smiled.

'Ah, that's more amusing. I want you to get together a team of men to harass the prisoner round the clock, twenty-four hours a day.'

Caputo coughed nervously.

'Forgive me saying so, chief, but I don't think we'll get anywhere that way with this son of a bitch. He's as tough as they come. To break him we'd have to use the most extreme methods, and that's bound to leave scarring and internal injuries, to say nothing of the risk of the guy dying on you.'

Zen pursed his lips judiciously.

'I don't think we quite understand one another, Caputo. I'm talking about verbal harassment.'

Caputo looked utterly perplexed.

'But he only speaks English!'

'The only English he speaks is "only spik Ingleesh". My bet is that he's as Neapolitan as you. Your job is to prove it. Set up a roster of men to go down there in shifts and abuse him in dialect. Tell him his mother performs fellatio on Arab carpet salesmen's dogs, that sort of thing. The idea is to get him to respond. It doesn't matter what he says, just the fact that he understands what's being said to him. OK?'

Caputo gave a laugh as sharp as a razor cut.

'I'll get Santanna on the job. When it comes to this sort of thing, he's a virtuoso.'

'Go to work on him until he cracks and says something in return. Then I want you to *really* go to work on him. I need a name, an address, anything we can pass on to the Questura to get this son of a bitch off our backs.'

He headed for the door.

'And if *la Piscopo* calls again?' asked Caputo.

Zen smiled thinly.

'Tell her I'm in Rome following up an important lead.'

Caputo gave an exaggerated wink.

'Right! Oh, before I forget, I managed to get those tickets for you.'

He handed Zen an envelope.

'My brother-in-law works backstage at San Carlo and gets comps to all the shows. Turns out he doesn't fancy this one, so if they're any use to you . . .'

Zen pocketed the envelope gracefully.

'Thanks, Caputo. Once we get this stabbing business sorted out, I think you're due for some leave. A couple of weeks sound good to you? You could spend some time with the wife and kiddies to make up for all this involuntary overtime.'

Caputo scowled.

'I'd rather come to work! But I have a few commercial interests which need a little personal attention. You know how it is.'

'That's the trouble with this country,' Zen agreed, putting the plastic cassette away in his coat pocket. 'If you don't do it yourself, it doesn't get done.'

Soldati d'onore

At about the time Aurelio Zen left his office, allegedly to go to Rome, two other policemen entered a superficially similar room in a building at the foot of the Vomero, just off Via Francesco Crispi, about half a mile from Zen's house as crows flew and footballs rolled. There was the same sense of excessive space, the same bleak décor, the same functional furniture, the same combination of chaotic clutter and impersonal neatness.

There, however, the similarities ended. For here, each desk sported a smart new Olivetti computer, all networked to each other and to a host of other such work-stations across the country. Phone calls were routed via the military communications system, with digital encoding to prevent interception. The windows were toughened against bullets and explosives, and incorporated a layer of metallic material designed to baffle electronic eavesdropping.

For this was the local headquarters of the *Direzione Investigativa AntiMafia*, an élite unit comprising hand-picked members of the *Carabinieri*, the police and the *Guardia di Finanza*, which had been created specifically to combat organized crime. The former regime's commitment to this particular struggle had always been a matter of some doubt, to say the least, and one of its most prominent and illustrious figures was currently facing trial on charges of having been, as many had long suspected, 'the Mafia's man in Rome'.

One of the first steps of the new government had therefore been to throw a conspicuous amount of money at the DIA, in an effort to demonstrate the difference between their predecessors' ambiguous and dilatory approach and the determination of these bold new brooms to sweep the country clean. Whether this determination also held good on a political level was of course another question, and one which the two men chatting quietly in the third-floor office had often discussed.

Not at work, though, in however quiet a voice. For rumour had it that when the building had been upgraded to incorporate the various technological marvels of which it now disposed, it had also been fitted with a series of extremely sensitive microphones which could pick up the merest whisper of sound in any corner of any corridor or room, toilets included. There had even been jokes concerning one of the officers on the team, whose bowel movements were of legendary volume, 'making a big noise for himself in Rome'.

No one had been able to confirm or deny the existence of this surveillance system, still less identify who, exactly, might have access to the results, but the prevailing wisdom held that it was advisable to avoid raising potentially sensitive issues while on the premises. The two men in question have no need to worry about this, however, for they are merely discussing their work, and in particular a new file which they have opened concerning one Ermanno Vallifuoco, who has just been reported missing by his family following his failure to return from a trip into town, supposedly to meet two business associates at a famous hotel on Via Partenope.

One problem is that each of these 'associates' claims to have spent the evening in question elsewhere, one at a restaurant (ten witnesses) and the other at home (fourteen, of whom five not directly related to the family), and that each denies ever having arranged to meet Vallifuoco in the first place. But what has brought the matter to the attention of the DIA is the fact that this is the third such disappearance in as many weeks, and two of the presumed victims are successful local businessmen linked to the Camorra and the other a prominent figure in local government.

Attilio Abate, the first man to vanish, failed to return after going out one night to walk his dog in streets surrounding his villa in Baia. The animal, a Great Dane, also disappeared. Abate was reputed to be one of the wealthiest men in the city, the owner of a company which had won substantial government contracts for the supply of military uniforms, bed linen and such items. At first a kidnap was suspected, although no ransom note was received. Then, ten days later, the second man went missing.

Luca Della Ragione had been a prominent member of the centre-right coalition which ruled the Campania region until the recent upheavals. Following the earthquake which devastated the inland region of Irpinia in 1980, money poured in from national and international sources, but for one reason or another a substantial proportion of this largesse not only failed to reach the tens of thousands shivering in their makeshift tent cities, but also vanished from the government's accounts. It had since been alleged that Luca Della Ragione was responsible for facilitating this financial conjuring trick, and that he also knew the whereabouts of the missing funds. The facts concerning these matters were likely to remain obscure, since he had also gone missing. Early one morning he had left the modern apartment block on Via Greco where he lived for a briefing with his lawyer before a court appearance, and had never been seen again. His car was found in the street, the alarm defused and the doors unlocked, but despite an extensive search and investigation there had been no further sign of Della Ragione. And now a third name had joined this select list . . .

'I suppose we'd better get out and circulate,' said one of the men, an aggressive-looking individual with a shock of jet-black hair and the build of a middle-weight boxer.

'I've already put out a few feelers,' replied the other. He was shorter and slighter, wiry and slightly feral in appearance, with a scar on his left cheekbone and an incipient bald spot nestling amid his curly, light-brown hair.

'And?'

'Nothing. No one's heard anything, or if they have they're not talking. But to be honest they seemed as mystified about it as everyone else. Only more worried, of course.'

Neither officer was in uniform, and their style of dress was completely different. The shorter one wore jeans, running shoes and an open-neck denim shirt. His companion was in a very expensive suit, a silk shirt and tie and black oxfords with a flawless mirror finish.

'Somebody must know something,' he said.

'Unless Ermanno had a hand in his own disappearance . . .'

'Even then, somebody must be hiding him out.'

'But not necessarily anyone known to us. He was under judicial advisement, just like Abate and Della Ragione. Like them, he has an interest in lying low until . . .'

He broke off, glancing at the wall. The two men exchanged a glance.

'Until the situation stabilizes,' the elegant one suggested. 'And there are plenty of other people who have an interest in postponing judicial enquiries into their cases until . . .'

'Until the situation stabilizes,' his companion concluded with a nod. 'Exactly. In which case there isn't a chance of us finding out anything useful. You can't play both sides against the middle if they *are* the middle.'

There was silence for a while.

'Marotta seems to have disappeared too,' the man in the Lacoste shirt said casually. 'Do you think there could be a link?'

The other looked sceptical.

'I don't see it. Marotta's just a gofer, when all's said and done. The other three are in the upper echelons of the Gaetano clan, the command and supply level. I could see why they might want to take them out of circulation, but Marotta? He doesn't know enough to be a danger to anyone but himself. They'd just hand him over and let him sweat it out.'

Another silence.

'Vallifuoco used to frequent prostitutes,' the man in the suit murmured as though to himself.

'So?'

'Maybe that's where he went last night, under cover of that business meeting.'

His companion considered this a moment.

'Maybe. We could look into the car, too. He drove a late model Jaguar, very distinctive.'

'One of the whores I spoke to said he had very particular tastes. Bondage, whipping, drawing blood, that kind of thing. Apparently he used a different woman every time. He blindfolded them and took them to a place he had somewhere near the station where he kept the gear he used for these sessions.

They could all remember what the place looked like inside well enough, but none of them has any precise idea where it is.'

'Maybe that's where he's hiding out.'

'That's where I'm going to start, anyway. And you?'

The other man shrugged.

'I thought I might look into the car. That's harder to hide than a man. Probably won't get anywhere, but it'll make the time pass more quickly.'

As before, they exchanged a glance of silent collusion.

'I wish I knew what was going on!' the man in the suit exclaimed in a tone of irritation.

The other shrugged again.

'We'll just have to wait and see. It might even be good news, who knows? Maybe there's been a change of heart. At management level, so to speak.'

They got to their feet.

'See you tomorrow, then,' said the elegant man.

'Good hunting.'

'You too.'

Giochiamo!

'So is it really beautiful?'

'It has its charms.'

'You're going to stay there for ever?'

'When's that? All I know is that in a few more years I can retire, and a few years after that . . .'

'You never used to be morbid, Aurelio.'

'Blame it on Naples. The place reeks of mortality.'

'I thought it reeked of rancid oil and bad drains.'

'It comes to the same thing in the end.'

They were sitting at a corner table in a restaurant near Rome's main railway station. It was called *Bella Napoli*, whence Gilberto Nieddu's original question. They had the place to themselves, this being just about its only virtue. The décor – all seashells, mandolins, dusty bottles of undrinkable wine, fishing nets and photographic murals of Vesuvius and the bay – had been applied with a heavy hand, and the food couldn't begin to redeem it. Gilberto had suggested that they stick to pizza, on the grounds that they surely couldn't screw that up.

'So did you find anything?' asked Zen, taking another bite which confirmed beyond doubt that, yes, indeed they could.

Gilberto Nieddu glugged some beer and lit a cigarette.

'It's a joke! When you called me from Naples, I thought we were talking about some cutting-edge product, so I started calling around. That meant putting on my disguise and creeping out to a bar, of course. Then I had to scare up someone with the equipment to run whatever it was you were bringing.'

He sat back, smoking contentedly.

'And?' prompted Zen edgily.

'That meant telling Rosa where I was going. One thing my attorney was very clear about was that I must never ever leave home without leaving an accurate itinerary and estimated time of arrival. Apparently some people in my position have been snatched off the street and pressured into doing some deal before their family or lawyer even knows what's happened . . .'

'But you didn't tell Rosa about me?' Zen interrupted.

'Of course not! We've all got our little problems, Aurelio. You respect mine and I'll respect yours.'

This was true enough, although in reality their problems were of a very different order. Zen's involved sneaking up to Rome without calling in to visit his mother. Since Signora Zen had become a sort of honorary granny to the Nieddu children, this in turn meant seeing Gilberto Nieddu without his wife finding out. If Rosa learned about Zen's visit, it would inevitably get back to Giustiniana and he would never hear the end of it.

Gilberto's problems were altogether more serious. But despite the fact that the Sardinian was one of his oldest friends, Zen found it hard not to feel slightly smug about them. Since leaving the police, Nieddu had built up a thriving business in the electronic surveillance field, specializing in industrial espionage. He had never lost an opportunity of gloating more or less openly to Zen about his successes out there in the 'real world', the implication being that it was at once lazy and unenterprising of Zen to keep slogging away at his safe but dead-end *statale* job when such rich pickings were to be had, for those with the get-up-and-go to pursue them, in the private sector.

But Gilberto was no longer gloating. A former client of his company, Paragon Security, had brought himself to the attention of the anti-corruption *Mani Pulite* team of judges in connection with a contract for the widening of a motorway in Lombardy. In the course of a lengthy interrogation, one of the regional politicians involved revealed that, in addition to the sums specified in the winning bid, several billion lire had also changed hands privately.

One aspect of the affair of particular interest to the authorities was how the entrepreneur in question managed to be so well-informed about the competing bids and bribes being offered by other firms, all of which, thanks to the seizure of his extensive records, were also under investigation. In the circumstances, the contractor felt no compunction in throwing a minnow like Nieddu to the judges, in the hope – vain, as it proved – of appeasing their feeding frenzy for a while.

It being just as onerous and risky to remove bugging devices as to install them, they were still in place. The truth of the contractor's allegations was proven, and Paragon Security itself came under investigation. Unfortunately, in addition to providing a range of services which were illegal in the first place, Gilberto Nieddu had also been fiddling his taxes. According to the declarations he filed, he had been earning barely more than Aurelio Zen's modest stipend from the State. The sums disbursed by his clients, though, were larger than this by a factor of about ten. The judges were naturally curious to learn how he proposed to account for this discrepancy.

'My only hope is Wojtyla,' Gilberto announced in a mournful voice when he met his friend at Stazione Termini that afternoon.

Zen looked askance.

'How he help you?'

'By dying. They still have an amnesty whenever a new Pope is elected. Anyone convicted of a non-violent crime with five years or less to serve gets out. My lawyer – who incidentally has already accounted for about half the assets I'd salted away where the judges can't get at them – reckons he can get me off with five to seven, less whatever I've served before being brought to trial. So it's a fine calculation. For example, if I get six, with nine months detention pre-trial, I want the big Polack to buy the dacha three months after sentencing. On the other hand if I get five, he should drop dead right away. It's about time, anyway. Rosa and her friends are all ready to convert to Islam. They say it's less repressive for women.'

He swallowed some more beer and lit another cigarette.

'On the other hand, of course, the case may never come to court. There seems to be a very encouraging political vacuum at the top these days. People are starting to realize that this 'Clean Hands' mentality is getting out of control. This sort of inquisitorial moralism is completely alien to our culture. Besides, if you really pursued it to its logical conclusion, you'd have to lock up eighty per cent of the population!'

'Thereby providing jobs as jailers for the other twenty,' Zen put in. 'Who says a managed economy doesn't work?'

Joking aside, Nieddu's position was anything but enviable. Although still at liberty, his office had been sealed, his assets seized and his business – so carefully built up over many years – ruined overnight. He was liable to be arrested at any moment, and meanwhile led a fugitive existence, shunned by his former friends and associates, waiting for the axe to fall.

'Rosa's doing the best she can,' he remarked in a maudlin tone, 'but at times she just goes to pieces completely. It's the effect this is going to have on the children we worry about most. To be honest, if it hadn't been for your mother giving us a break from time to time, I don't think we'd have been able to make it. She's a real treasure!'

'Certainly,' said Zen neutrally.

Nieddu produced a grey plastic cassette from his pocket and passed it across the table.

'Well?' asked Zen.

Nieddu rolled his eyes up to the ceiling.

'After all that, it turned out to be just a video game! One of those cartridges you buy and plug into a machine hooked up to your TV. Come to think of it, you wouldn't know. You don't have kids.'

Zen reached out idly and picked up the cigarette packet lying on the table.

'That's all? Just a game?'

'What were you expecting?' asked Nieddu.

His friend shrugged.

'I don't know.'

'Why are you so interested in it?'

Zen gestured evasively.

'It's a long story,'

He opened the open pack of cigarettes and took one.

'May I?'

Nieddu, who had no idea that Zen had supposedly given up smoking, waved freely.

'So tell me about this game,' Zen said, pushing his failed pizza aside.

'What is there to say? It's like any other. The scenery and cast may change, but the object is always the same. You're trying to beat the system, access higher levels and rack up as many points and lives as possible.'

Zen smoked in silence, nodding soporifically.

'Sounds like the story of my life,' he murmured.

'In this case you're a rogue cop trying to clean up a city which has been taken over by the mob. You also have to protect these beautiful women that the bad guys are out to get, and of course watch your own back. At least, that's the opening scenario. I didn't have time to find out what happens once you get past the first level.'

'Ah, I don't expect either of us will ever do that,' Zen commented enigmatically.

'You still haven't told me why you're so interested in it,' Nieddu reminded him.

Zen sighed.

'Someone got in a knife fight in the port. We don't know who he is or what he was doing there. I hoped this might supply some of the answers.'

Nieddu seemed surprisingly interested in this inconsequential story.

'The game cassette was in his possession?'

'That's right.'

'Was he entering or leaving the port at the time?'

'Leaving.'

'Were there any foreign ships at the time? Especially Japanese or American?'

Zen frowned.

'What are you getting at, Gilberto?'

Nieddu suddenly relaxed and gave one of his huge infectious laughs.

'You're right! No reason I should do your job for you. I've got enough problems of my own as it is.'

Zen held up the grey plastic cassette.

'You think this was being smuggled in? Why would they bother to do that if you can buy it over the counter?'

Nieddu stood up.

'Ah, well, that's the question. Anyway, I must be going. I promised Rosa I wouldn't be late.'

He got out his wallet and made a show of offering to pay the bill, but Zen snatched it away.

'This is the least I can do in return for your help, Gilberto. I only wish I could do something about your real problems. Perhaps I'll get one of my Neapolitan contacts to ask San Gennaro to intercede for you. I'm told he's very effective.'

Gilberto Nieddu laughed once again.

'Actually, I think that a miracle may already have occurred.'

Zen looked at him curiously.

'What do you mean?'

Nieddu shrugged.

'Oh, I don't know. I just have a feeling that my luck is about to change.'

The two men exchanged an opaque glance. Zen started towards the door, then turned back.

'Let me have another cigarette, will you?'

Nieddu handed him the pack.

'Can I have a light too?' Zen added. 'I seem to have left mine at home.'

Nieddu laughed yet again, this time with a marked edge.

'You'll forget your own name next, Aurelio!'

I due creduli sposi

Another evening, another restaurant. This one also served Neapolitan specialities, but here no attempt had been made to create a supposedly characteristic décor evoking the city as it appeared through the misty eyes of expatriate nostalgia: colourful, chaotic, cheap and cheerful. For this establishment *was* in Naples, or more precisely in Posillipo, one of the most beautiful and exclusive neighbourhoods on the bay, situated at the tip of a small headland shaded by palms and lemon trees and overlooking the sea.

At a table right up against the railings at the very edge of the terrace, Gesualdo Troise and Sabatino Capuozzo sat looking about them with a distinct air of unease.

'Fancy place,' said Sabatino. 'Fancy prices too, I bet.'

Gesualdo shrugged.

'We'll have to get used to it. This is the kind of thing the girls have been brought up to take for granted.'

'Funny, when you think where the money came from.'

A waiter, severely correct in his starched jacket, appeared at their table. Despite their unexceptionable suits and ties, he eyed them with barely concealed disdain, as aware as they themselves that they were out of their depth here. Gesualdo informed him shortly that they were waiting for some friends to join them. The waiter removed an invisible speck from the immaculate tablecloth and ejected it unceremoniously over the railing.

'*Siente, cumpagne mije,*' murmured Sabatino.

The waiter turned around with an expression of astonishment at this unwonted familiarity. Then he caught sight of the pistol. It was in a shoulder-holster just visible in the hollow which Sabatino had deliberately created by leaning forward so that his jacket bulged open.

66

'These friends are young ladies from a very important family,' Sabatino told him seriously. 'We want them to have a good time, understand?'

'Of course,' the waiter replied in a robotic tone.

'We may eat, we may not, but we want the best of everything. Good stuff, prompt service, no bullshit. If the evening's a success, we won't forget you.'

'Even less if it isn't,' added Gesualdo.

The waiter nodded rapidly.

'Don't worry, sir. I'll take care of everything myself.'

He departed rapidly into the elegant converted villa on the hillside behind them containing the bar and the internal dining room. Gesualdo sighed loudly.

'That's going to cost us another Caravaggio.'

Sabatino flashed his wallet, bulging with 50,000-lire banknotes bearing the likeness of this artist.

'What else would I spend it on? Nothing's too good for Filomena. She deserves the best there is.'

From a side pocket of the wallet, he took a strip of photographs, much creased with wear.

'God, she's adorable!' he sighed.

Gesualdo raised an eyebrow. Reaching into his jacket, he produced a studio photograph framed in cardboard and enclosed in a plastic slip-case.

'"She deserves the best there is," he says, and then drops a whole two thou at a passport machine. This cost me a hundred thou, but it's worth every lira.'

He turned the photograph towards his friend.

'Doesn't she look lovely?'

Sabatino smiled wryly.

'If anyone had told me a year ago that we'd be sitting here mooning over a couple of girls' snapshots, I'd have said he was crazy.'

Gesualdo nodded.

'I never expected this to happen to me. I never really believed it happened to anybody, except in the movies.'

'And just think, if their car hadn't broken down that time, we would never have met them.'

'Or if we hadn't taken that short cut because the traffic was so bad. You didn't want me to make that illegal left turn, remember? And I said, "If we get arrested, it won't be for a traffic violation!"'

'Well, you didn't want to stop and help them change the tyre. "It could be a trap," you said. "They get tourists that way all the time."'

Gesualdo sighed.

'Yet the moment I got out of the car and saw her standing there, I knew that was it. For life.'

'Me too,' agreed Sabatino.

The exalted look abruptly drained from Gesualdo's face.

'Except that their mother will never consent to the idea of them marrying the likes of us.'

'It must be awful for them, having to sneak out every time they want to see us.'

'And it's horrible for us having to lie to them the whole time, not being able to introduce them to our families and friends. It's almost enough to make me want to chuck the whole thing in.'

Sabatino looked at him in astonishment.

'The girls, you mean?'

'Of course not!' Gesualdo replied indignantly. 'This line of work, I mean. Pack it in and apply for a regular job.'

Sabatino smiled at him.

'You'd go out of your mind with boredom by the end of the first week. And then there's the money.'

Gesualdo nodded.

'I suppose you're right. Another few years and we can go straight.'

'Filomena said she'd marry me now, even without her mother's consent.'

'Orestina told me the same. But you know we can't. Not with the risks we run every day.'

'And which they'd have to share. The opposition can get pretty vindictive when things don't go their way. Remember when Don Fortunato's brother fell from grace? They couldn't get to him, so they killed his sister, his wife and his eldest kid.'

'The only thing to do is stick it out and hope they wait for us.'

He glanced at his watch.

'Where are they, anyhow? They should be here by now.'

As if on cue, there was a sound of voices from inside the restaurant building. The two men turned round hopefully, but the lone figure which emerged from the garden door of the villa was a man. With a purposeful but unhurried stride he crossed over to the table where Gesualdo and Sabatino were sitting.

'Good evening, gentlemen.'

His accent was harsh and alien. The two men looked up at him warily.

'Signor Gesualdo?' the man asked, looking at Sabatino.

Gesualdo got to his feet.

'That's me,' he said shortly.

'Ah, excuse me! And you must be Signor Sabatino,' the man exclaimed. 'Allow me to introduce myself. Alfonso Zembla, a friend of the Squillace family. May I?'

He sat down. After a momentary hesitation, Gesualdo followed suit. The newcomer held up his hands apologetically.

'I'm sorry to force myself on you like this,' he said in a tone of embarrassment. 'I don't mean to intrude, but . . . It's difficult to know where to begin. You see, your girlfriends . . . I'm afraid I have bad news.'

Gesualdo reached over the table and clutched the stranger's arm.

'Are they dead?'

'No.'

'Injured?'

'No.'

'*Pregnant?*' breathed Sabatino.

'Not that, either. The fact is, they've just heard that they've won a scholarship to study English at a school in London. Two other students had to cancel at the last minute, and Orestina and Filomena were next on the list. But they have to leave tonight.'

'Tonight?' both men cried together.

Aurelio Zen nodded sternly.

'They have to register for the course tomorrow morning. That means catching the last flight out tonight.'

Utterly lost for words, Sabatino looked helplessly at Gesualdo, then back at Zen.

'You mean they've left already? Can't we at least say good-bye? Where are they?'

'They're waiting outside in the taxi that's to take them to the airport. They were afraid to break the news to you themselves – they were afraid you'd be angry – so they asked me to do it.'

He consulted his watch.

'There's still a few minutes to spare. I'll have them come in, shall I?'

Without waiting for a response, he turned and signalled to the waiter, who had been hovering at the entrance to the restaurant. Zen got to his feet and withdrew discreetly. As he reached the doorway to the building, Orestina and Filomena appeared, soberly but expensively dressed in the military-style greatcoats which were currently in fashion.

'Not a word about our bet, now!' Zen murmured.

The two women swept past without a word. Zen took a seat at the bar inside and ordered an aperitif which he sipped while watching the brightly lit scene outside on the terrace.

Side by side, the women approached the table where their lovers were sitting. They seemed nervous and hesitant. The two men got to their feet and confronted them with expressions of confusion, dismay and self-pity. For a moment no one said anything, then each couple started speaking rapidly, the men questioning and complaining, the women explaining and justifying. The occasional phrase drifted in through the open door, wafted on the breeze laden with the scent of herbs and flowers.

'. . . so sudden . . .'

'. . . just heard today . . .'

'. . . such a dangerous city . . .'

'. . . not any more than here . . .'

'. . . with no friends, no family . . .'

'. . . perfectly capable of looking after . . .'

'. . . attacked or robbed, perhaps even . . .'

'. . . in a very safe area right in the . . .'

'. . . won't see you for . . .'

'. . . only a few weeks . . . .'

Finally they fell silent. The men gripped their lovers' arms, the women leaned forward to be held and kissed. The dissonant rumble of a horn sounded outside in the car park.

'That must be for us!' cried Orestina, pulling free of Gesualdo's embrace. 'It's time to go.'

She sounded shocked, as though the reality of departure had only just come home to her. Zen walked out on to the terrace.

'Come on, girls! The taxi's waiting!'

The two young couples hugged each other protectively.

'The flight closes in thirty minutes,' Zen insisted. 'Pasquale says he can't guarantee getting you there in time unless you leave right away.'

Gesualdo grasped Orestina tightly.

'Promise you'll call me every day.'

'Of course!' she replied.

'Call me twice, if you can,' Sabatino told Filomena.

Watching from the doorway, Zen felt torn between a desire to laugh at the intensity of their emotion, and an inexplicable melancholy quite out of keeping with the realities of a situation which, after all, he himself had engineered.

It was only when the women finally extricated themselves from their lovers' arms and turned to go that he finally understood that what he was witnessing was not the callow amateur dramatics of four self-obsessed young people who have to part for a few weeks. Although none of them was aware of it, they were saying goodbye not just to each other, for a while, but to something infinitely more intimate and precious, and for ever.

Un poco di sospetto

Gesualdo and Sabatino sat quite still at their table, staring at the ground as though in shock. They were still there when Aurelio Zen returned, having escorted Orestina and Filomena out to the waiting taxi.

'Where are they?' muttered Sabatino, looking up with a start.

'They've gone,' Zen told him.

'It's all so sudden!' Gesualdo exclaimed.

He seemed to be talking to himself. Zen sat down between them.

'Pull yourselves together, lads! It's not the end of the world. In fact, it might even be helpful.'

'Helpful?' said Gesualdo aggressively, all his emotion bursting out. 'And what's your interest in all this, anyway?'

Zen handed them each one of the cards he had had engraved in the name Alfonso Zembla.

'If you drop by here this evening between nine and ten, I'll tell you. And I'll also tell you a really easy way in which you can get yourself into the good graces of your sweethearts' mother.'

The men took the cards, but it was clear that their thoughts were elsewhere. Silence fell. Over to the east, above the city, an airplane lumbered laboriously into the pale azure sky, its engines straining at the seemingly impossible task of lifting such a massive weight. Gesualdo and Sabatino followed it with their eyes, willing it to succeed. The plane climbed steadily up through the clear, still air, out over the calm waters of the bay, its lights winking brightly against the deeper blue of the gathering dusk, then turned slowly in a wide circle over the shadowy outline of the peninsula and islands, heading north.

Gesualdo rose, followed by Sabatino. Without a word to Zen, they walked off across and into the restaurant. Zen clicked his fingers to summon the waiter.

'Bring me the same again,' he told him. 'And a phone.'

When the phone arrived, on a long white cable, he called Valeria.

'They're on their way,' he said.

'How did it go?'

'The two lads seem to be taking it very hard, but that could work to our advantage. People who exaggerate their emotions are usually the first to change them.'

Outside the restaurant, Gesualdo and Sabatino walked over to their parked cars.

'I still can't believe it,' said Sabatino, shaking his head slowly.

'Maybe because it isn't true,' suggested Gesualdo.

Sabatino stopped dead, staring at him.

'What do you mean?'

A shrug.

'I don't know. But I don't quite buy this. The girls take off without any notice, supposedly to study English. How do we know where they've gone?'

'We can call them,' said Sabatino.

Gesualdo shook his head.

'They didn't leave a number, did they? Or an address. Just the name of some school that may not even exist, for all we know.'

'Filomena said she'd call me twice a day!' protested Sabatino.

'Yes, but from where? They could be anywhere in the country, or abroad for that matter. This could all be a ruse to get them out of our influence. I sense the fine hand of their mother in all this. And this Alfonso Zembla character gives me the creeps. Where did *he* spring from?'

'"A friend of the family," he said. I've never heard Filomena mention him before. And what's he doing here in Naples? With that accent, he has to be from somewhere in the North.'

He took out the card Zen gave him and inspected the address.

'You think we should go?' he asked his friend.

'Of course. If this is some kind of set-up, Zembla has to be in on it. Maybe we can worm it out of him. He didn't seem that bright to me.'

Sabatino unlocked his car.

'Maybe we're getting a little carried away here,' he said with a loosening-up gesture of his right hand. 'That's the trouble with being in this line of work. You end up thinking that everyone's as devious as the people we hang out with.'

'I hope you're right.'

Sabatino got into his car.

'I'm going round to Dario's to play cards for a while, put my ear to the ground about this other business. You want to come?'

Gesualdo shook his head.

'I've got an appointment.'

'Business or pleasure?'

'Business. I'll swing by and pick you up around nine.'

'Take care.'

'You too.'

Gesualdo drove out of the car park along a steep, narrow, switchback street that ended at the main road a few hundred metres up the hillside. There he turned right, coasting down the cobbled corniche whose extensive views out over the bay have proved fatal to so many drivers. Dipping down to water level at Mergellina, he drove along the front past the gardens of the Villa Communale and back into the city.

In the inverted ghetto of Posillipo, where the wealthy and powerful have paraded their wealth and power for well over two thousand years, Gesualdo had felt ill at ease, an interloper. The shocking news of the girls' departure was fully in keeping with other subliminal messages he was picking up, a kind of white noise which the place generated along with the obedient hum of luxury cars, the murmur of conversation between people who never need to raise their voices to be heard, the silence of exclusion and the discreet hushing of a tame, respectful sea.

Here, plunged into the deafening clamour and random trajectories of the streets, he was at home once more, back in the innards of the city he knew so well. He turned out of Piazza dei Martiri into a gateway in the wall of a nineteenth-century *palazzo*. Inside a concrete ramp led steeply down into a cavern, its dimensions too huge and complex to be grasped at once. The vaulted ceiling, barely visible in the gloom, must have been over fifty feet high. The space below extended back at least twice that distance, irregular in shape and divided by walls of bare stone left to support the streets and houses on the hill above.

Gesualdo angled his car into a vacant slot in the middle of one of the rows of vehicles parked there, for a fee, by office workers and other commuters. Unlike them, however, he did not walk back the way he had driven in, towards the steps leading up to street level, but the other way, into the deepest recesses of the subterranean car park. The ground underfoot was dusty with particles of stone scuffed up from the soft volcanic tufa forming the walls, floor and ceiling of this gigantic excavation, one of a series of such cavities underlying the entire city.

It was the Greeks who first realized that the stratum of solidified lava beneath their new city, Neapolis, was at once easy to extract and work, and strong enough to resist collapse. Both they and the Romans exploited this fact to install a complex system of subterranean aqueducts, reservoirs, road tunnels and storage spaces for grain, oil and other goods. The temperature at these depths was consistently cool, the humidity constant.

But the boom period for the underground city dated from the Spanish conquest. In one of the earliest attempts to enforce zoning regulations within the city walls, the invaders prohibitively taxed the importation of building materials. The response of the inhabitants was to reopen the ancient tunnels and caverns, this time as secret quarries, and to use the tufa to extend or amplify their homes. The fact that they were thus undermining the very houses they were constructing apparently struck no one as ironical.

The branch of the cavern which Gesualdo was following narrowed progressively to form a giant ravine no more than ten feet across, but even higher than the main body of the cave. The lower walls had been widened, presumably to accommodate the vehicles whose tire tracks were imprinted in the fine dust covering the ground. The passage ended at a pair of rusty iron doors, from behind which a variety of industrial noises were audible: drilling, sanding, hammering. Occasional brief flashes of incredible brilliance enlivened the prevailing darkness.

Gesualdo pressed a button mounted beside the doors. After a long pause, a muffled voice inside said something incomprehensible. Gesualdo leant forward, pressing his face to the metal.

'Roberto sent me,' he shouted.

Another long pause ensued. Then there was the sound of a bolt being drawn back, and a man's face appeared between the two doors. He was wearing welding goggles, through which he inspected the intruder cautiously.

'It's about a car,' said Gesualdo.

Troppo vero

When the phone rang the first time, Zen assumed it must be work. On his return from the trip to consult Gilberto Nieḍdu in Rome, he had called by the port and dropped off the grey cassette with the duty officer, a young man named Pastorelli who had merely saluted Zen and returned to a volume of Mickey Mouse comics printed on what looked like crudely recycled toilet paper. After returning the video game to the plastic bag containing the suspect's other belongings, Zen had departed as inconspicuously as he arrived.

By dint of staying out of the house most of the next day, he had managed to avoid hearing anything further about the progress – or, more likely, the lack of it – of the case to which he was supposedly devoting his every waking hour. He realized that this ostrich approach to problem-solving was widely regarded as immature and escapist, but where, he demanded of the hypothetical sneerers, had all his clear thinking and tireless energy got him in the past? To Naples, was the answer, and when in Naples . . .

Sooner or later, nevertheless, he had to go home to meet the new tenants of the lower flat and see them properly installed. It was while he was overseeing this operation that the phone started ringing upstairs. Obedient to his 'what I don't know can't hurt me' philosophy, he decided to let the machine take it. It was not until some time later, on one of his trips up to his own flat in search of decorative materials to fake the influence of a woman's hand below – and also to remove various personal effects which might reveal more about him than he wished strangers to know – that he finally bothered to listen to the message.

'So you were in town yesterday and didn't even bother to come and see your poor mother who you've abandoned here like some old coat you've no more use for now you've gone native in the sunny south with some slut you've picked up like that time in Venice with Rosalba's baby who may I remind you happens to be my God-daughter apart from anything else which makes you her great-Godfather but of course that didn't stop you from going right ahead and ditching Tania who I'd just begun to think of as part of the family and someone who might one day take the place of your poor wife Luisella who just happens to be in Rome for a week and actually took the trouble to come round here and visit me unlike some I could mention even though you walked out on her fifteen years ago the same way you do on all the women in your life including your mother who I'd have thought might feel entitled to a little consideration seeing as how you wouldn't even be here today if it hadn't been for me carrying you in my belly all those long months and in wartime too with the shortages and the fear and my husband disappearing the way he did which is I suppose where you get it from not that that's any excuse and I certainly don't see why I should be punished for something I suffered enough from at the time God knows instead of which you hide there behind the answering machine like the coward you are while I sit here all alone and unloved at my age in a strange city with no one to care for me – *sola, perduta, abbandonata!*'

This was the recorded version. When he called her back, Zen was treated to a live encore, preceded by a lengthy recitative explaining how she heard about his visit from Rosa Nieddu, who 'accidentally let it slip' when she came by to drop off the girls that morning so that she could drive Gilberto to the airport and how at first she couldn't believe what she'd heard and then Rosa tried to pretend she hadn't said it and then broke down and confessed everything and they had both burst into tears and hugged each other.

'Ah, the female mafia on the job again!' murmured Zen, feeling drenched in oestrogen as though in cheap scent.

Fortunately his mother was not listening.

'Then later on Luisella called to say she needed to get in touch with you about the divorce settlement . . .'

'What? I haven't seen her for ten years! We haven't lived together for . . .'

'But you're still married to her, Aurelio, and now she's met someone else and wants to have children before it's too late. I hope you don't mind, but I did just say that as you've made all that money from that American family I'm sure you'll have no trouble agreeing to any suggestions which her lawyers may make.'

'Are you out of your mind, mamma?'

'Then that evening Tania dropped round so naturally I told her about you coming all the way up here to chat about video games with your pal Gilberto and not even bothering to come and see your poor mother who you've abandoned here like some old coat you've no more use for now you've moved to the sunny south and gone native . . .'

And so on, for some time. And when Zen finally succeeded in getting the conversation back on track, it promptly ran right over him.

'So then Tania told me her news. You'll never guess what's happened!'

'I suppose she wants to get married so that she can divorce me and get her hands on the American money you no doubt told her about too.'

'She *does* want to marry you, Aurelio, but not for your money. It's for the child.'

'Whose child?'

'Yours, of course! She's pregnant.'

During his previous sojourn in Naples, many years ago, Zen had investigated a particularly unpleasant killing in which an informer was tied to a table and his skull perforated by an electric drill. Zen's present sensations appeared to approximate, however feebly, the experiences of the victim. He did a number of rapid mental calculations involving dates, times and places. It was, he concluded, just possible.

'You didn't tell them where I am, did you? Don't give them this number! Don't even tell them I'm in Naples!'

'Why shouldn't I tell them? Luisella's your wife and Tania's the mother of your child – my grandchild. They're family, Aurelio.'

'For God's sake, mamma! They're just trying to get their hands on my money now I finally have some after all these years. Women are all the same!'

'Don't you use that tone of voice with me, Aurelio! None of this would have happened if you'd had the simple common decency to pay me a visit when you were in town. I don't expect much, God knows, only a few minutes of your time once every couple of weeks. Is that too much to ask?'

Many years' experience of interrogations had left Aurelio Zen with a keen sense of when and how to turn the tables.

'Why don't you come down here?' he suggested.

The flow of aggrieved verbiage ceased. There was a shocked silence.

'To Naples?' his mother demanded at last, her voice a whisper. 'Are you crazy?'

'It's not as bad as it's made out, mamma. I've been pleasantly surprised by the . . .'

'First you drag me down to the South, now you expect me to move to Africa!'

'Not to live, of course. But you might think about spending a few days here some time . . .'

'If anything, I'll go back to Venice! I can't see any less of you than I do already, and if I've got to live all alone I might as well do it there as here . . .'

And so on, for another five minutes. As Zen listened, he realized for the first time the extent to which he had already become 'meridionalized'. He saw it all with a different eye now, this dark, disturbing stuff boiling up like mud churned up by a power boat roaring up a shallow canal – with a clear, unforgiving Southern eye. These were extracts from another narrative, another life, redundant here.

Nevertheless he went through the usual motions, assuring his mother that he would call more often and visit her in person just as soon as the demands of the extremely vital and urgent case he was presently working on permitted. He told her that he loved her and missed her and would never ever come to Rome again without coming to see her, however rushed he might be, because she was more important to him than anything or anyone else. He told what she wanted to hear, then hung up and went to tear the cord out of the wall. He couldn't leave it here in his absence any-way. The last thing he needed was for Gesualdo and Sabatino to be fielding calls for someone called Aurelio Zen.

But before he could disconnect the instrument, it started to ring again. It's mamma, he thought, calling back for further reas-surance. His heart sank at the prospect, but it was idle to pretend that he wasn't there.

'Yes?'

'Good evening, *dottore*. This is Pastorelli.'

'Well?' barked Zen.

'Many apologies for the interruption, *dottore*. I know we've been given very strict instructions never to disturb you at home, but I can't get hold of Giovan Battista . . . of Inspector Caputo, that is. He's out somewhere, his wife said, and she doesn't know when he'll . . .'

'So?'

'Well, the thing is, we have a bit of a problem. It's in relation to that case involving the stabbing of that Greek sailor on the night of the . . .'

'Has he died?'

'Who?'

'The Greek!'

'No, no. That's to say, I don't know. We've had no word as to his condition.'

'Then why the hell are you wasting my time, Pastorelli? If you're lonely, go upstairs and chat up the whores.'

'It's the prisoner, *dottore*.'

'What about the prisoner?'

'He's gone.'

'Gone?' boomed Zen. 'Who authorized his release?'

'No one, *dottore*. He escaped.'

Come? Perchè? Quando? In qual modo?

Pasquale had gone off duty after dropping the Squillace girls at the airport. He apologized profusely for not being able to drive Zen in person, but promised he would ring around and send someone reliable, thus sparing his client the indignity of having to call a taxi company himself, like some nobody without any standing or contacts in the city. Before leaving, Zen went across the alley and explained to the toothless Don Castrese that he was expecting friends to call that evening and that he might be delayed. He left a key and instructions to admit two young men answering to the names Gesualdo and Sabatino.

The cab dispatched by Pasquale was waiting for Zen in Via Cimarosa. The driver, a squat, tough-looking woman of indeterminate age and few words, confirmed his destination and did not speak again until they arrived at the port. It was the first time that Zen had had occasion to visit his place of work after dark, and he was astonished at the transformation. The shutters of the windows on the top floor of the police station were all closed, but cracks of light escaped here and there and the sound of disco music mingled with voices and laughter floated down through the soft evening air.

Pastorelli, a short intense-looking man with a permanently worried expression, was waiting in the entrance hall, visibly perturbed. Zen made no attempt to mitigate the man's embarrassment or to respond to his explanations and excuses, merely leading the way upstairs to his office as though it were quite normal for him to be there. Not until he was ensconced behind his desk did he deign to address a word to his subordinate.

'As duty officer in charge of this post, you are personally accountable for ensuring that the statutory regulations are enforced and a proper degree of security maintained.'

He lifted the phone.

'In fact, I think we might be able to set a precedent here. You know how hard it is to get fired from the police. Many attempts have been made, but they nearly always result in mere demotion or transfer. But if I call the Questura and report that you have not only been turning a blind eye to the fact that a brothel is operating on the premises, but have allowed the suspect at the centre of the most important case this section has ever handled to escape from under your nose, I'm pretty sure that you'll be on the street tomorrow – if not in jail yourself.'

Pastorelli blanched visibly but said nothing.

'On the other hand, I'm not sure that's in my own best interests,' Zen went on, setting down the receiver again. 'So we may have to pass up this chance to make the record books and settle for the usual cover-up. Where's Caputo?'

'On his way, sir. His wife passed on the message and he called in to say he'd be here as soon as he can.'

Zen took out the pack of *Nazionali* he had bought earlier that day and lit up.

'The only way to lie effectively is on the basis of the truth,' he observed philosophically. 'If I'm going to condone a cover-up, I don't want it blown because some essential detail was concealed from me. You will therefore tell me exactly what happened, step by step, holding nothing back.'

Pastorelli nodded earnestly.

'I came on duty at five,' he began.

'Was the prisoner still here then?'

'I didn't check. The night shift is always very quiet . . .'

He broke off as a particularly raucous laugh from the top floor rent the night air.

'Go on,' said Zen.

'The prisoner's meal was taken down to him at seven-thirty, as per regulations. Pasta, chicken, bread, half a litre of wine.'

'Except that the prisoner decided to dine out this evening.'

Pastorelli looked down at the floor.

'When Armando didn't return . . .'

'Who's Armando?'

83

'Bertolini, sir. He's the other man on nights this week. He took the prisoner his meal tray. About eight I wanted to step out for a coffee, so I went looking for him to man the front desk. The corridors and offices on the first floor were all dark, and I knew he wouldn't have gone upstairs . . .'

'Get on with it, Pastorelli! Where was he?'

'In the prisoner's cell, sir. Handcuffed to the bars and gagged with strips torn from his undershirt. His uniform was missing.'

Zen rolled his eyes up to the ceiling.

'He said that when he'd come down with the meal, the prisoner was rolling about on the floor of his cell, apparently in agony and claimed that he'd been poisoned. Bertolini knew this was a very important case, and of course you keep hearing rumours about people who know too much getting poisoned in jail, so he sort of lost his head . . .'

'And instead of reporting back to you, went right ahead and tried to administer first-aid himself, at which point the prisoner made a miraculous recovery and hit our Armando over the head with the chamber-pot, right?'

'No, sir. It was a stool.'

A maniacal light appeared in Zen's eyes.

'Ah, a stool! That changes everything.'

'It does?' queried Pastorelli with a puzzled expression.

Zen smiled horribly.

'You know, Pastorelli, you remind me of some cartoon character. One of those lovable, gormless, anthropomorphic rodents. If you do end up getting fired, I bet we can find some lonely old lady who'd be happy to keep you as a pet.'

He crushed out his cigarette on the floor.

'So the prisoner tied up Bertolini and took his uniform. How did he get out?'

'Sir?'

'You were on duty at the front desk from the time Bertolini took the meal down until you went looking for him. Is that correct?'

'Yes, sir.'

'Did anyone enter or leave the building in that time?'

'No, sir.'

'And I take it you had the wit to search the premises since then, to check he's not hiding out somewhere.'

'Yes, but . . .'

Pastorelli hesitated.

'Spit it out,' Zen told him.

But at that moment the door swung open and Giovan Battista Caputo appeared, waving a newspaper, his face wreathed in smiles.

'We're off the hook, *dottore*!'

He laid the newspaper on Zen's desk.

'Tomorrow's *Mattino*,' he said. 'You can get it early, if you know where to go.'

He ran a stubby forefinger under the banner headline.

POLITICAL TERRORISM RETURNS, it read, and in slightly smaller type below, NEW ORGANIZATION BEHIND THE MYSTERY OF THE 'ILLUSTRIOUS DISAPPEARANCES'?

Inset in the text were three photographs, one larger than the rest, showing three men, all in their fifties, all wearing suits and ties. One was visibly ducking away from the photographer's flash, another was smiling and relaxing at a party, the third and largest was staring deadpan into the camera, as though sitting for an enforced portrait.

Zen skimmed rapidly through the accompanying article. Apparently the local media had received a communiqué from a previously unknown group calling itself *Strade Pulite*, claiming responsibility for the recent disappearances of three leading social and commercial figures in the city:

Two years after the political events which promised so much, it is clear that nothing has changed but the names. The work of the judges and investigators continues to be obstructed and blocked at every turn. The list of those accused of corruption and criminality grows ever longer, but so far not one of them has been brought to trial, much less condemned and sentenced. In short, the usual cover-up and procrastination is taking place, while the guilty continue to walk the streets of our city, as free men!

Since the law cannot – or will not – touch them, we have

85

decided to take the law into our own hands. Three of the most scandalous examples of civic putridity have already been removed: Attilio Abate, Luca Della Ragione and Ermanno Vallifuoco. Their fate and their present where-abouts are of no more concern than those of any other item of garbage. It is enough that they defile the streets of our city no longer.

But our work has only just begun. There are many other instances of such ordure still to be dealt with. We know who they are, as does every Neapolitan who has studied the sad history of our city in recent years. They are the men who grew fat on the sufferings of the earthquake victims in 1980, the men who grew rotten on the money which the Christian Democrats handed out to save their henchman Cirillo from the clutches of his kidnappers, the men whose greed and arrogance have made our city a national and international byword for public and private corruption, waste and inefficiency.

For years they flouted the law with impunity, secure in the protection of their allies in Rome. Berlusconi promised to make a new start, a clean sweep, but as always this turned out to be just another proof that 'Everything must change so that nothing will change'. And nothing has, until now. But now things *are* changing! We have seen to that, and we will con-tinue to do so. Our enemies – the common enemies of every right-thinking Neapolitan – cannot escape us. We go about our work as invisibly as the men who clean our gutters and remove our rubbish. Indeed, our job is the same: to return the city to its citizens, pristine and purified, a source of civic pride once more. *Strade Pulite per una città pulita!*

Zen pushed the paper away.

'"Clean streets for a clean city." Well, it's a good slogan. Sounds as if some Red Brigade cell went to a PR firm who told them to drop the Marxist rhetoric and get snappier copy.'

He looked at Caputo.

'But what's it got to do with us?'

'It'll buy us time, *dottore*. Some foreign sailor getting knifed in the port is going to look small time in the context of a full-blown terrorist campaign dedicated to wiping out all the local politicians' nearest and dearest cronies.'

Zen nodded.

'I suppose you're right.'

He turned to Pastorelli, who was looking distinctly uncomfortable.

'You were about to tell me something when Caputo walked in. Let's have it.'

'Well, sir, the thing is, I searched the building, like I told you. I didn't find the prisoner, but I did notice that his belongings had been tampered with.'

'What?'

'You remember you gave me that video cassette yesterday evening and told me to put it back with the other stuff. Well, I did as you said, but when I checked the room just now the stuff was all over the floor. All except the cassette, that is.'

Zen put his head in his hands and stared at the desk.

'How do the clients of that operation on the top floor come and go?' he demanded. 'Obviously they don't use the front entrance.'

'There's a fire escape at the side,' Caputo volunteered. 'It's nice and secluded, and we have excellent security at the door. There's never any trouble . . .'

'What about the normal entrance from the main staircase?'

'That's entirely closed to the clientele, *dottore*. There's no risk of anyone getting into the building that way.'

'I'm not interested in anyone getting in,' Zen snapped. 'I'm interested in someone getting out. Someone in police uniform.'

Caputo looked grim.

'I'll go and check,' he said, turning away.

'No! I need you here. You go, Pastorelli. But first, who knows that the prisoner has escaped?'

Pastorelli frowned.

'Well, Bertolini obviously. Then there's me, and you . . .'

'Besides us and Bertolini, you idiot!'

'Nobody.'

'Are you sure?'

'I phoned you and Giova . . . Inspector Caputo. That's all.'

'OK, get going.'

With an expression of infinite relief, Pastorelli fled. Zen turned to Caputo.

'When you escorted the prisoner to my office the other day, you stopped to pick up his belongings on the way, right?'

Caputo frowned.

'How did you know?'

'Because you wouldn't have wanted to carry them all the way down to the cells and back. And because that's how the prisoner knew where they were being kept.'

Caputo gave one of his toothy grins.

'Of course. So it's important, this cassette?'

Zen gazed into the middle distance.

'Not according to my sources. But if the prisoner risked recapture in order to take it with him, it begins to look as though they must have been wrong.'

He turned to face Caputo.

'I need a doctor.'

Caputo's eyes widened.

'You feel ill?'

'Not for me, for the prisoner.'

Caputo goggled still more.

'But *dottore*, the prisoner is gone!'

Zen resumed his abstracted expression.

'Nevertheless, he needs to see a doctor. I'm sure you can think of someone suitable, Caputo. *Un medico di fiducia.* Someone you can recommend without reservation. Understand?'

'Of course!'

'Someone who can be trusted to do whatever might prove necessary,' Zen pursued, 'even if the procedures demanded might prove to be slightly irregular. And who, above all, can be trusted to keep quiet about it.'

Caputo's predatory grin intensified.

'For the right consideration, *dottore*, this guy'd perform an abortion on the Virgin Mary. But don't worry about the money. He owes me a couple of favours, and that makes him nervous. He'll be glad to help.'

Zen smiled softly at Caputo.

'Have I ever told you how much I like it here?' he murmured.

Sulla strada

Via Duomo, later the same evening. Running almost due north from the port, this street is dead straight and relatively broad by the standards of the city, but the traffic was as stagnant at that hour as sewage in a backed-up drain. Double rows of parked cars to either side forced the moving vehicles into two narrow lanes just wide enough for a stationary file in either direction. Meanwhile pedestrians, the diminutive lords of this petrified jungle, picked their way through the revving, honking, impotent mass as though negotiating the impressive, irrelevant ruins of a mightier but extinct civilisation.

But one car seemed to be making some headway, despite everything. It was obviously expensive, a foreign import of some sort, painted a brilliant red. But there were plenty of Volvos and BMWs and Mercedes stalled in the traffic jam, reluctantly rubbing bumpers with such undesirable company as traders' three-wheeled Ape vans, old Fiat 500s on their third 100,000 kilometres and the usual slew of beaten-up cars, buses, taxis, TIR lorries – even a refuse collection truck. What caused the crush to loosen in front of this particular vehicle was the flashing blue light attached to the roof, and the official police wand insistently waving from the driver's window.

Thus empowered, the red saloon nosed through the traffic at all of 10 mph to just south of the cathedral, where it abruptly veered left into a narrow side-street, ignoring the 'No Entry' sign. Half-way down the block it pulled up outside a seven-storey house just like all the others and sounded its horn in a series of long blasts. Windows and curtains above opened, but the driver continued to lean on his strident, demanding horn. At length a young man appeared at a window on the second-floor. He waved to the driver of the car, who signalled back. The horn fell silent.

'Who is it?' demanded the other man, seated inside the apartment before a table strewn with playing cards.

'Gesualdo. I've got to run.'

'Work?'

The first man shrugged.

'Oh, Sabatì! Just as I was finally starting to win! That's a shitty excuse.'

'We just need to check someone out. Come along, if you want. Then we can come back and finish the game.'

His companion hesitated a moment.

'Whereabouts?'

Sabatino took out a printed card.

'Via Cimarosa.'

'Wow! You bastards are moving up in the world.'

They ran down the steep, narrow stairs to the street, where three vehicles now stood nose-to-nose with the red saloon blocking their passage.

'Oh, Dario!' called the driver. 'Who invited you along?'

One of the waiting cars blasted its horn insistently. Dario stood back and stared at the offending driver with slitted eyes.

'This is a one-way street!' the man yelled. 'Clear the way immediately! You're breaking the law six times over!'

At an exaggeratedly leisurely pace, Dario strolled over to remind the instigator of this rash protest that it wouldn't make that much difference if they made it seven by rendering his car, if not his person, unserviceable pending lengthy and expensive professional intervention. Meanwhile Sabatino admired the red saloon, whistling appreciatively.

'So where did you get this?'

Gesualdo smiled.

'Friend of a friend. But what's really interesting is where *he* got it.'

Sabatino glanced at him, but Dario was already on his way back from putting the fear of God into the driver who had so ill-advisedly attempted to enforce the traffic regulations single-handed. Gesualdo said nothing more. With a mighty roar, he reversed at high speed along the alley into the continuing stalemate on Via Duomo. Reaching out of the window, he turned on the blue flasher held on the roof by its magnetic base and handed the police wand to Dario.

'Wave this around a bit.'

Dario looked at him doubtfully.

'Are you sure that's a good idea?'

'Works like a charm. Just try it and see.'

'But suppose some of our friends are about. If they get the idea that you're a cop . . .'

Gesualdo laughed sarcastically.

'Next time I see them, Dario, I'll let them know that you think they're dumb enough to think that if I really was a cop, I'd drive around advertising the fact.'

Dario shrugged.

'I guess you're right.'

But just before they reached Piazza Amore, Sabatino leant out of the window and grabbed the flashing light off the roof.

'Kill the wand!'

'What's up?' asked Dario.

Sabatino pointed. Locked in the grid of traffic headed the other way was a *real* police car, with a couple of uniforms in the front.

'All we need now is for them to start taking an interest,' murmured Gesualdo nervously.

Fortunately the policemen's view was blocked by a large orange truck in front, and they hadn't noticed the presence of their counterfeit colleagues. In fact they didn't seem to be taking much interest in anything. They hadn't even bothered to make use of their own lights and siren to carve a passage through the jam, for some reason, seemingly content to lumber along at the same speed as the common public. As well as the two uniformed officers, there was a man in civilian clothes on board, sitting all alone in the back. He seemed to be about to get out of the car, perhaps having realized that at this point it would be quicker to walk.

But as the red Jaguar passed by, the line of traffic going the other way suddenly started to move, then to pick up speed. For a moment it seemed as though some plug had been pulled, and that everything would now be easy. Then, without any warning, the whole thing ground to a halt once again. The refuse truck stopped dead, its brake lights bathing the police car in an eerie red glare. The uniformed driver groped for the brake pedal, but he was still speaking to his colleague in the front passenger seat and hit the clutch instead. The police car slammed into the tailgate of the truck, not fast enough to do any serious damage, although the civilian in the back went sprawling into the space behind the front seats while the two cops, who naturally hadn't bothered to buckle their seat-belts, shot forward and struck their foreheads on the windscreen and the steering wheel respectively.

The one in the passenger seat recovered first. He glanced at the driver, who had blood streaming from his nose.

'That son of a bitch!' he yelled in dialect. 'I'll squash his balls like tomatoes!'

He got out of the car and strode towards the front of the truck, some sort of municipal maintenance vehicle by the look of it. But when he was more than half-way there, the door of the cab swung open and three men in overalls jumped out and turned in a line, facing him.

What happened next is unclear. The policeman may have started to say something, but no one remembered that. All they remembered – the few who had not been looking the other way at the time, or whose view had not been blocked by another vehicle – was the gunfire, the abrupt volley of rapid, hammered shots which 'could have come from anywhere'. Almost everyone remembered the policeman falling, the gunmen sprinting away, abandoning their truck, the screams, panic and general confusion. On the other hand, no one at all seems to have noticed the man in civilian clothes struggle out of the back of the police car and run off down a narrow alley as fast as he could go, his handcuffed arms swinging stiffly from side to side.

Due bizzarre ragazze

By this time, the red Jaguar was over half a mile away. Thanks to a judicious use of the police wand and the flashing light, which allowed him not only to disregard the rules of the road but to intimidate those similarly bent on ignoring them, Gesualdo had been able to indulge to the full his penchant for massive acceleration, emergency braking, breath-taking near-misses, controlled skids and all the other techniques associated with the chaos theory of urban driving.

None of this seemed to have improved the mood of the two men in the front of the car. The brief effervescence of male camaraderie had gone flat, leaving a thin, sour, strained silence. Both Gesualdo and Sabatino appeared to be sunk in a mood of sullen apathy, punctuated by frequent sighs, which baffled and slightly alarmed their passenger. Maybe it was a mistake inviting myself along, thought Dario De Spino.

By now he had known the two men for almost a year, but was frequently forced to admit to himself – though not to others, for knowledge was his business – that what he didn't know about them easily outweighed what he did. He had met Sabatino first, actually tried to pick him up in a bar! It rapidly became clear that Sabatì was not that way inclined, but it also became clear that he and Gesualdo liked hanging out with Dario, in a spirit of casual, bullshitting camaraderie, and that they were connected to some very big players indeed.

Exactly *which* players, Dario had never been able to determine exactly, although he wouldn't admit this to anyone else either. On the contrary, being seen with Gesualdo and Sabatino had upgraded his own image considerably in quarters where such enhancement can make the difference between a sweet deal and a kiss-off – or something far worse.

So it wasn't just altruism which made Dario wish to raise his companions' spirits by any possible means. The world in which he had been born and had his being was rich in portents, omens and auguries. Read them wrong and you were dead, often literally. Maybe the lads were simply suffering from indigestion, or maybe someone had, God forbid, put the evil eye on them. In either case, he needed to find out, and fast.

'So how's business with you two?' he asked a trifle too breezily. 'Personally I've been doing a little distribution work for one of the big names in the pharmaceutical sector.'

No harm in hinting that he too had powerful contacts whose identity he could not, needless to say, reveal. In fact the deal was a one-off involving a couple of kilos brought in by a friend of a friend, in both senses of the word, to be marketed through various gay discos, the discretion of whose clientele was assured.

No response.

'What a life!' he went on. 'Up at all hours, from one end of the city to the other, the phone ringing off the hook, trying to keep track of inventory, and God help you if you botch a sale! The only perk is the built-in wastage inevitable in any transportation and repackaging operation.'

Still no response. Dario leant forward between the two front seats.

'Here you go, lads. Something to lift your spirits.'

Gesualdo did not take his eyes off the road. Sabatino glanced down at the plastic sachet of crystalline white powder in Dario's outstretched palm. With a violent motion of his hand he slapped it away.

'What do you think you're doing?' yelled Dario, scooping the sachet up off the floor. 'That's pure coke!'

The silence from the front seats merely intensified.

'What the hell's the matter with you two?' Dario demanded.

The only reply was a massive sigh from Gesualdo.

'What's up?' asked Dario.

'Nothing!'

'What's wrong?'

'Just drop it, will you?' snapped Gesualdo.

Dario leant forward again, scanning the street ahead. He was really worried now. If the car had been going slowly enough, he would have opened the door and made a run for it. But there was no chance of that, the way this maniac was driving.

'Gesuà! Sabatì! For God's sake, what's happened?'

'It's personal,' muttered Sabatino.

The Jaguar squealed round a corner, right into the path of an oncoming bus. With a flick of his wrist, Gesualdo cut into an alley on the other side of the street.

'Our girls have left Naples,' he said.

Dario stared at him, then burst into relieved laughter.

'Is that all? They'll be back.'

'Maybe.'

'Where have they gone?'

'To study in London.'

'Lucky them! They'll come back with all kinds of certificates and qualifications and land some great job.'

'Not here, though,' Sabatino replied gloomily. 'Somewhere up North, where all the classy jobs are.'

'Or maybe they'll meet someone in London and not come back at all,' said Gesualdo.

Dario laughed again.

'In that case, lucky you!'

Sabatino turned around.

'What's that supposed to mean, you idiot?'

Dario shrugged broadly and winked.

'There are plenty of other women around.'

'Not like Orestina and Filomena.'

'What have they got that the others haven't?' demanded Dario. 'One's as good as another, since none of them is any good except for one thing. Anyway, that's beside the point. They'll be back all right, and before you know it you'll be knee-deep in mortgage payments and credit-card bills, not to mention a pack of brats. This may be the last chance you ever get to kick off the traces. So instead of making life hell for yourselves and everyone around you, why not get out there and enjoy yourselves?'

'Enjoy ourselves?' repeated Sabatino incredulously.

'Right! Get out there and play the field for all you're worth. Just like your precious females will be doing in London.'

Gesualdo brought the car to a screeching halt and swung round to face Dario.

'Don't you dare insult two of the purest, most faithful women who have ever lived! You have no idea what they've had to go through from their family for taking up with the likes of us.'

'That's probably your main attraction,' commented Dario cynically. 'If you'd been a couple of *guagliune per bene*, they wouldn't have given you a second look. In short, you're the most interesting men they've ever come across here. But in London? Do you think they're going to waste their time there weeping and worrying about you two? Give me a break! Women need to be the centre of attention. If you aren't around to give it to them, they'll find someone who is. It only makes sense for you to play by the same rules.'

But Gesualdo had already climbed out of the car, followed closely by Sabatino. The front doors slammed with percussive finality.

'Wait for me, lads!' called Dario.

'We've got private business here,' Gesualdo told him coldly. 'Either wait or make your own way home.'

He and Sabatino disappeared down a set of stone steps running steeply downhill between walls overhung with foliage. Dario looked after them for a moment, then shrugged and lit a cigarette. As he did so, he noticed a taxi standing opposite, apparently just paying off its fare. Dario walked over and started to negotiate with the driver, a no-nonsense babe somewhere in her fifties.

'Oh!'

Dario looked round. The speaker was the passenger who had just got out of the taxi.

'Eh?' retorted Dario.

The man came closer, staring at Dario insistently.

'Maybe I could use you,' he said.

He was tall and spare, with a pale face, grey eyes and a thin wedge-shaped nose. Dario laughed dismissively.

'Sorry, you're too old.'

'I'd make it worth your while.'

'I don't do it for money.'

They exchanged a look.

'Oh!' shouted the driver. 'You want a ride or what?'

Dario regarded her haughtily.

'Not with you,' he said.

There followed a brief but colourful exchange of views on single-gender sexual practices and the personal charms of older women, after which the taxi roared away. Dario looked at the stranger.

'What do you want?' he said.

'Someone I can trust.'

Dario laughed shortly.

'Is that all?'

The man produced a number of large denomination banknotes, as well as an engraved card in the name of Alfonso Zembla. He handed both to Dario.

'I live just down the hill. Your friends Gesualdo and Sabatino are on their way to my house now.'

'Who said they were my friends?'

'I watched you drive up together in that red saloon. Nice car. They didn't seem to be too pleased with you, to be perfectly honest, and yet they left you there with about fifty million lire's worth of automobile to steal or trash. Who but friends would do that?'

Dario shrugged.

'So?' he demanded.

Zen paused a moment.

'Would the reason why they weren't pleased have less to do with you than the fact that their girlfriends left town today?'

Dario made a wry face.

'God!', he said.

'They're making a fuss about it?'

'You'd think it was the end of the world. I mean we all know breeders get hung up on relationships, but I've never seen anything like these two. When I suggested that maybe a little flexibility was in order, they accused me of dragging their darling fishes into disrepute and left me to walk home!'

Zen nodded. Taking Dario's arm, he led him across the street towards the flight of steps.

'It sounds as if it's high time they were taught a lesson, and I think you're the man to do it. After the way they've treated you, it would be satisfying as well as lucrative.'

'What do you have in mind?'

'I'm a friend of the Squillace family. They're horrified at the idea of their girls getting mixed up with a couple of low-lifes like your friends, and they're willing to pay good money to ensure it doesn't happen. Now as luck would have it the flat below mine has been let to a couple of young ladies who have just arrived here and are desperate to – how shall I put it? – place themselves under the protection of someone who can help them get on in the world. And they're not too particular how.'

Dario nodded rapidly.

'You aim to fix them up with Gesualdo and Sabatino?'

'Exactly. The problem is that your friends know I'm in with the Squillaci, so they don't trust me. Which is where you come in. I need you to act as go-between, monitoring the situation, smoothing out any difficulties that may arise and generally doing your best to get our star-struck young lovers to fall head over heels for someone new. If you bring it off, the Squillace family will make it well worth your while.'

He paused as they came to a small square halfway down the steps, overlooking the sea. Navigation lights twinkled in the velvet immensity of the night.

'These neighbours of yours,' Dario began. 'Are they young? Pretty? Do they know how to turn it on?'

'They've got everything it takes to drive a man crazy. But why don't you come and see for yourself? My house is just down there.'

Dario shrugged.

'Why not?'

They heard the music first. It reached up to them, sinuous and insinuating, rhythmic but unsettling, a long melisma skidding around between keys without ever settling down. It got ever louder as they approached, booming and bending off the high stone walls of the alley. Then the house itself came into view. The first floor was a blaze of lights, the shutters and windows thrown open and the strange, oriental music blaring out.

'Oh, *ragazze!*' Zen called loudly.

Two heads appeared simultaneously at the windows, a blonde to the right, a brunette to the left.

'Let me introduce Dario De Spino,' Zen continued. 'If anyone can fix you up, he can.'

A squeal of excitement from above.

'How wonderful!'

'What it is to have friends!'

Zen unlocked the front door. The note he had left earlier was no longer there.

'So what do you think?' he asked De Spino as they climbed the stairs.

'They're the oddest looking creatures I've ever seen! And that accent! Where the hell are they from?'

'Albania.'

'Albania!'

'They left earlier this year. Paid someone a fortune to smuggle them over to Bari. But there was no work there, so they've come up to Naples to try their luck.'

'So how come they speak Italian?'

'Watching television. It was never effectively jammed, apparently.'

He pushed open the door of the lower apartment. Dario De Spino entered the room, staring wide-eyed at the two women who stood facing him. They were dressed in late-sixties outfits which no doubt represented the height of underground chic in Tirana: polyester tank-tops, extremely short miniskirts and calf-length white boots. Their hair was long and straight, their make-up primitive but copious.

Zen rubbed his hands together and turned back to the doorway.

'Well, I'll leave you three to get acquainted.'

'I'm Libera,' said the brunette, advancing on Dario De Spino. 'And this is Iolanda. We're so pleased to meet you. We've just arrived in the city, and we don't know a soul here.'

'If only we could get in touch with the right people,' sighed Iolanda. 'People with connections. It's hard for two girls all alone, with no friends or family to help . . .'

The voices faded as Zen walked upstairs to his own flat. The door was open and the lights on, but there was no sign of anyone home. Then he continued up the spiral staircase giving access to the roof extension and there they were, standing out on the terrace, smoking cigarettes and gazing up at the twinkling lights of a passing plane. Given the delays considered normal at Capodichino, it might even be the one entrusted with the safety of their darling girls.

Che figure interessanti

Twenty minutes later, as Aurelio Zen walked up the steps and down the street to the turn-of-the-century *palazzo* where Valeria Squillace lived, it was with a sense of a job, if not well done, at least well begun. Putting Dario De Spino on the payroll had definitely been an excellent inspiration, and the crucial negotiations with Gesualdo and Sabatino had gone much more smoothly than he had feared.

Initially the two men had seemed distinctly suspicious of 'Alfonso Zembla', and had asked a great many questions about his life, work, residence in Naples and relationship to the Squillace family. For all of ten minutes they had interrogated him like a couple of cops, while Zen fed them a mixed diet of innocuous facts, half-truths and outright lies. Yes, he was from the North, from Venice. He worked in the port of Naples as a customs inspector, and was distantly related to Valeria Squillace on her father's side.

As for this sudden interest in Orestina's and Filomena's private lives, he explained that he had become a sort of uncle to the two girls, who confessed things to him that they would not tell their mother. He understood the latter's doubts and anxieties about this double liaison, so unsuitable on the face of it, but considered them unfounded. That was why he was taking advantage of a combination of circumstances which had arisen to give Gesualdo and Sabatino a chance to redeem themselves in the eyes of the girls' mother.

As an act of charity, he explained, Signora Squillace had responded to an appeal on behalf of the Albanian refugees who were flocking to Italy, seeking work and a better future. The nuns who sponsored the appeal were housing and feeding many hundreds of these immigrants in their own facilities, but the demand exceeded their capacities and they had appealed for help to many of the city's wealthier families, including the Squillaci, who had responded positively to similar appeals in the past.

Zen hinted obliquely at some dark secret which Signora Squillace felt obliged to expiate by allowing some vacant rental property she owned to be occupied temporarily by deserving cases selected by the nuns. It was only after doing so that she had seen a newspaper report suggesting that some of these supposed 'refugees' were in fact criminals and prostitutes who had left Albania to escape justice, and who were continuing to carry on their trade in Italy.

Her anxieties had been alleviated to some extent by the knowledge that he, Alfonso Zembla, was on the premises to keep an eye on what was going on. Unfortunately an exceptional situation which had arisen at work meant that for some time he was going to have to spend a considerable amount of time away from home, starting tonight . . .

'What sort of situation?'

The question came from Gesualdo. The tone was dry, almost ironic, as though he already knew the answer. He really would have made an excellent interrogator, thought Zen.

'An undercover operation,' he replied. 'I can't say any more. It's all strictly hush-hush.'

Zen was gratified to see that the two men exchanged a significant glance. He had chosen his professional cover partly to explain his presence in the port area, if they should find out about it, but partly with a view to giving them a further incentive to comply with his request. Given their presumed line of work, the prospect of having an ally in the Customs might be expected to exercise a powerful appeal.

Now it was time to emphasize the other benefits which they stood to gain.

'What I want to be able to do is tell Valeria – Signora Squillace – that I've left the place in safe hands, and she has no reason to worry that it's being used as a whorehouse, or worse. So we kill two birds with one stone. I can concentrate on my job, while you two get the credit for defending the Squillace family property against the depredations of the Muslim hordes.'

'We can't just sit around here all the time,' Sabatino protested. 'We've got work to do, too.'

'That's no problem. The main thing is that you spend the night here, and check up on the situation whenever your other responsibilities permit. I take it that your families can spare you for a few days? That's all it'll take, just until this emergency situation at work blows over . . .'

A lot more negotiation, manoeuvring and mutual mendacity had followed on both sides, but in the end the two men agreed, albeit somewhat grudgingly, to what Zen proposed. He had given them a brief tour of the flat, pointing out such details as the tricky gas tap and the trip switches which went if you attempted to use more than one electrical appliance simultaneously, reminded them to double-lock the door and turn off the lights when they went out, then picked up the overnight bag he had packed earlier and left before they had time to change their minds.

Some weeks earlier, when they had first discussed this idea, Valeria had mentioned that since he was putting himself out in this way on behalf of the family, the least she could do in return was to provide him with a roof over his head. He had assumed that she was thinking in terms of a hotel room, but when the issue came up again she had pointed out that with her daughters away there were two vacant bedrooms in her apartment, and that he was welcome to stay there.

It had never for one moment occurred to Zen that this invitation was the result of anything other than expediency, and perhaps the thrift which notoriously characterized wealthy families. What with the costs of the girls' trip to London, to say nothing of Zen's incidental expenses, which Valeria had agreed to underwrite, this was going to end up costing her several million lire. What more natural than that she should wish to save the additional extravagance of hotel accommodation for her collaborator?

· It was only when Valeria came to the door to greet him that another possible scenario occurred to Zen. It was indeed thrust upon him, in the form of the formidable and breathtakingly visible bosom which nuzzled him in the ribs as Valeria leaned forward to give and receive their usual – and, as he had always thought, entirely conventional – peck on the cheek. Her black gauze gown, cut very low both front and back, left just enough to the imagination to arouse interest. A pervasive scent, subtle but heady, completed these discreet provocations.

'So how did it go?' she asked, bolting the door behind Zen and taking his bag.

'Fine, excellent, perfect, great, no problem,' he burbled incoherently.

Valeria produced a smile he had never seen before, like someone unwrapping a fragile family heirloom from its cocoon of tissue paper.

'You're a wonder!' she said.

The Squillace apartment could not have offered a greater contrast to the building in which it was situated, a ponderous and brooding edifice seemingly cobbled together from discarded designs for a museum, railway station or opera house. Its pointlessly grandiose dimensions suggested the pretensions and insecurity of recent riches rather than real power and permanence, an impression strengthened by the large quantity and low quality of the decorative details, which betrayed a vulgar terror of the unadorned and the asymmetrical.

But once inside the apartment, everything was light, bright, sparse and stylishly luxurious. The overall tone was Milan: ranks of cupboards in white polyester resin with bare wood fittings, lots of glass and steel shelving and tables, long low sofa units, bare parquet floors with one or two oriental rugs, pale grey walls enlivened with a few large modern oils.

'We used to entertain a lot when Manlio was alive, so we needed the space,' Valeria said as they entered the salon, which stretched some thirty feet across the entire width of the apartment, divided into a sitting and dining area. Through the open windows, a scattering of lights and a vast blankness hinted at the fabulous view which the place must command by day.

Valeria guided Zen to a corner of the sofa set and seated herself beside him.

'But it's not worth moving now,' she continued. 'As soon as the girls get married, I'll go home.'

'Where's that?'

'Ferrara.'

He looked surprised.

'I didn't realize you were from the North.'

'Oh, yes, and *of* it, too. I only moved down here because of Manlio. For the girls it's different, of course. They were born and brought up here. To them it's their home.'

'So how did you meet your late husband?' Zen asked politely.

'At a wedding. He was the best man and I was one of the bridesmaids. The groom was a cousin of Manlio who looked after certain business interests he had in Emilia-Romagna. Manlio proposed to me two weeks later.'

She looked at Zen intently.

'That's who it is!' she exclaimed, laying her hand on Zen's arm.

'Who what is?'

'I knew you reminded me of someone, but I couldn't think who. Of course, it's Orlando! You could be twins. I've got a photograph somewhere, I'll show you.'

She got up to fetch it, but at that moment the telephone sounded, a confident rich burble. The call wasn't for Zen, although plenty of people were desperately trying to contact him at that very moment. But his own phone was out of action, and he had been careful to avoid telling anyone where he was staying.

Valeria was on the phone for some time, evidently talking to her daughters in London. She had, Zen realized, a good body, but he still wasn't interested. No more romantic complications for him. He was very comfortable with the role he had been playing since coming to Naples: the philosophical observer who looks on with wry amusement at the follies of others but is too wily and cynical to risk becoming entangled himself.

She turned towards him, catching him eyeing her, and smiled unexpectedly.

'I'm sure it'll all seem better in the morning, darling. Anyway, I've got to run, there's someone at the door. Try and get some sleep, and give me a call in the morning. Bye!'

She hung up and drifted back towards Zen.

'So how are they finding London?' he asked.

'They say it's just as dirty as Naples, the traffic's even worse, there are more beggars and it's cold and raining.'

'But they're going to stick it out?'

'Filomena sounded a bit homesick. She's always been the weaker one. She gets moody quite easily. But Orestina's made of sterner stuff, and proud too. And in the end Filomena will go along with whatever her sister decides.'

She stood over him, smiling.

'Now, then, would you like something to drink? Some tea? A nightcap?'

'Tea would be wonderful. And then I must get some sleep. I have rather an important case on at the moment, and I'll need to be up early.'

'Is it something to do with this *Strade Pulite* business?' Valeria asked, heading off towards the far end of the room.

'No, no. That has nothing to do with me.'

He got up and followed her across the dining area into a luxuriously equipped kitchen.

'Well, I don't know who's behind it,' Valeria remarked, filling a kettle, 'but I wish them the best of luck. The people they claim to have abducted are the very ones poor Manlio worked with for years and trusted like his own family, and who then left him to fend for himself against the judges without lifting a finger to save him!'

She set the kettle on the stove.

'Which reminds me, come in here and I'll show you that picture.'

She led the way into a small room furnished with a desk, filing cabinet and a small set of bookshelves. The air smelt faintly of cigar smoke.

'This was Manlio's office,' Valeria said. 'I don't need the space, so I just left everything as it was, what was left of it. The *Guardia di Finanza* came and took everything away.'

She turned and pointed to a large framed photograph mounted on the wall behind the desk.

'That's the one.'

The picture showed a convivial group of men in what looked like a restaurant. There were ten or more of them, all men, all looking towards the camera, all smiling or laughing.

'See that man in the centre?' said Valeria, pointing with one fleshy heavily ringed finger. 'The one sitting at the end of the table? That's Orlando Pagano. Actually he's a little heavier than I remembered, but don't you think he looks like you?'

Zen narrowed his eyes obediently. There was a certain resemblance, he supposed, although the man in the picture was both fleshier and swarthier than Zen himself.

'Here's Manlio,' Valeria went on, pointing. 'And this is the supposed victim of that Strade Pulite group, Ermanno Vallifuoco.'

Vallifuoco was a complacently corpulent man with an expression of inscrutable serenity. Manlio Squillace was leaner and slighter, with a pencil moustache and gleaming eyes. Zen leant forward, scrutinizing the picture intently.

An unearthly sound made itself heard next door, a long rising whine like some primitive lament.

'The kettle!' said Valeria, hurrying out. 'Would you like some cake? I baked it myself, an old Ferrarese recipe.'

Zen did not reply. He was still staring at the photograph, but not at the illustrious victim of terrorism or the late-lamented Signor Squillace. His attention was focused on a man who, judging by his distance from the head of the table, had been one of the less important guests, a minor character brought in to make up the numbers in this boisterous scene of underworld conviviality. He had been forced to look sharply back over his left shoulder in order to face the camera, and even so was partially obscured by his neighbour. But enough of his face was visible to leave no doubt in Zen's mind that he was none other than the man who had knifed the Greek sailor a few days earlier and then mysteriously disappeared from his cell at the police station.

Sogno o son desto?

The chic austerity on display in the 'public' areas of the Squillace apartment was gleefully abandoned once past the door to the family's own rooms, which sported an amazing range of high-tech, low-taste gadgets, gimmicks and gizmos ranging from novelty telephones to auto-flushing toilets, from remote-control light fixtures to a set of interactive operas on CD-ROM.

So it came as no particular surprise to Zen, when he went to the bathroom early next morning, to find a miniaturized waterproof television set attached to a bracket in the shower cubicle. The idea struck him as both idiotic and irresistible – we may be half the men our fathers were, but they couldn't watch TV in the shower – and he turned it on in the middle of the local news. What with the hiss of the water and the assorted noises associated with his ablutions, it was some time before he tuned in to the story which the gorgeously coiffed presenter was reading.

'. . . approached the truck following the collision, when a group of men – estimates vary as to the exact number – leapt out and opened fire. The officer was killed instantly. The assailants then ran off into the neighbouring Forcella area, abandoning their vehicle. Another official travelling in the police car was unharmed, but in the confusion a prisoner they were transporting is thought to have escaped. A search was instituted, but so far all attempts to trace the authors of this savage crime have been unsuccessful. The victim has been named as Armando Bertolini, twenty-nine, resident in Fuorigrotta and married with one . . .'

Valeria Squillace was assembling the coffee machine when the apparition occurred: a naked man, dripping wet, sprinting past the kitchen and down the hall. She dropped the *caffetiera*, spilling grounds all over the floor and hurting her foot quite badly. Even

108

once the pain had subsided, she had no idea what to make of it. She wondered for a moment if the whole thing was a dream. But the splashes of soapy water on the parquet, not to mention the pain in her toes, were real enough.

Back in Filomena's bedroom, where he was sleeping, Zen searched frantically for the phone, which took the form of a pink plastic rabbit. Judging by the décor, it was very hard to believe that Filomena Squillace could possibly be old enough to give her mother any cause for concern. Every available surface was piled high with stuffed toys and brightly coloured knick-knacks decorated with cartoon animals and wide-eyed infants. The only hint of sexuality came in a series of posters featuring a variety of intense-looking young men struggling to look less wholesome than they actually were.

Zen perched naked on the bed and pressed a series of buttons protruding from the rabbit's chest and pressed the creature's head to his ear. The number rang for a considerable time before being answered with a tentative '*Sì?*'.

'Who's this?' demanded Zen into the grille on the rabbit's stomach.

'Who's calling?'

'Is this the port police?'

'I think you have a wrong number.'

That was quite possible, given the fact that the keys were cutely disguised as buttons on the bunny's outfit. Zen muttered an apology and was about to hang up when the voice at the other end said, 'Is that you, *dottore*?'

'This is Aurelio Zen. Who's speaking?'

'Oh, thank God! This is Caputo.'

'Why the hell didn't you answer properly?'

'I thought it might be the Questura. They've been after you all night.'

There was a faint knock at the door, but Zen did not register it.

'When did this happen?' he demanded.

'Last evening, while we were driving Pas . . . the prisoner to the hospital. We got in a fender-bender with this rubbish truck. Bertolini went to give them hell and suddenly these guys jump out and riddle him with bullets. I put in a call for backup . . .'

'And Pastorelli?'

'He ran off. I haven't heard from him.'

The door opened and Valeria Squillace appeared with a cup of coffee.

'OK, listen, Caputo,' Zen said. 'I'll be there as soon as I can. Until then, the arrangements we made yesterday still stand. Got that?'

Valeria stood looking on with a small, fixed smile. Perhaps he's some sort of nudist, she was thinking, although he didn't seem the type.

'Don't go into any details,' Zen continued. 'Refer all supplementary questions to me.'

He put the rabbit back on the bedside table and turned to Valeria. It was only then that he realized that he was naked.

'I haven't had time to get dressed,' he explained apologetically. 'One of my men was killed in a gunfight last night. I'm rather shaken up.'

Valeria set the coffee down on a dresser just inside the door. She was wearing a thick ivory-coloured towel robe. Judging by the expanse of shoulder, leg and upper chest visible, she wasn't wearing anything else.

'How horrible,' she said with the same fixed smile.

Zen didn't bother making any belated attempts to cover his genitals, but naturally Valeria studiously avoided looking anywhere in that direction. Nevertheless, she somehow got the impression that one particular item was rather more prominent than it had been when she first came into the room. Whether or not this was in fact the case, the mere idea was enough to produce a spectacular blush which served to emphasize the contrast between her body and the garment loosely wrapped around it, secured by a single twist of belt. This only made matters worse, and the next time she didn't look there was no further doubt.

They were saved by the telephone, which began chirping and beeping and ringing and buzzing from its various locations all over the house. Valeria's rictus vanished along with her blush. She turned briskly away, closing the door behind her. With an effort, Zen pulled himself together and started to get dressed.

When he emerged, ten minutes later, the salon was filled with sunlight streaming in through the open doorway leading to the balcony. Valeria, now also decently clad, leaned over the railing. A light breeze ruffled her hair.

'Good morning,' she said, as he appeared. 'Did you sleep well?'

'Very well, thank you,' he replied, taking her cue that this was to be their first meeting that morning.

'That was Orestina. Apparently their evening ended better than it began. They met some people who invited them to something called a "rave". I'm not sure what that is, exactly, but they seem to have had a good time.'

From the balcony, there was a magnificent view extending right over the city to the coastline near Pompeii and the brooding mass of Vesuvius. From the gardens and terraces below, a heady mixture of scents awakened by the sunlight rose up to envelop them. In the middle distance, Zen could clearly see the cranes and warehouses at the port. And that grey block, slightly to the left, was the Questura.

'Well, I'm glad someone is,' he said resignedly.

Cara semplicità, quanto mi piaci

The Greco, at the foot of Via Chiaia, seemed to Dario De Spino the right sort of venue for his purposes. Its slightly faded *gran caffè* elegance, the sense of tradition and history, the waiters in their starched uniforms, to say nothing of the view of the former Royal Palace and of the San Carlo opera house – all this was calculated to impress the pants off these two babes who'd grown up in some mosquito-ridden hovel in Hoxha's Albania. They'd think they'd died and gone to heaven!

Not that Dario was interested in removing their pants himself, although he had been known to dip into the other side of the gender pool from time to time, both by way of demonstrating his versatility and confirming that he was better off where he was. But his resources in that respect were already overstretched, what with Mohammed out at Portici – a thirty-minute commute each way, on top of everything else – and the demands of social life here in town. With his extensive range of business interests, it was essential to remain on good terms with a large number of people, many of whom could get distinctly snippy if he didn't make a pass at them every so often.

No, Dario's interest in the *albanesi* was, he would have been the first to admit, purely professional. And from that point of view, the outing had already been a success. Even in the bizarre gear they had brought with them from that Stalinist hell-hole, they were getting plenty of attention on the street. By the time Dario had taken them to the sweat-shop in Via Spagnoli and fixed them up with some of the fake designer duds they run up there, he would need a cattle prod to keep the young studs at bay. It also wouldn't do them any harm to see the conditions in those airless *bassi*, where children, young women, mothers and old crones stitched and sewed from morning to night for piece rates that would make the plaster Madonna on the wall weep tears of blood. If they took exception to Dario's proposition, once he finalized it, he could ever so gently remind them of the alternative.

But that was still some distance in the future. For now, all he wanted to do was to wean them away from the idea this Alfonso Zembla had given them that their long-term salvation lay with Gesualdo and Sabatino. The trick was to demonstrate that he was a much more important and well-respected figure, and, given his actual reputation, this needed to be approached with some care. Which was another good reason for choosing the pricey Caffè Greco, where it was extremely unlikely that they would run into anyone he knew – or that still more embarrassing class of people he did not know, or had forgotten, but who turned out to remember him only too well.

There was little risk of that sort of unpleasant encounter here. As he escorted the girls in, they caught sight of themselves reflected in the antique mirrors in their ornate frames, and gasped. At one end of the marble bar an elegant gentleman in a superb suit of slightly old-fashioned cut was holding forth to two younger underlings each carrying about a million lire's worth of tailoring themselves. Carefully choosing a moment when none of the trio was looking his way, Dario nodded respectfully.

'Buon giorno, cummendatò!' he murmured. 'Comme state? Sto' bbuono, grazzie.'

He turned to his two charges with a confidential air.

'One of the top men in the Regional Council. If Vitale sneezes, half the city catches a cold. I would introduce you – he's a great admirer of female beauty, even at his age – but I know those two with him and I can guess what they're talking about. It'll be all over the papers tomorrow, but for now discretion is the key word. No, don't stare!'

This to Libera, who was ogling one of the younger men with a directness Dario attributed to her unspoilt innocence. Who knows, he might actually have a couple of virgins on his hands here! From everything you heard, the Albanians had a code of behaviour which made the Sicilians look frivolous. Libera's ingenuous eye-contact certainly had a remarkable effect on the recipient of her attentions, who was now listening to the elderly buffer – whoever the hell he might really be – with little better than half an ear. Dario slipped a 5,000-lire note to a passing waiter.

'Give that to the barman. The name's De Spino. He's to treat me like a regular, but with respect.'

The girls could hear this, but of course they understood the local dialect about as much as Dario did Albanian. And the results were certainly gratifying.

'Dottor De Spino!' the barman called out as they approached, his expression a perfect mime of deferential goodwill. 'What a pleasure to see you again. And such charming young ladies! What may I have the honour of serving you?'

They ordered coffee in various forms, all minutely prescribed as to strength, quantity, heat, and presence and abundance of milk and foam. This ritual took the best part of a minute, following which De Spino broached the matter in hand.

'Yes,' he mused, as though the idea had just occurred to him, 'I could introduce you to so many people, people who really count, moving in the top ranks of society. Whereas those two lads upstairs . . . They're pleasant enough fellows, but frankly they wouldn't be allowed past the door in the sort of houses I'm talking about.'

'I thought they were friends of yours,' replied Iolanda pertly.

Dario De Spino smiled in a wise, worldly, mildly self-deprecatory way.

'A man like me has to mix with all manner of people,' he murmured, waggling his hand to illustrate the degree of social flexibility involved. 'Many of them think that they are my friends. If I allow them to cultivate this illusion, it is because it suits my purposes.'

A shrug of vast condescension.

'Gesualdo and Sabatino are useful to me in various ways. They are of the people, you understand, the lower orders, and move naturally and widely in that milieu. Then again, they are linked to one of the most powerful criminal clans in the city. That makes them extremely helpful for facilitating . . . various enterprises.'

The effect on his listeners was all he could have wished.

'You mean they're *gangsters*?' gasped Libera, open-mouthed.

Dario gave a pained look, as if gently reproving her crassness.

'Everyone in Naples is more or less a gangster, my dear. It's a question of degree. So far as I know, neither Sabatino nor Gesualdo has been blooded . . .'

'Blooded?' repeated Iolanda with a look of alarm.

'A technical term,' Dario returned, inspecting his finger-nails. 'I mean that as far as I know they haven't killed anyone yet. Not in the line of work, at least. Their private lives are, of course, another matter. But there is no question that they are intimately associated with various figures whose activities are – how shall I put it? – of considerable interest to the authorities.'

He smiled apologetically.

'But enough about them! What interests me is you, and your problems. The question is, where do we go from here?'

He did not have to spell out what 'here' meant. It was clear from his companions' disconsolate expressions that they appreciated the position only too well. Their attempts, the night before, to make contact with the two young men recently installed upstairs had ended in the most abject failure.

Libera made the initial approach, appearing at the door of the upper apartment to solicit Gesualdo's assistance with a time-honoured line:

'Excuse me, but our lights have gone out.'

Gesualdo summoned Sabatino, and the two men came downstairs, located the fuse-box and threw the switch which De Spino had deliberately tripped. Catching sight of their friend as the lights came on, they gasped.

'What the hell are you doing here?' demanded Sabatino.

'You're not the only ones who have friends all over town,' Dario responded, holding up his hands. 'Let me introduce you. This is Iolanda . . .'

'And I'm Libera,' said the brunette. 'So pleased to meet you. We've just arrived in Naples and we're just desperate to find work.'

'We'll do anything rather than have to go back to Albania,' wailed Iolanda. 'Anything!'

'These two know all sorts of people,' De Spino put in. 'Right, lads? I'm sure they'd be only too happy to give you a leg up on the situation, so to speak.'

But Gesualdo and Sabatino had not seemed at all happy. On the contrary, they had been brusque to the point of rudeness, and immediately retreated upstairs again after making it very clear that they wanted nothing whatever to do with the tenants of the lower flat or their problems.

'I've got quite enough on my plate as it is!' said Gesualdo when De Spino came to plead for his charges. 'It may be difficult for you to appreciate, Dario, but some of us have work to do. On top of which, as I thought I made clear to you in the car, I'm feeling emotionally shattered at the moment.'

'Besides,' said Sabatino, 'how would it look for us to get hooked up with a couple of single women, however innocently, on the very day our *'nnammurate* left town?'

In vain Dario De Spino had tried to persuade them that their scruples were ridiculous in the new Italy of the nineties, when the tired old ideas of life as a perpetual guerilla war between the sexes were at last being broken down.

'Why don't you take them under your wing?' Gesualdo had retorted. 'You know as many people as we do, and your reputation certainly can't suffer from hanging out with a couple of illegal immigrants with legs up to here.'

As a matter of fact, Dario had already decided that he was going to do just that, but in his own good time. First he wanted to collect the commission which the Squillace family were offering if he managed to get Gesualdo and Sabatino off their backs, which in turn involved getting Libera and Iolanda on to theirs. The question was how.

'They're so cold!' complained Libera, producing a cigarette from her bag and looking around helplessly. The young man she had been eyeing earlier immediately sprinted over with an outstretched lighter. He seemed inclined to linger, but De Spino gave him a look which soon sent him back to his companions.

'The other Italian boys we've met have been all over us,' Iolanda commented. 'But those two . . .'

A light suddenly appeared in Libera's eyes.

'They're not . . . how do you say? . . . *faggots*, are they?'

'They're as normal as you or I,' Dario assured them blandly. 'They're just distracted by their personal and professional responsibilities. The problem is how to get their attention.'

Iolanda finished her coffee and set the cup down with a bang.

'I think we should try killing ourselves,' she said.

Passi subito!

In retrospect, there were plenty of clues to what was about to happen, but, as so often, Zen did not spot them until it was too late.

To avoid awakening the suspicions of Pasquale – who knew him as Alfonso Zembla, a humble employee of the port authority – he had asked to be dropped outside the Central Post Office and then walked around the corner into Piazza Matteoti. Like so many streets and squares in Naples, this piazza has been renamed more than once, most recently to celebrate the most famous victim of the Fascist era. In this case the renaming also constituted a symbolic act of restitution, for the square in question is the one which Matteoti's opponents had chosen as the heart of their administration, and is lined with monumental buildings erected to serve the needs and proclaim the might of the new Italy.

Similar structures are to be found all over the South, even in quite small and seemingly insignificant towns. Elsewhere, Mussolini appeared above all a dramatically unique figure, unlike anyone who had preceded him on the political stage. Whether you supported or opposed him, his novelty was undeniable. But to Southerners he was a familiar figure, a *capo* who ran the toughest mob in town and ruthlessly disposed of anyone who got in his way; a man who demanded and commanded respect, fear and grudging admiration. Those who supported him would be protected, those who did not would be destroyed.

This was a code all Southerners had imprinted in their genes, and after decades of fine talk and patronizing neglect from the proponents of liberal democracy, it was a relief to have someone finally cut through all the bullshit and tell it the way it was, the way they knew it always had been and always would be. And they were rewarded, for the Duce kept his side of the bargain. In return for the overwhelming support they received south of Rome, the blackshirts extirpated every other species of banditry which had plagued the area for centuries, capital investment flowed south, jobs were created, and the secular temples of the new regime began to rise. Police stations received particular attention. The *Polizia dello Stato* was the creation of Mussolini, who was always suspicious of the loyalty of the *Carabinieri* with their royalist, élitist traditions.

When it came to constructing a suitable headquarters for the Fascist police chief, named after the ancient Roman quaestor, no expense had been spared. In Naples, the result was a building resembling a monstrous enlargement of one of the granite blocks from some aqueduct or amphitheatre. This trick of perspective may have been partly responsible for Zen's failure to spot the clues until it was too late. Riveted by this spectacle of petrified power, he failed to take proper notice of various persons in his immediate vicinity. The beggar, for example, his left arm picturesquely drooping inside his shirt, his haggard and unshaven face piteously appealing to the Christian instincts of the passers-by. Or the street kids, the *scugnizze*, swarming all over the wide pavement in a continually shifting envelope of ordered chaos. And to one side, at the street corner, a skinny male in his late teens revving the motor of a scooter and scanning the scene with apparent idleness, as though awaiting the arrival of a friend or lover.

Such were the individual elements, but it was only in retrospect that Zen was able to describe the way in which they meshed together, and to identify the purpose of the machinery or the signal which set it in motion. Everything happened very quickly. First a sudden manoeuvre of the *scugnizzi* blocked his path with their boisterous, high-spirited chase game. While he waited for them to disperse, the beggar closed in, beseeching charity with some long incoherent narrative. Zen had barely started to reach for his wallet when both he and the beggar were surrounded anew by the street kids, none of them more than twelve years old, settling around them like a flock of starlings, uttering weird high-pitched yelps. Something flew over Zen's head, away towards the man seated on the scooter, and at the same moment a grip like pliers closed on his rump in an agonizing pinch.

He whirled around indignantly, but the offender had already melded back into the juvenile collective, which was on the move again, streaking away across the piazza into the ambient *bassi*, there to dissolve without trace in the porous tenements and alleyways. With a shrug of resignation, Zen turned back to settle accounts with the beggar, but he too had vanished. He was about to continue on his way when the noise of a revving engine attracted his attention, and there was the beggar, inexplicably clinging to the pillion of the scooter with *both* hands as the machine roared off around the corner and disappeared. It was only then that Zen realized that something else had gone – his wallet.

The uniformed policeman cradling a machine-gun outside the Questura denied having seen anything with a massive shrug which suggested that such incidents were very common, principally the fault of the victim, and in any case too trivial to warrant his attention. Zen proceeded to pull rank, thus at least giving himself the satisfaction of seeing the man cringe, only to realize that one of the items in the missing wallet was his police identification card.

More serious consequences of this loss soon became apparent. Without any tangible proof that Zen was who he said he was, the guard on duty at the rear of the entrance hall refused to admit him to the upper reaches of the building, which were strictly reserved for high-ranking servants of the Italian public and hence off bounds to the public itself. Matters were not helped by the fact that the only form of identification remaining to Zen was the small box of printed cards identifying him as Alfonso Zembla.

'But I'm here on official business!' he protested to the guard. 'They've been trying to get hold of me all night. Let me phone through and they'll confirm it.'

As if bestowing an immense favour, the guard waved negligently at the internal phone at his elbow. Zen got through to the operator and was connected to Vice-Questore Piscopo's office.

The deputy police chief was not available herself, but an under-ling confirmed that no one could be admitted to the official presence without suitable identification.

'But this is ridiculous!' spluttered Zen.

'It has perhaps escaped your attention that a new terrorist group is operating in this city and has already claimed three victims,' the voice replied icily. 'All agencies are on triple-red alert as per a ministerial communiqué. There are no exceptions.'

Under the patronizing gaze of the guard, Zen replaced the phone and retreated to the centre of the cavernous entrance hall to consider his next step. He had been very careful to have no contact whatsoever with the Questura since his arrival in Naples, and as a result there was no one in the building who knew him by sight and could vouch for him. He could get Caputo to come downtown, but that would leave no one to cover for him down at the port, and, besides, with the Questura on triple-red status following the *Strade Pulite* attacks, it was by no means certain that the mere word of an underling like Caputo would be enough to convince the authorities that Zen was indeed worthy of admission to the inner sanctum of power.

He was still debating these and other possibilities when a presence made itself felt at his elbow.

'Having problems, *duttò?*'

The speaker was slim, slight and dapper, and might have been aged anywhere from forty to sixty. He was wearing an odd collection of items, each showing signs of long use and careful maintenance: an antique three-piece grey suit, a wrinkled white shirt buttoned tight at the collar, a green V-neck pullover and a camel-hair overcoat mottled by age or damp and worn unbuttoned. The man's hands were covered by white cotton gloves. The left carried an old but immaculately blocked felt hat, the right a small ivory case. One gloved finger flicked up the silver lid, revealing a stack of business cards. With a resigned sigh, Zen took one. The inscription, elegantly printed in relief, read 'Professore Gennaro Esposito: Magician, Astrologer, Clairvoyant'.

'I don't believe in magic,' said Zen.

The ivory box snapped shut and vanished.

'That's just to present myself,' Professor Esposito replied

calmly. 'I've virtually retired from practice, anyway. The competition is fierce these days, and if you don't advertize on television no one takes you seriously. But that's neither here nor there. The question is, what *can* I do for you?'

Zen gave the man a sour look.

'Not a damn thing, unless you can magically spirit me up to the fourth floor.'

'To see whom?'

'The Questore's acting deputy. A certain Piscopo.'

The professorial eyes rolled impressively.

'Ah!'

Zen nodded.

'Impossible, even for retired magicians.'

A wave of the splayed gloves.

'We're in Naples, *duttò*. Everything is improbable, but nothing is impossible. Even the price is not exorbitant. I can offer you two options. The first, at thirty thousand, will take about an hour, give or take, depending who's on duty today. Or if you decide to go for the express service, I can have you there faster than you could walk up the stairs. That costs fifty thou, but it's worth the extra.'

Zen smiled wearily.

'I'm sure it is. Unfortunately I can't take advantage. The reason I'm cooling my heels here in the first place is that my wallet just got stolen, along with my identification card and all the cash I had on me.'

The man studied Zen with renewed interest.

'You're a policeman, *duttò*? In that case, I can offer you the professional discount. Five per cent off the normal service fee, ten off the express.'

'I still haven't got it.'

'No problem.'

The gloved fingers darted out, grazed Zen's wrist and vanished again with his watch.

'With your permission, *duttò*, I'll keep this for security.'

The man turned away, melting into the crowds of people entering and leaving and queuing and jostling all around. Zen stood there, looking helplessly about him. First his wallet, now his watch. It was time to leave while his shirt was still on his back. But he seemed powerless to move. Despite his sarcasm about the professor's magical powers, it was almost as if a spell had been cast upon him.

'This way, *duttò!*'

He turned round. Professor Esposito was beckoning to him from the checkpoint at the back of the hall where Zen had been refused entrance earlier. He made his way through the throng towards the impassive guard, who gave no sign of ever having seen him before. His guide led him to a set of three elevators and inserted a key into the right-hand one. The doors slid open.

'The Questore's private elevator,' Esposito whispered conspiratorially, ushering Zen inside. 'Goes direct to the top floor. Like I said, you'll be there quicker than climbing the stairs!'

La sorte incolpa

'No, that's not the problem. It's that you're unlucky.'

The speaker – a woman, judging by the pitch of her voice – was in police uniform. She was smoking a small cigar and wearing dark glasses. The large room was dim, the shutters closed.

'Anyone can be unlucky,' Zen replied.

Vice-Questore Piscopo rapped her cigar, unloading a neat package of ash into a steel ashtray on her desk.

'Once, yes,' she replied. 'Several times, even. But there is a logic in this, as in everything else. Occasions do not contradict the rule. Statistically, you have proved to be unlucky.'

She lifted a paper from the file in front of her.

'There's a pattern here, *dottore*, which I recognized long before hearing of your latest problem – I refer to your allowing your wallet to be stolen. A pattern which none the less might have enabled me, in a certain sense, to predict it.'

A pause.

'In Milan, you wrongfully arrest a man for the Tondelli murder and twenty years later he tries to kill you after his release from prison. In Rome, you single-handedly "solve" the Moro kidnapping, unfortunately too late to save the victim. Same thing two years later, in Perugia, with the Miletti family. In Sardinia, you concoct a convenient solution to the Burolo murders to satisfy your contacts at Palazzo Sisti – who then disappear from the political spectrum within a year or so. As if to demonstrate the degree of your incompetence, you then go on to make absurd allegations against a leading regional politician, now mayor of Venice and a close ally of our own minister. And now this.'

Zen said nothing. In the ten minutes since he had been admitted to the room, Vice-Questore Piscopo had said nothing relating to the case in hand. It had been, he now realized, a mistake to mention the theft of his wallet. He did so by way of excusing his failure to appear earlier, but it merely made him look incompetent and helpless, and confirmed the thesis which the authorities had apparently formulated as regards his record in general. When Piscopo finally got around to mentioning the incident of the night before, her interpretation was fully in accord with the line already established.

'On the basis of our investigation, we can rule out the possibility of a planned attack. The killers aboard the stolen municipal vehicle were unaware of the presence of the patrol car carrying your men until the traffic accident, in itself completely unpredictable, occurred.'

Zen gazed at the reflective lenses.

'Who were they?' he asked.

'The gunmen?'

Another gesture indicating that this case had already been filed away in a capacious category labelled WEIRD STUFF THAT HAPPENS WHEN AURELIO ZEN IS AROUND.

'According to witnesses, there were anywhere from four to eight men aboard the refuse truck. All were dressed in blue overalls, like regular municipal employees, but we have questioned all the personnel concerned with this work and are satisfied that they are not involved. The truck itself went missing from the municipal depot two months ago.'

The Questore's deputy puffed on her cigar.

'Which leaves the question of what your men were doing there in the first place.'

Zen felt himself stiffen up. The woman's uniform, an unusual affectation in one of so elevated a rank, left him feeling as naked as he had been when Valeria came into the room that morning.

'Three days ago,' he began laboriously, 'a stabbing occurred in the port . . .'

'I am only too aware of that, *dottore*! We have been subjected to the most insistent pressure for a solution ever since.'

Zen nodded, as though she had acknowledged a shared bond.

'Yesterday the prisoner – who was still unidentified and who refused to make a statement of any sort – complained of severe abdominal pains. I summoned a doctor . . .'

'You were *on duty*?'

The question was laden with ironic emphasis.

'Naturally. The gravity of the case clearly demanded that I set aside all other matters and devote myself to finding a solution without regard to personal comfort or to bureaucratic norms.'

'And yet we have been trying without success to contact you for over forty-eight hours now. Your subordinates certainly did a masterly job of covering for you, but I must say that we all had the impression that you took a distinctly – how shall I say? – *relaxed* view of your duties.'

'Unfortunately my home telephone line is temporarily out of action,' Zen replied. 'I called SIP, but you know what it's like trying to get any emergency work done at the weekend.'

'So the prisoner complained of abdominal pains and you summoned a doctor.'

'Exactly.'

'A police doctor?'

Zen hesitated fractionally.

'There was none available. And since it was clear that the prisoner was in considerable pain, and given the importance of this case, I summoned a civilian doctor who was able to come immediately. He confirmed that the prisoner was suffering from gastro-intestinal complications and required urgent medical attention. He signed a medical report to this effect, a copy of which I will forward in due course. I immediately authorized the release of the prisoner into the custody of two of my most experienced officers, with orders to convey him to hospital and remain at his bedside until the necessary medical intervention had been completed. It was while they were carrying out these duties that the attack took place.'

Vice-Questore Piscopo nodded and smoked, smoked and nodded.

'So not only do we still know nothing about the principal suspect and material witness in a case with enormous international repercussions, but the individual himself has escaped from custody.'

She opened her hands in mock appeal.

'What would you call that, *dottore*, if not bad luck?'

'A carefully planned and ruthlessly executed ambush,' Zen replied, 'designed specifically to free the prisoner before he could be made to talk.'

Piscopo snorted contemptuously.

'Why would anyone bother to set up an ambush for some knife-wielding thug?'

Now it was Zen's turn to express ironic surprise.

'I didn't realize that you had succeeded in identifying him, *dottoressa*. And if he has a criminal record, as you suggest, it is very odd that we have received no positive response to our request for fingerprint and photographic identification.'

'Of course I haven't identified him. I was merely . . .'

'There is however another possibility,' Zen went on, 'which would explain both the ambush and the lack of documentation.'

'And what might that be?'

'This man isn't a lone wharf rat, as everyone has assumed, but a close associate of one of the most powerful clans of organized crime in the city.'

There was a long silence, during which Piscopo's glasses seemingly became even more opaque.

'Which?'

The word was as hard as a jagged chip chiselled off a block of marble.

'Ermanno Vallifuoco,' Zen replied.

The policewoman pulled at her cigar and discharged a dense cloud of blue smoke.

'Ermanno Vallifuoco has been taken out of circulation.'

'Yes, I read about that.'

A silence. Vice-Questore Piscopo scrunched up the print-out of Zen's career and tossed it into a metal waste basket.

'In a way, you're a pair,' she declared. 'Ermanno Vallifuoco represented the old Naples, just as you, Dottor Zen, represent the old Italy.'

'And have I too been "taken out of circulation"?'

The mouth beneath the dark glasses did not smile.

'Less effectively, unfortunately.'

Le cose che han fatto

'She said that?'

'Those were her very words.'

'And you believe her?'

A shrug.

'Then why hasn't Orestina said anything about it to me?'

'Filomena said they'd sworn not to tell us,' Sabatino explained. 'She just blurted it out while we were talking this morning. She sounded a bit exhausted and emotional – apparently they'd been up most of the night – and she said she couldn't lie to me.'

Gesualdo, who was driving, made an unnecessarily vicious left turn.

'Oh, she couldn't, eh?'

Sabatino glanced at his partner in surprise.

'What's wrong with that?'

'And those little bitches bought into it?' yelled Gesualdo over an excruciatingly loud and dissonant blast of his horn at the mental incompetent at the wheel of the car ahead, who had very nearly caused an accident by suddenly stopping, without the slightest warning, at a stop light.

'For them, it meant a free trip to London,' Sabatino remarked in a conciliatory tone. 'Besides, Filomena said they knew they could trust us, so it didn't make any difference anyway.'

'*Strunze 'e mmerda! Chi t' 'a date 'a patente?*'

This to the driver in front, who was still blocking the street, even though the light had changed to green several nanoseconds earlier.

'So Orestina didn't mention this to you?' asked Sabatino.

Cutting out in front of an oncoming bus, the red Jaguar roared past the offending vehicle.

'We talked about other things,' Gesualdo replied combatitively.

'Like what?'

'Like none of your fucking business.'

'Oh, *those* things . . .'

Two blocks later, the Jaguar's precipitate progress ended in the constipated streets feeding into Piazza Garibaldi and the souks around the main railway station.

'Who set it up?' demanded Gesualdo. 'That Alfonso Zembla, I suppose.'

Sabatino waved negligently, the lordly dispenser of privileged information.

'He's got nothing to do with it. Apparently it's all their mother's doing. Her idea is that the girls are just in love with the idea of being in love for the first time, and that if they spend a few weeks away they'll forget all about us. But it seems to have worked the other way round . . .'

A pause.

'. . . at least as far as Filomena's concerned. She said she's missing me so much she couldn't sleep all night.'

With a wary eye out for policemen, Gesualdo attached the flashing blue light to the roof and started to inch through the blockade.

'And what about you?' he asked aggressively. 'Did you tell your faithful Penelope about us moving into a house with two Albanian sex bombs who're willing, quote, to do anything to get ahead, unquote?'

Sabatino shrugged.

'Well, no . . .'

'Why not?'

'She wouldn't understand. You know how women are.'

Gesualdo shook his head.

'On the contrary.'

They rounded the piazza and entered the squalid streets behind the station.

'Odd that Orestina didn't trust you,' murmured Sabatino as though to himself.

'Still odder that you didn't trust Filomena,' Gesualdo shot back.

'It's not a question of trust! I've done nothing to be ashamed of.'

'So far.'

Sabatino gave his partner a look.

'What's that supposed to mean?'

Gesualdo brought the Jaguar to a halt at the kerb.

'Well, now we know that the whole thing's just a trick . . .' he sniffed.

'What difference does that make?'

There was no answer.

'So is this it?' asked Sabatino at length.

Gesualdo opened the car door.

'This,' he said, 'is it.'

They crossed the street and entered one of a few remaining tenements which had survived both the war and the subsequent reconstruction. A steep internal staircase led to a dingy but spotlessly clean landing with an open window overlooking a small courtyard. Behind one of the two doors which opened off it, a child was crying insistently. Gesualdo rapped at the stout wood panelling.

'Who is it?' a woman called out.

Gesualdo cleared his throat respectfully.

'Good morning, *signora*. Excuse the disturbance. I'm a friend of Roberto.'

He glanced at Sabatino before adding, 'It's about a car.'

Dove sia nessun lo sa

On the bench in the cavernous entrance hall of the police station, a laurel wreath the size of a tractor tyre rested against a wall mottled by dust which had collected in the pockmarked plaster. Red ribbons and the Italian flag flanked a grainy snapshot of Armando Bertolini as a raw recruit in uniform. The card below read: 'To Our Fallen Colleague, More in Sorrow Than in Anger, the Officers and Men of the Port Detachment'.

The building was completely silent and seemingly deserted. Zen walked upstairs, bellowing Caputo's name. His voice echoed hollowly. Then running footsteps sounded above, and the slight but virile figure of his subordinate appeared on the landing.

'What's going on?' demanded Zen, puffing slightly with the exertion of climbing the stairs. 'This place is as dead as some country railway station in Calabria.'

Caputo mimed deference tempered by grief.

'Most of them have taken the day off, chief. In the circumstances, it seemed only natural. Everyone's shocked by what happened to poor Armando. Even upstairs has closed.'

'What are you talking about?' Zen wheezed, having attained the landing. 'I've been given to understand that the upper floor of this building is disused.'

Caputo nodded.

'But today it's even more disused.'

'They've shut the whorehouse? Jesus!'

'As a mark of respect, *dottore*. It's only for one night, mind you, and Monday is always slim pickings.'

'I'm glad to hear that a spirit of pragmatism still prevails, Caputo.'

He led the way down the corridor to his office. When the door had shut behind them, he turned and looked his subordinate in the eye.

'Now then, what really happened?'

Caputo opened his mouth, closed it again, and shrugged.

'Like I told you on the phone, chief, we were driving along quietly, minding our own business and looking for a suitable opportunity to let Pastorelli pretend to escape . . .'

'No, I mean what *really* happened?'

'I already told you, chief! These guys in the refuse truck jumped out and gunned down Bertolini before any of us could . . .'

'You're not listening, Caputo!'

Zen's face was a mask glowing with obscure passions.

'For the last time, what really happened?'

Caputo's eyes were fixed hypnotically on Zen's.

'Really?' he murmured, as though breaking a taboo by uttering the name of a divinity.

A pause, a shrug.

'The talk is that it was probably a hit team from one of the clans using a municipal vehicle as cover. When the accident occurred, they realized the operation might be jeopardized and decided to take the initiative. Either that or they just panicked. That's all I could find out. No one seems to know anything for sure. It's odd.'

Zen continued to hold Caputo's gaze for a long while in silence. Then he turned away abruptly.

'And the stabbing case?'

Immediately Caputo perked up.

'We've got movement on that one, chief! The Americans got back to me. They've identified the person whose fingerprints appeared on that cassette.'

'Excellent! Who is he? I need to speak to him immediately.'

'His name's John Viviani. But there's a problem.'

'A problem?'

Caputo's grin erupted and vanished with equal suddenness.

'His ship sailed last night.'

'Ah.'

'But the real problem is that this Viviani isn't aboard.'

'So where is he?'

'No one knows.'

It took Zen five minutes more to get the whole story. Ensign John Viviani, a junior officer on the aircraft carrier, had been granted shore leave the previous day with orders to return to his vessel by three in the afternoon. When the ship sailed at six that morning, Viviani had still not returned. He had been listed as absent without leave and his details circulated to the relevant authorities, but so far no trace of him had been discovered.

'What about Pastorelli?' demanded Zen.

'He finally called in. He got the cuffs off with the key we gave him and is lying low at home.'

'All right, here's what we do. Bertolini's killing is out of our hands. The Questura will handle that. As far as the stabbing goes, our line remains the same. The prisoner was being transported to hospital when a totally unforeseeable attack took place, as a result of which he fled without trace. Our investigations are on-going and we have no comment to make. Got it?'

A swift nod.

'Got it, chief.'

'I'm going to go and make some, er, parallel enquiries.'

But it turned out this wasn't so easy. When he got downstairs, Zen discovered a guard on the main door of the police station, a man he had never seen before, kitted out in battledress and machine-gun. Undeterred by Zen's imperious manner, he demanded to see his ID.

'I am Vice-Questore Aurelio Zen, in command of this detachment. And who might you be?'

'Landi, Proculo,' the man replied. 'Anti-Terrorist Squad.'

He nodded towards a jeep parked outside, containing four men similarly equipped and armed.

'In view of the threat posed by the assault yesterday,' Landi continued, 'we've been posted here until further notice with strict orders not to let anyone enter or leave without proper identification.'

It took Zen only a second to sum up the realities of the situation. The Questura had taken over. His little fiefdom, such as it had ever been, was no more.

He walked back upstairs and tapped on an office door.

Inside, Giovan Battista Caputo was in the middle of a telephone conversation in dialect. Zen turned idly towards a notice-board on the wall, feeling like a foreigner again, an alien intruder to be isolated and repelled. It was some time before he emerged from this slough of self-pity sufficiently to realize what he was looking at. The notice-board was covered in various official communications relating to events in which the local force was expected to take a professional interest. Most had been there for some considerable time, judging by the colour of the paper.

But there were two new ones, freshly circulated by the Questura. One featured a mug shot of the escaped prisoner in the stabbing case, with a warning that he was to be regarded as armed and dangerous. The other featured a military-issue photograph of Viviani, John, a US naval officer presumed missing after failing to report to his ship. It showed a pleasant, open-faced lad in his twenties with crew-cut hair and the wary look of someone trying to appear tougher and more competent than he really felt himself to be. Zen detached both from the board, folded them carefully and put them away in his pocket.

'Don't waste your time, chief!' Caputo told him, hanging up the phone. 'Those guys always turn up after a couple of days on the town, once they sober up or run out of money.'

'I need to get out of here the back way,' Zen said. 'Like our prisoner did.'

Caputo barely raised an eyebrow.

'No problem.'

Zen went over to the desk and dialled a number.

'I'm coming home,' he said.

'Home?' queried Valeria.

'I need some money. My wallet got stolen. Do you have some cash? I'll pay you back.'

'How about lunch?'

A pause.

'If you're hungry,' added Valeria.

Unseen, Zen smiled.

'I'm always hungry.'

'Just the sort of man I like.'

Una donna che non val due soldi

Which was more than the whore at Via Francesco Proscopi 53c felt about either of the young men with hard eyes and tough bodies who had so rudely talked their way into her home.

She didn't like them calling her a whore, for a start-off, and particularly not in front of Daniele, who had immediately picked the word up and was now trumpeting it proudly about the apartment as he no doubt would later about the entire neighbourhood: '*Puttà! Puttà!*'

Still less did she like them using Roberto's name to get past the door, when it was clear within seconds – but too late – that they had no connection with this local fixer and power-broker beyond knowing his name. Heaven only knew who they *were* connected to. Someone powerful, for sure, or they wouldn't have dared throw their weight around in this arrogant way. There was a name out there, all right, but she preferred not to think too much about who it might be.

But all this paled into insignificance compared with what happened next. She had admitted bringing the car to the underground depot run by Lorenzo, who ran the place for Roberto, who in turn ran all manner of things for . . .

'Where did you get it?' demanded one of the men.

He was the one she had been most afraid of all along – wrongly, as it now turned out. For no sooner had she repeated the line she used with Lorenzo – 'I saw it on the street, unlocked and with the key in the ignition' – than the other man, to whom she hadn't so far paid much attention, grabbed Daniele as he ran past, still yelling '*Puttà!*', and hauled him up to perch on his knees. Then, still smiling, he took out a pistol and aimed it at the back of the child's head, which he was holding in such a playfully tight grip that Daniele had no idea what was happening.

'*Puttà!*' he yelled, encouraged by this welcome male attention. '*Puttà!*'

'For Christ's sake, Sabatino!' the other man hissed, loud enough to be heard.

So that's the deal, she thought, the good cop and the bad cop. Not that they were cops, of course, but the pattern was the same.

'*Oh, puttà!*' shouted the one called Sabatino, mimicking her son's voice and grinning from ear to ear. 'Where did you get it?'

If only there was a simple answer, she would have told them. But there wasn't. She'd seen the news, and knew now who the owner of the car was. And she knew – or rather, like everyone else, didn't know – what had become of him. All she was sure of was that some gang of terrorists was involved, and that the lean, cruel, unknown young man across the room had just cocked the revolver pointing at the nape of her son's neck, his blank eyes boring into her like some scary trick's cock.

'From a client!' she blurted out.

'When?'

'Friday night.'

'Who was he?'

'I don't know! I hardly saw him.'

'*Puttà!*' yelled Daniele merrily.

His mother started to weep. For the first time, the child looked alarmed. Sabatino slid his pistol back inside his jacket.

'Go and play outside,' he said.

Daniele glanced at his mother, who nodded.

'But no tricks!' warned the other man.

The woman held her arms open to her son, who came running.

'Go and see Aunt Clara,' she told him. 'But don't say anything about these men being here.'

'Same as usual?' lisped Daniele brightly.

His mother sighed and nodded gravely.

'Same as usual.'

Daniele turned bravely away, pleased to be helpful. He went out, closing the door behind him, same as usual, leaving his mother alone with the strange men.

'I'd never seen him before,' the woman said. 'He asked for some very . . . unusual services. But the money was good, so I agreed. I got into his car and we were about to drive off to his place when the accident happened.'

'Accident?'

This from the other man, the one whose name she didn't know.

'A truck hit us from behind,' she replied, shrugging. 'One of those yellow ones that pick up the rubbish. My trick got out to argue with the driver. And that was the last I saw of him.'

'Oh, come on!' Sabatino jeered aggressively.

There was no telling what might have happened if the other man's mobile phone had not started beeping. With an expression of annoyance he flicked up the mouthpiece and started speaking quietly, turning away so as not to be overheard. That broke their rhythm and gave her a chance to regroup, not that she had any idea what to do with it.

'Did anyone else see this?' demanded the one calling himself Sabatino, more to stop her overhearing what his partner was saying than in hope of a positive answer.

'No, I was the only one on that . . .'

She broke off with a frown.

'That's odd!'

The reply was brutal:

'What's odd?'

She looked up at him. This was the moment. They would either kill her now or not. At least Daniele would be safe.

'There're two *femmenielli* who usually work the opposite corner. But you know what? They haven't been there, the last couple of nights. I never thought about it until now. They've disappeared, just like . . .'

The other man snapped his mobile phone closed and stood up.

'Let's go!'

Sabatino frowned.

'What is it?'

'De Spino. He wants us now.'

They headed for the door. There the one who was not called Sabatino turned and stared levelly at the woman.

'Not a word of this to anyone else, or we'll be back. If not for you, then for your kid.'

She sat trembling as the door closed behind them. De Spino, she was thinking. She couldn't place anyone by that name except Dario, but he was just a small-time fixer and scam artist. It was a joke to think that someone like that could get a pair of ruthless thugs like these to drop everything and come running. It must be another De Spino. The old order was breaking down, and new men she had never heard of were taking over. She was out of tune with the times, with the new Italy. Soon no one would want her, even on the street.

It was only then that she realized that the two men had said nothing about the money Lorenzo gave her for the car. A slow smile spread across her tired face. Maybe it was time to pay a call on Grandma in Avellino. She was always complaining that she never got to see Daniele. They would be safe enough there up in the mountains for a while, by which time the whole episode would hopefully have been forgotten.

Qualche cosa di nuovo

It was not yet two when Zen left the Squillace apartment, replete with several bowls of *pasta e ciceri*, a celebration of making the most of what you have: chunks of chickpea bathed in oil and pasta under a dusty blanket of aged Parmesan. The sanctity of lunchtime might have been eroded farther north, where people hastily gobbled sandwiches at work just like Americans, but here in Naples the traditional three-hour *ora di pranzo* still commanded widespread respect. The streets outside were quiet, the corridors and stairs of the building deserted. It was therefore a surprise to Zen to find the porter already on duty.

He had already had one unnerving encounter with this Cerberus, who evidently took his responsibilities extremely seriously. When Zen had appeared on his way in, an hour or so earlier, he had leapt out of his wooden sentry box in the hall and quizzed him with an air of haughty scepticism as to his business there. As agreed, Zen explained that he was Signora Squillace's cousin from Milan, down here on business for a few days. The porter telephoned upstairs to check that Dottor Zembla was indeed known and expected, and only then, with some evident reluctance, allowed him to enter.

So the sight of the porter patrolling the hallway was not at first a welcome one. But it immediately became clear that the attitude of this functionary had changed dramatically. Perhaps he too had had a good lunch, or perhaps a few glasses of wine had softened his mood. At all events, he greeted Zen with deference and even warmth, and escorted him in person to the street door with a variety of bland but amiable comments about the weather.

Zen had summoned Pasquale before coming down, and the familiar yellow Fiat Argenta was already waiting at the kerb.

The porter hurried over to open the rear door for Zen, and made a great fuss about accepting the tip offered in return for these courtesies. Then he closed the door behind Signora Squillace's suddenly honoured guest, and looked across at two young men sitting in a red Alfa Romeo parked on the other side of the street. The driver, wearing a white sweater with the sleeves rolled up to reveal his tattooed arms, said something to his companion, in dark glasses and a Lacoste T-shirt, who put down the magazine he had been reading. Gravely, deliberately, the porter nodded once.

Inside the cab, Pasquale reached back and handed his passenger a blue plastic bag marked 'Carmignani Toys – Since 1883'.

'Don't worry, *duttò*. It isn't a toy.'

Zen opened the bag and looked at the box inside. It showed a photograph of a mobile telephone.

'Already?' he said in astonishment.

'Eh, eh! We make a sale, we deliver the product.'

Zen sighed.

'Unfortunately I can't pay you, Pasquale. My wallet got snitched outside the Questura and I can't get to the bank until tomorrow. I've already had to borrow some money from a friend to pay someone else off.'

'*Gesù, Gesù!* A few years ago, I could have made a few phone calls and your wallet would have been returned within the hour with every last lira intact. But that was the old days, before they locked up Don Raffaele. Nowadays everything's chaotic. There's no respect, no organization! I'll put the word about, *duttò*, but I'm afraid you can kiss your money goodbye.'

'The money's not that important. The real problem is that my police identification card was in there too, and without that . . .'

He broke off, realising his slip.

'So you *are* in the police!' exclaimed Pasquale triumphantly. 'I was sure of it.'

Zen gestured awkwardly.

'I didn't want to . . . inhibit you. Sometimes when people know you're a policemen, they feel less free to offer certain services of an irregular nature.'

Pasquale put the car in gear.

'Very thoughtful, *duttò*. I appreciate your delicacy. So your ID was taken too. Is that all?'

'All? It'll take months to get a new one.'

The taxi accelerated violently away.

'*Ma quante maje?*' Pasquale demanded rhetorically. 'A few days at most.'

Zen laughed.

'You've obviously managed to avoid too many dealings with officialdom very successfully, Pascà. From the day I put in my application for a replacement card, it will take a minimum of . . .'

'Twenty-four hours, *duttò*! Maybe even less, depends on the workload. I'll need a photograph, of course.'

A pause.

'You're offering to get me a fake?'

Pasquale took both hands off the wheel and turned around indignantly to protest.

'A fake? Do you think I'd try and fob you off with a fake? This is the real thing, *duttò*, indistinguishable from the original. Handmade in Aversa by some of the best artisans in the business. The printing, the paper, the stamp – all genuine! A work of art that's even more authentic than the original!'

'How much?'

'We can talk money later,' Pasquale said expansively, glancing in the rear-view mirror. 'Nothing excessive, though. And think of all the trouble you'll save yourself.'

Zen did so.

'All right,' he said, holding up the plastic bag. 'But I already owe you for this.'

Pasquale shrugged.

'Forty-eight hours, same as cash. After that I might need to apply a little interest, just to cover my outgoings. But if you want to run a line of credit, I can get you the best terms in town. What name would you like on the card?'

As they sped down the slope of the Vomero, Zen replied that his own name would do nicely, thank you very much, and then mentioned the other little matter which he was hoping that Pasquale might be able to help him with. But Pasquale did not seem to be listening to Zen's story of a missing American sailor with his usual deferential concentration. His replies were perfunctory and abstracted, and he kept glancing in the rear-view mirror. His driving had become uncharacteristically erratic, too, involving apparently unmotivated stops, last-minute turns down side-streets, and several complete rotations of a roundabout.

'Have you got an escort, *duttò*?' he asked at length.

'An escort?'

'Couple of men detailed to follow you about in a red Alfa. No, don't look round!'

Zen shook his head.

'Hmm,' said Pasquale.

They drove along the seafront to Via Partenope, where Pasquale abruptly pulled up in front of one of the luxury hotels facing the bay.

'Get out here,' he told Zen. 'Make as though you're paying me off. Then go into the hotel and walk straight through the lobby to the rear exit. I'll meet you there.'

Bemused but compliant, Zen got out and pretended to hand Pasquale some money through the window. On the other side of the street, a red Alfa Romeo had come to a stop opposite them. Zen turned and entered the hotel while Pasquale roared away, ignoring the pleas of a waiting couple who needed a ride to the airport. Through the revolving door, a wide strip of carpet led across a marble lobby with lots of uncomfortable-looking reproduction antique chairs. A doorman in livery loomed. Zen handed him a 10,000-lire note and pointed outside, where the youth in dark glasses and the Lacoste shirt was trying to cross against the ferocious traffic.

'That rent boy's trying to blackmail me,' Zen whispered. 'He's threatening to tell my wife if I don't pay him twice what we agreed. Can you kindly stop him pestering me?'

'No problem, sir,' the man replied suavely. 'But in future, kindly consult the concierge. He can provide someone whose discretion is guaranteed, twenty-four hours a day, with room service if desired.'

As Zen retreated towards the lifts, the doorman moved to block the path of the youth in the Lacoste shirt, who was now marching towards the revolving door. But instead of retreating in awe of this formidable personage, the intruder merely paused briefly and murmured something in his ear. The effect was electric. The doorman appeared to shrink visibly, like a leaking balloon. His look became glassy and his limbs seemed unsteady.

The youth walked by as though he were not there and ran swiftly past the registration desk and around the corner to the stairs and lifts. The right-hand lift was open and ready for use, but its companion, according to the illuminated indicator, was ascending past the second floor to come to rest at the third. The youth sprinted up the stairs, taking the shallow carpeted steps four at a time.

Just beyond the lifts and the stairs, an illuminated green sign suspended from the ceiling read 'Emergency Exit'. Below the sign was a closed door fitted with a metal push-bar. On the other side stood Aurelio Zen, looking down the narrow alley behind the hotel. At the far end, a yellow Fiat taxi was just turning in from the main street.

'Who do you reckon they are, *duttò*?' asked Pasquale once they were under way again.

'I can't imagine. Probably they mistook me for someone else. Anyway, we've lost them, thanks to you. Now then, as I was saying, I have another commission for you.'

He handed Pasquale the poster of John Viviani he removed earlier from the notice-board at the police station.

'This man went missing yesterday. Run off copies of this poster and distribute them to as many of your colleagues as possible. If any of them recognize him, and above all if they pick him up, have them get in touch. I'll make it worth their while.'

Pasquale nodded absently.

'Very good, *duttò*. Just the same, I wish we knew who those two in the Alfa were.'

He glanced suspiciously at a car coming in the oncoming lane. It was also red, and the two men aboard were young and tough-looking. But the car was some sort of flashy import, the men were dressed differently, and, in any case, they were going at high speed in the opposite direction and showed no interest whatsoever in the yellow taxi.

Stelle, un bacio?

'It worked, didn't it?'

'Oh, sure! If you'd held her feet over the gas burner, that would have worked too. Jesus!'

'The woman was obviously frightened.'

'I don't blame her, with some maniac holding a gun to her son's head!'

'For Christ's sake, Gesuà! I mean she was frightened of talking, frightened of getting involved. So I gave her something to be even more frightened of, and it worked. As for the kid, he never even knew what was happening. He thought it was all a big game.'

Gesualdo shook his head and said nothing.

'Anyway, since when have you been so particular about the methods we use?' demanded Sabatino. 'We shouldn't be driving around in this goddamn Jaguar, for a start-off. It's about as conspicuous as a carnival float, and we now know that it's hot as well. The last thing we want is someone tying us into the Vallifuoco hit.'

'On the contrary, that's exactly what we want.'

Sabatino shrugged and stared out of the window.

'She said it was a refuse truck, right?' he said at length.

'What?'

'The vehicle that rammed them from behind before Don Ermanno got a chance to do the same or worse to her. They did a nice job fixing the damage, by the way.'

'Lorenzo only hires the best. He has to, given his clients and turn-around times. Anyway, what about the truck?'

'Two things. First off, what the hell was a city garbage crew doing around there at that time of night? Those guys knock off strictly at six, even assuming they bother to show up for work at all.'

Gesualdo considered this in silence.

'And the second thing?'

'That shooting last night on Via Duomo,' said Sabatino. 'We damn nearly got caught up in that ourselves, you know. Talk about luck. We must have passed the spot just before it happened. Anyway, that was a refuse truck too.'

'So?'

'So, what's this new terrorist group calling itself?'

Gesualdo snapped his fingers.

'"Clean Streets". Christ, I think we may be on to something!'

He frowned.

'But we won't be the only ones. The police are bound to make the same connection. It's just too obvious.'

'It *is* just too obvious,' murmured Sabatino. 'I wonder why.'

Gesualdo didn't seem to hear.

'And meanwhile,' he said, bringing the car to a halt at the top of the Scalini del Petraio, 'instead of following this thing up and grabbing a piece of the action while we can, we have to drop everything to go and hold Dario's hand. Jesus!'

Sabatino sighed and got out of the car.

'You were the one who took the call, Gesuà. If it'd been me, I'd have told him to look after his own problems.'

'He sounded so desperate. Said it was a matter of life and death.'

'If he's pissing us about, it will be. His.'

They ran down the steps three at a time, through the little square where a boy was chasing a chicken which had escaped from its wire enclosure, and on down the final precipitous alley to their temporary home. Dario De Spino was standing at the door, rubbing his hands anxiously.

'Thank God you're here!' he blurted out. 'They're threatening to kill themselves! I would have called the cops, but I didn't think you'd want them snooping around. Besides, their papers aren't in order and I don't want to make matters worse.'

'Who?' demanded Gesualdo.

'Why, your new neighbours on the first floor, of course!'

Sabatino blasphemed loudly.

'You dragged us all the way over here for that? Let them kill themselves, if that's what they want.'

145

'Of course they won't kill themselves!' snapped Gesualdo. 'That's all talk. Your problem, Dario, is you don't understand women.'

'Certainly not these ones,' De Spino replied with a touch of pique. 'Albanians aren't flexible like us. Everything's gloom and doom, blood and guts. They scare the hell out of me, to tell you the truth.'

'That's your problem,' returned Sabatino. 'You're the one who decided to take them under your protection. If they've gone hysterical, you deal with it. It's got nothing to do with us.'

De Spino shook his head pityingly.

'You're trying to ingratiate yourself with the Squillace family by keeping an eye on the property, right? Well, how do you think it's going to look if two illegal immigrants top themselves in the place on your shift, eh?'

Gesualdo pushed impatiently past.

'Well, since we've come all this way, we may as well take a look.'

He led the way upstairs and knocked on the door of the lower apartment. There was no reply. He tried the handle, but the door was locked. Sabatino leant out of the window at the end of the landing. A narrow ledge ran from this to a balcony outside the rear bedroom. With the air of someone to whom such feats are part of the job, he climbed out of the window and stepped out along the ledge, pulled himself over to the balcony and looked in through the window.

'Holy Christ!'

'What is it?' demanded Gesualdo.

'Break the door down!' Sabatino yelled urgently, clambering back in through the window.

They put their shoulders to it, and when that didn't work Gesualdo pulled his pistol and shot the lock off. Then he kicked the door open, ran across the room and threw open the door to the bedroom. Libera and Iolanda were lying stretched out on the floor, each grasping a length of wire bared at one end and plugged into a wall socket at the other. Their eyes were closed and their mouths agape, tongues extended.

Gesualdo circled the bodies cautiously and unplugged the

lengths of wire from the wall. The other end was still grasped tightly in the victims' fingers. He pried these open, revealing extensive blackening. Meanwhile Sabatino was feeling for a pulse.

'This one's alive!' he said, bending over Libera.

Gesualdo put his hand on Iolanda's bosom, then leant down and proceeded to administer the kiss of life. Sabatino did likewise with Libera. After a long interval, the victims began to show feeble signs of animation. The two men immediately redoubled their efforts, squatting astride the women's supine bodies and pumping their chests vigorously.

Dario De Spino, all this while, had been looking on from the doorway. He appeared to be holding his breath, for some reason, as a result of which his face had turned bright red.

Possibil non par

Professor Esposito had arranged to meet Aurelio Zen in Piazza del Duomo, but when Pasquale dropped his passenger off there was no sign of the professor. Pasquale was sceptical as to the chances of his ever reappearing.

'Your watch must have cost – what? – three, four times what you owe him? Why should he let you redeem a pledge which is worth more than the debt it secures?'

This verdict was delivered with the gravity and assurance of an economist explaining why the government's fiscal policies are doomed to failure. Zen had no answer to its implacable logic, but he decided to wait for fifteen minutes anyway. Before dismissing Pasquale, he broke the mobile phone out of the box and, as a test, dialled his answering machine, which was taking calls for the disconnected phone.

There were two messages. The first was from Gilberto Nieddu, asking him to get in touch 'as a matter of the gravest urgency'. The other was from someone called Luisella, who just said she would call back. Zen switched off the portable and was about to put it away when he realized who Luisella was. He closed his eyes and uttered a curse.

'How's that, *duttò*?' asked Pasquale with a worried look.

'This thing brings bad luck,' muttered Zen, holding up the mobile phone.

Pasquale seemed to take this complaint literally.

'I'll change it for another, if you want. But what's the problem, exactly?'

'My ex-wife just called me.'

'Ah!' said Pasquale, as though everything was now clear. 'That's not the phone, *duttò*. That's the moon.'

'The moon?'

148

'It'll be full tonight.'

Zen shrugged.

'That happens every month, Pasquale. I haven't heard from my wife for seven years. Why now?'

'Because it's also the solstice, *duttò*. When the solstice and the full moon fall on the same day, even San Gennaro is over-matched.'

With this thought, Pasquale went off to circulate the poster of John Viviani amongst his fellow *tassisti*. Professor Esposito still had not appeared, so Zen dialled Gilberto Nieddu's number in Rome – or rather the number of a printing shop in the outskirts of the city belonging to a distant relative whom Nieddu had roped in on a 'Sardinians versus the Rest of the World' ticket when times got tough.

Zen left a message and his number with this cut-out, then held the line until Gilberto was put through.

'Aurelio! Thank God you called.'

From the tone of his friend's voice, Zen gathered that his message had been something more than mere hyperbole.

'What's happened?'

'It's your mother, Aurelio. I don't want to alarm you unnecessarily, but . . . well, she seems not to be at home.'

Behind Zen's back, a chorus of car horns played a brassy big-band fanfare.

'That's impossible! She never leaves except to come and visit your kids.'

'Exactly. That's when we first suspected something was wrong. She was supposed to come over this morning, but when I called for her there was no answer. Then Maria Grazia, the housekeeper, showed up and we went inside. It was empty, Aurelio. No Giustiniana, no note, no nothing. I was hoping that perhaps you knew where she was.'

Zen felt his head spinning.

'Look, I can't come up to Rome just now. Maybe tomorrow, I don't know. Can you make a few enquiries? Ask the porter, the other people in the building . . .'

'I wish I could, Aurelio, but I have to go abroad. I'm flying out of Fiumicino in a couple of hours. A business trip.'

'But you told me you'd had to surrender your passport.'

'Oh, and one final thing,' Nieddu said in an oddly strained voice. 'You remember that video-game cassette you brought me to look at?'

'What about it?'

'I've just discovered there was some sort of mix-up. Apparently the one I gave you back wasn't the same one you gave me. There were a bunch of them lying around in this place I went to test it. I suppose I must have picked up the wrong one.'

'Are you joking? Jesus Christ, Gilberto! So where's the original?'

'Don't worry, it's in safe hands. Well, I've got to go, Aurelio. I hope your mother gets in touch soon. *Ciao!*'

The line went dead. Zen frantically redialled the number in Rome, but there was no reply. He was trying Gilberto's home number when a figure standing meaningfully close caught his attention. Professor Esposito bowed politely.

'I'd given up on you,' Zen said ungraciously. The news of his mother's disappearance had shaken him more than he had yet appreciated. He imagined her having slipped out of her mind, as effortlessly as a dust-ball carried through an open window by the draught. She might even now be wandering around the traffic-ridden streets and addict-haunted parks of the capital, babbling to herself and accosting strangers under the illusion that she was back home in Venice, where everywhere was safe and everyone knew everyone.

'We had an appointment,' the professor remarked in a puzzled but slightly hurt tone.

'The cab driver who brought me here said you'd never show. "The watch is worth more than what you owe him," he told me. "Why should he bother to give it back?"'

Professor Esposito looked pained.

'Evidently he must be a low and ignorant class of person. It is true that I could have realized a short-term profit on the transaction by retaining your watch, but only at the cost of forfeiting your custom in the future and injuring the good name I have been at such pains to build up over the years.'

Zen nodded vaguely, but he wasn't listening. He had to find his mother, but he also had to find the escaped prisoner – and, above all, the US naval ensign who had gone AWOL. If what Gilberto had told him about the video-game cassette was even half true, then John Viviani was potentially in deadly danger.

'"Never make an enemy unnecessarily, nor neglect an opportunity to make a friend,"' observed Professor Esposito sententiously, '"for enemies can harm you and friends help you in ways and on occasions that you can never imagine." Francesco Guiccardini.'

He slipped his hand into his overcoat pocket and produced a watch which he handed to Zen.

'I happened to notice it had a tendency to lose time, so I took the liberty of showing it to a friend of mine who cleaned it thoroughly. Then I thought, Gennà, Gennà, what have you done? Is it likely that the *dottore* wouldn't have got the watch fixed himself, if he wanted to be on time? If he has omitted to do so, it can only be because he wants it to run slow so as to provide an excuse when he's late for some professional or social appointment. And now you've ruined everything for him. What an idiot you are, Gennaro!'

Zen thanked the professor for this thoughtful and ingenious hypothesis, but assured him that he had just never got around to getting the watch repaired. He then handed over the money he owed. The professor bowed again.

'You have my card,' he said. 'If you ever have any other little matters which need sorting out, you know where to find me.'

'Actually . . .'

Professor Esposito was instantly all attention.

'Yes?'

Zen shook his head.

'No, it's nothing.'

Neither man moved.

'That card of yours,' Zen said at last. 'It mentioned various services of an, er, supernatural variety.'

'Yes.'

'Would they include tracing someone who has disappeared?'

Bisogna consolarle

The kiss of life having proved effective, Gesualdo was all for calling a doctor to check the two girls' condition, and then an ambulance to take them straight to hospital 'and off our hands'. But the mere suggestion was enough to set off another crisis.

'First I cut her throat!' screamed Libera, grabbing a breadknife and holding it to Iolanda's neck. 'Then my own!'

'It's just the effects of the electricity,' Dario De Spino told the men. 'They're still in shock, so to speak.'

Libera waved the knife about as though executing a sculpture carved from the humid mass of the afternoon air.

'No doctors! No hospitals!' she spat menacingly. 'No authorities! No papers!'

'They'd only deport us,' Iolanda explained in a calmer tone. 'And back home they'd lock us up in a concentration camp! No one ever comes out of those places alive.'

'Better a quick and honourable death here!' yelled Libera, brandishing the knife.

'OK, girls, OK!' said Sabatino with a big grin, holding up his hands in token of surrender. He had no doubt that these crazy Albanians are quite capable of carrying out their crazy threats. He could still remember the stories his father used to tell about blood feuds up in the mountains near Avellino, things no one would believe possible now. Yet that had been just fifty years ago, a few hours drive from the city.

'We can't risk it,' he whispered to Gesualdo. 'If these two cut their throats, the cops will be all over the place. We'd be out of circulation for a year at least, and you know what that would mean for our promotion prospects. There're plenty of hungry young bastards out there who'd be only too glad to take our places.'

Gesualdo shrugged unwillingly.

'Whatever you say.'

Sabatino turned to the two girls.

'Eh, no problem!' he announced with a big smile. 'We'll just for-get this ever happened, right? And if there's anything we can do to help, within the limits of what's possible, just tell us and we'll be only too glad to bear it in mind. Meanwhile you can stay here . . .'

'And you,' Libera said, dropping the knife with a clatter and taking his hand, 'will stay too.'

Sabatino looked at her, then at Gesualdo.

'Maybe one of us had better stick around for a while to calm them down,' he said rapidly in dialect. 'You get back to work, Gesuà. I'll join you as soon as I'm free. It won't take long, but in a case like this it's just as well to be on the safe side.'

His partner stared at him for a moment in a way that could have meant anything or nothing.

'Whatever you think, Sabatì,' he said tonelessly.

Turning to go, he found Iolanda standing in front of him, gaz-ing at him intently. For a moment he paused, as though expect-ing her to say something. Then, with a shrug of impatience or relief, he bustled out. Libera caught Iolanda's eye and jerked her head sharply towards the door. With a grimace, Iolanda went after Gesualdo.

Dario De Spino coughed tactfully.

'If you'll just excuse me for a moment, I must make an urgent phone call. Remember Don Giovà? One of his conquests wants me to fix up her son with a job on the cigarette-smuggling boats.'

Catching Sabatino's eye, he tapped the side of his nose and added in dialect, 'Have fun!'

'What was that he said?' asked Libera as De Spino closed the door, leaving them alone.

'He told me to look after you,' said Sabatino.

'And will you?'

Sabatino gestured awkwardly.

'There's not much I can do, but . . .'

'Dario mentioned someone called Don Giovanni,' Libera rat-tled on. 'Maybe he could help.'

'No, no, he's finished.'

'Finished?'

'He used to be a player around town, but he was a big womanizer. That was his downfall.'

Libera sighed loudly.

'Ah, it's useless! Here are my sister and I, stranded in a foreign land with no one to help us. We have no work, no money, no hope. Our last chance was that you and your friend might take pity on us.'

Sabatino shrugged.

'Eh, eh! Life is tough everywhere these days.'

Libera turned away, biting her lip.

'You're so cold! I'm desperate, and all you do is laugh at me.'

Sabatino reached out and grasped her hand.

'I'm not laughing.'

They exchanged a long look. Libera gently disengaged her hand.

'Words are cheap.'

'I mean it!' Sabatino insisted. 'Why do you think I went to all that trouble to get rid of Gesualdo? He's cold, all right. But not all of us are, and certainly not me. I want to help you. I want you to be happy!'

He rubbed the fingers which had been gripping her hand. They seemed to be smeared with some sort of greasy black substance which smelt vaguely familiar, paint or polish . . .

'Prove it,' said Libera, staring at him defiantly.

Sabatino took a bunch of keys from his pocket, removed one from the cluster and handed it to Libera. She stared at it as though she had never seen such a thing before.

'What is it?' she asked.

'A key, of course.'

Libera looked him in the eyes.

'Yes, but what does it open?'

Sabatino reached inside his jacket and produced a pen. Taking Libera's hand in his, he wrote something on the velvety skin of her inner wrist.

'Come to this address at eight this evening,' he said, 'and you'll find out.'

Che loco è questo?

Professor Esposito's tall, angular figure was familiar enough in the back streets north of Via Sapienza, where he was regarded with a mixture of awe and mockery. Everyone had some tale to tell about the legendary powers, both worldly and supernatural, of '*o prufessò*, which ranged from predicting the winning number in the lottery to locating a lost will by direct communication with the dear departed, from fixing up someone's worthless nephew (who was nevertheless *pate 'e figlie*, with a family – God help them – to support) with a safe municipal job, to obtaining tickets for Napoli's big game against Juventus which had been sold out for months. One story even claimed that the professor had brought back to life a child who had swallowed rat poison, simply by passing a magnet over its inert body!

The professor's physical appearance, on the other hand, was a subject of general derision, mingled perhaps with a tinge of fear. His height would not have been considered exceptional farther north, but here, especially accentuated by his extraordinary skinniness, it created a freakish effect reflected in the nicknames which seemed to stick to him like dough thrown at a wall: Piece of Spaghetti, Stilt-Walker, the Lighthouse, Number Twenty-Nine. This last referred to the number popularly known in the local bingo game of *tumbulella* as 'the source of all trouble', an allusion to the male sexual organ.

On this occasion, though, Professor Esposito's progress through the narrow, crowded alleys of this part of Spaccanapoli caused even more consternation than usual.

'*Mamma bella d''o Carmine!*' exclaimed an old woman selling contraband cigarettes from a tray on her ample lap. 'The professor has duplicated himself!'

To a casual glance this might indeed appear to have been the case, for at his side was another man of equal height and scarcely greater bulk. They were similarly dressed, too, in long overcoats and grey felt hats, and their stride – long and hurried by local standards – was evenly matched.

'Some long-lost brother?' mused the cobbler, looking up from his work outside the one-room home where five children were playing a noisy game of tag.

'Why not? There's no shortage of foundlings in Naples!' commented his customer, playing on the original meaning of the name Esposito.

But when the professor finally reached his own home, on the third floor of a tenement above a second-hand book shop, he introduced his companion to the woman there – who might with equal likelihood have been his sister, his wife or his mother – as Don Alfonso Zembla. He then dismissed her curtly, with instructions that he was not at home to anyone.

'Not even Riccardo?' the woman queried.

'Least of all Riccardo!' retorted the professor, making the two-fingered gesture against the evil eye.

Once the woman had gone, he set about closing the shutters and the windows, leaving the room in semi-darkness.

'I needn't bother with the costume,' he remarked as though to himself.

His visitor looked puzzled.

'Costume?'

The professor opened a large trunk in the corner and lifted out a long robe in a satiny crimson material.

'There's a hat and boots to go with it,' he said. 'It's useful when you're dealing with the *popolino*, common folk who are ignorant and credulous. With a man like you there's no need for cheap tricks.'

'I don't see why that makes any difference,' his visitor objected. 'If you get results, your clients will believe in your powers, costume or no costume. And if you don't, fancy dress isn't going to help.'

The professor closed the trunk with a curt shake of the head.

'With all due respect, *dottore*, there you betray a complete misunderstanding of this science, which is not Newtonian but, if I may use the expression, post-Einsteinian! What is true for a given person in a given situation is not necessarily true for that person in a different situation, or for another person in the same situation, and still less if both are different.'

He lit an oil lamp and placed it on the table, beckoning his visitor to be seated at one end.

'If some illiterate market trader comes to consult me and sees me looking like this, he'll think, "This is no magician, no seer, this is an accountant or a teacher." He won't believe what I tell him, so it's a waste of time for me to tell him anything at all. The relationship is doomed from the start. With you, on the other hand, it's exactly the opposite. There's no point in me dressing up and going through a lot of mumbo-jumbo, because you would just think, "This man is obviously a fake or he wouldn't need to bother with all this nonsense." Am I right?'

Zen nodded. The professor seated himself at the other end of the table.

'Very good. Now then, what can you tell me about the missing individual? Have you a picture, or better yet some object belonging to him or her? An article of clothing, a piece of jewellery . . .'

'This is all I have.'

He took out the Missing Persons bulletin on the escaped prisoner and passed it up the table.

'I don't even know the man's name . . .' Zen began.

'I do.'

Zen stared at Professor Esposito, who was scowling at the photograph.

'His name is Giosuè Marotta, also known as '*o pazzo*.'

'"The madman"?'

'"The joker", rather, although there's nothing particularly amusing about Don Giosuè. He boasts of having killed over a hundred men. Eighty is probably nearer the mark, but his technique is more remarkable than his sheer output. He works in various media, but his speciality is the garrotte. They say he can make the process last as much as fifteen minutes.'

Zen gaped at him.

'You mean this man is well-known?'

Professor Esposito shrugged.

'Notorious, in certain circles.'

'But we had him in custody for days, and were unable to identify him!' Zen protested. 'We sent his prints and that mug shot over to the Questura. They said they had nothing on him.'

'Naturally. These people are not film stars or politicians. In the circles I just referred to, fame is inversely proportionate to how much is known about you, especially officially. With the very top people – Don Gaetano or Don Fortunato – the only data extant are the time and place of birth, and both are almost certainly false.'

Zen acknowledged the point with a nod.

'Have you any idea where this Marotta is now?' he asked.

The professor stared at the photograph for a long time. Outside in the street, above a cacophony of car horns, shouts, whistles and revving engines, a lone cock crew three times. Inside the room all was still except for the buzzing of a fly circling in the hot air above the lamp. It plunged sideways and fell, spiralling down to land on its back on top of the mug-shot of Giosuè Marotta, legs waving feebly.

'In Hades.'

The voice appeared to come from a great distance.

'You mean hell?' queried Aurelio Zen, frowning.

There was a long silence.

'That's the best sense I can make of it,' Professor Esposito said with a sigh. 'The images are very faint. Good reception is almost impossible without an object of reference, something imprinted with the subject's personal aura. But I see him somewhere deep underground, with flames and figures milling around. Do you know *The Last Judgement* they have up at Capodimonte? Or you may be familiar with the Roman copy by Michelangelo. In the glimpse I had, Don Giosuè might have been posing for one of the figures towards the bottom of the picture.'

Zen made no attempt to hide his disappointment.

'That doesn't help me much.'

'A time may come when it all makes sense,' the professor replied blandly, pushing the photograph back down the table. 'May I offer you a refreshment of some kind?'

Zen hesitated a moment.

'As a matter of fact, there's someone else I'm anxious to trace.'

'Then you're in luck, *dottore*. This week only I'm offering a thirty per cent discount on the second consultation. Who is it this time?'

'My mother. But I have no photographs, no personal belongings, nothing.'

The professor smiled.

'Stand up and come here.'

Zen obeyed. Professor Esposito undid the two middle buttons of his client's shirt and inserted the little finger of his right hand into Zen's belly-button.

'Where your mother is concerned,' he remarked, closing his eyes in concentration, 'you yourself are the only object of reference required.'

Cor di femmina

'What's the matter with you?' demanded Libera as Iolanda walked in looking, as her companion tactfully added, like a cigarette butt fished out of a urinal.

'Mind your own fucking business!' was the angry reply.

'It *is* my business, darling,' Libera reminded her. 'They've both got to come across or we don't get paid.'

'If it's the money you're interested in, you can kiss it goodbye right now!' snapped Iolanda, throwing herself down on the sofa, legs akimbo.

'What else would I be thinking about?' Libera asked innocently.

'Well, forget it! Gesualdo is straight as a die.'

Libera put her head on one side and nodded slowly.

'Not even a hint of any action?'

'Not a damn thing. You want to hear about it?'

'I'm all ears, darling!'

She came to perch on the edge of the sofa. Iolanda sighed mightily.

'I caught up with him on the steps outside and gave him the big sob story. Pretended to weep and be nervous and tongue-tied, the whole production.'

'Well done. And?'

'At first he took a really tough line. Said he couldn't help me, it was nothing to do with him, and he was sure De Spino would fix us up with something. "I can imagine what that creep has in mind," I told him. "Do you want to force my sister and I out on the streets?"'

'The very idea!' murmured Libera.

'He seemed to soften a bit at that. I mean, he's basically a really decent guy, you know? That's what makes it so tough.'

She looked away distractedly. Libera's jaw hardened.

'You're not falling for him, are you?' she said insinuatingly.

Iolanda flashed her a furious look.

'Don't be so fucking stupid!'

'All right, dearie, all right. No need to get your tackle in a twist. So what happened?'

Iolanda sighed again.

'He said he felt very sorry for us. I told him to stuff his pity. And he said . . .'

'Yes?'

'He said it wasn't just pity.'

Libera's eyes opened wide.

'He did?'

'So of course I went ahead and made a total fool of myself. I told him I'd always known there was something between us from the first moment I'd set eyes on him, and that someone so handsome couldn't be cold and selfish, blah, blah. And then it all came out.'

'What did?'

'A big speech about how he was engaged to be married and would never do anything that might hurt his future wife and the mother of his children. Then he turned on his heel and walked off without a word or a look, as though I was a piece of dog shit . . .'

She started to weep.

'And now he's probably on the phone to that bitch in England, giving her an earful about how beautiful and sweet and feminine she is . . .'

Tears rolled down her cheeks and splashed on to her blouse. Libera embraced her briefly and patted her back.

'Never mind, dear. You'll get over it.'

Iolanda sniffed.

'What about yours? Same story, I suppose. Bastards! They're all the same!'

Libera inspected her nails.

'Well, maybe not quite *all*.'

'What do you mean?' snapped Iolanda.

Libera tossed her hair and laughed archly.

'Oh, nothing in particular.'

Iolanda stared at her intently. Her tears had dried up.

'You expect me to believe that he fell for you?' she demanded with a harsh laugh. 'Oh, sure! And you started your period too, I suppose. Another miracle of San Gennaro!'

Libera shrugged modestly.

'Miracles sometimes happen, nevertheless.'

'Stop pissing me about!' exclaimed Iolanda. 'Let's face it, there's no way those two are ever going to come across for the likes of us.'

'I suppose you're right,' replied Libera. 'That must be why he gave me this . . .'

She displayed the key, dangling on a chain around her neck, and the address inked on her wrist. Iolanda stared at them in silence.

'That cunt,' she said at last.

Rolling up off the sofa, she strode rapidly to the door.

'Where are you going?' Libera asked in a tone of alarm.

'Back to the streets! At least there I can turn an honest trick and make some honest money.'

Libera ran and grabbed her.

'Are you crazy? Do you want to throw away the money Zembla promised us when it's practically in our hands?'

'I've had it, understand? All this bullshit about love is driving me round the bend.'

She threw herself back on the sofa and burst into tears.

'I'll fetch Dario,' said Libera, heading for the door. 'I'm sure he'll have some ideas. Stay right here!'

'I feel like I'm being torn apart,' Iolanda muttered to herself. 'And there's no one I can confide in or ask for advice, no one at all. To fall for a client! The shame of it! I'll be the laughing-stock of Naples.'

She sat up and sniffed loudly.

'But it won't happen. I'll just forget the bastard, wipe him out of my memory for ever . . .'

Her face collapsed as she started to weep again.

'Only I can't! Whatever I do, I think of him. Whatever I look at, I see his face.'

The door swung open and in came Libera with Dario De Spino, who had been having a nap in the upstairs flat.

'I hear we have a little problem,' he said with an encouraging smile.

'Piss off, you asshole!' shouted Iolanda.

'Now, now, calm down, *signorina*. Your sister tells me that she's managed to win over Sabatino, but that you can't seem to make any impression on Gesualdo. Is that right?'

With a shriek of impotent rage, Iolanda hid her head under the sofa pillows.

'Don't take it so personally, darling,' said Libera, gesturing languidly. 'You don't really think that any man could resist a woman like me, do you? I don't want to boast, but . . . well, the fact remains that some of us have got what it takes, while others . . .'

'You bitch!' screamed Iolanda, hurling an ashtray at her head.

Libera stepped back just in time and the projectile flew past and out of the window.

'*Grazzie assaje, duttò,*' called an elderly male voice from the house opposite. 'First the cigarettes, now the ashtray. Too kind, I'm sure. But listen, next time just give me a call and I'll come over and pick it up, OK?'

'Ladies, ladies!' De Spino remarked in a soothing tone. 'We mustn't let a little setback like this ruin everything. Don't worry, we can still wrap up this little scam before I find some more, ah, permanent employment for you.'

Un ladroncello

Gesualdo was shaking down a small-time *scippatore* and sneak thief when Sabatino caught up with him. The proceedings had started with Gesualdo reminding Ciro that he was behind with his payments for the para-legal intervention which had kept him out of Poggioreale after being caught in a *Carabinieri* sting operation designed to clean up the centre for the G7 conference.

Under pressure – a discreet knee in the crotch, a teasing glimpse of a holstered pistol, the pitiless glint in his interlocutor's eyes – Ciro had conceded that there was indeed a substantial discrepancy between the terms mutually agreed at the time (100,000 lire per week for six months) and the actual reimbursements which had been effected (0 lire per week for two months). But it was not him that was at fault, he protested, it was the market.

'They promised us rich pickings once the politicians went home! The tourists were supposed to start coming again, they said. The city was going to be a major holiday destination, its bad old reputation a thing of the past, right? You know what? It's worse than ever! Because they cracked down so hard while the big shots were here, everyone had to make up for the lost income afterwards. There was a spate of muggings, the foreign press ran scare stories and now there's almost nobody worth robbing in town! I'm sorry, Gesuà, but there's only so much I can do. This is a market economy, like they say. When times are bad, we all have to tighten our belts.'

Gesualdo grinned at him.

'You don't need to do that, Ciro. If you don't come up with the cash by the end of the week, we'll tighten your belt for you. So fucking tight that your lungs are sticking out of your mouth like bubble-gum while your intestines fill your pants at the other end. Understand?'

'You'll get the money, no problem! Just give me a couple of days. Trade is starting to pick up again. If only the cops hadn't made a big deal of cleaning up the streets, everything would be just fine.'

Gesualdo nodded.

'Speaking of which, what have you heard about that?'

The thief shifted his ferrety gaze this way and that.

'About what?'

'About "Clean Streets".'

Ciro shrugged hastily.

'Nothing. Nothing at all.'

Gesualdo ran his forefinger along the side of Ciro's throat.

'I just thought I'd mention it,' he said casually. 'Because if you do hear anything, it might help in regard to the arrears we were just talking about. Question of a couple of notches on the belt, so to speak. The *capo* is in a bit of a snit about this. Don Ermanno was a close associate of his.'

Ciro's expression of terrified confusion grew even more marked.

'But . . .' he began, and then thought better of it.

'But what, Ciro?'

'Nothing.'

Gesualdo laughed heartily, as though at a shared joke, and embraced the thief. Ciro emitted a loud groan, covered by Gesualdo's laughter, and collapsed in a limp heap on the cobbles. Grasping his ears good-naturedly, Gesualdo hauled him to his feet.

'For the love of Christ!' the thief moaned.

'To every thing there is a season, Ciro,' Gesualdo remarked pleasantly. 'A time to live and a time to die, a time to talk and a time to shut up. This is a time to talk.'

Ciro nodded.

'It's just – forgive me, I'm obviously ill-informed – but I've been told – no disrespect intended . . .'

Gesualdo stared at the man's sweating face.

'What have you been told, Ciro?'

'I didn't believe it, understand? Not for a moment, but . . .'

'What were you told?'

Ciro swallowed hard.

'Last night over cards, Emiddio 'o Curtiello said that it was Don Gaetano – may God preserve him! – who had given the nod to the whole thing in the first place.'

He stepped back with the look of a gambler who has placed his bet and awaits the verdict of the wheel. Gesualdo looked at him levelly for some time. Then he smiled slowly and nodded.

'Get the money to us by Friday,' he said.

'Friday? Gesù, can't you make it Sunday at least, Gesuà.'

A thought seemed to strike him. He reached into his pocket and produced a laminated card which he handed over.

'Here, I lifted this this morning, right outside the Questura!'

Catching the look in Gesualdo's eye, he added hastily, 'The mark had no money to speak of, but this is the genuine article all right. Not one of those cheap fakes they're turning out in Aversa.'

Gesualdo glanced contemptuously at the card in Ciro's hand, and suddenly became very still. He seized it and scrutinized the writing and the picture carefully.

'Keep it as a token of goodwill!' Ciro told him, eager to regain the initiative. 'All you need to do is change the photo and you're an honorary Vice-Questore. Eh, Gesuà? Well, I must be going. *Ciao!*'

Before Gesualdo could react, he jumped on to his motorbike and roared off. Sabatino, who had arrived a few minutes earlier and had been watching the encounter from a bar on the other side of the street, came over to join his partner.

'I trust you put the fear of God into him,' he said lightly.

Without replying, Gesualdo handed the plastic card to Sabatino, who looked at it with an expression of total shock.

'Holy shit!' he murmured.

Che strepito!

Aurelio Zen strolled along Via Chiaia over the saddle between the Monte di Dio and the lower slopes of the Vomero, and continued up the gentle slope of elegant Via Filangieri. He walked slowly, taking in the myriad dramas and comedies unfolding all around him, a guarded smile on his lips, compact and self-contained.

As the street veered to the left, becoming Via dei Mille, he paused to inspect the watch which Professor Esposito had returned to him. He had already done this several times, in an attempt to determine whether or not the watch was really his. Even after another inspection, he remained in some doubt about this. The make, style and general appearance were apparently identical, yet the watch somehow felt different from the one he had worn for so many years, and which had previously belonged to his father. Of course, this might be just the effect of the cleaning and repair which the professor's friend had effected, free of charge.

An elegant young couple brushed past him, one to either side, each speaking animatedly into a mobile phone. Maybe they're talking to each other, he thought, the ultimate yuppie relationship. Well, now he too could play these games.

'Valeria? Aurelio Zen.'

'Who?'

'Alfonso Zembla, I mean.'

'What's all that noise?'

'I'm just passing a stall selling bootleg cassettes. Wait a moment . . . Hello? Hello?'

'Hello?'

'Ah, there you are. I'm calling from my new mobile phone. The city's full of dead spaces, I'm finding.'

'It's lucky you rang, Alfonso. I just got a call from someone who wants to get in touch with you.'

'Was it my mother?'

'Pardon?'

'My mother. She's gone missing.'

'No, this was a man. He didn't leave a name, but he's going to call back later.'

'I went to see a *mago* and asked him where she was. He told me the Three Furies were on my trail.'

'Furies?'

'He stuck his finger in my navel and had a vision of the Erinyes. Do you know about them? Female divinities who punish crimes against close relations. Obviously the professor has a classical turn of mind. The other missing person I asked about he located in Hades.'

'Have you got a fever, Alfonso?'

'I'm fine. You haven't forgotten that we're going to the opera this evening, have you?'

'Of course I haven't. If you're not back here in time, I'll meet you at the San Carlo.'

'Right. And listen, if anyone calls for me, just give them the number of my mobile. Have you got a pen?'

'Even if it's your mother?'

'There's no escaping the Furies, the professor says.'

In Piazza Amadeo, close to the lower terminus of the other funicular railway up the Vomero, he entered a café and ordered a beer. His plan was to drop by the house on Scalini del Petraio and find out whether his hired professionals had managed to make any impression on the Squillace girls' *innamorati*.

It's Gesualdo who is going to be the problem, he thought. Sabatino looked like someone who could be talked into almost anything, certainly into bed, but his partner had that sanctimonious façade which conceals a mass of unresolved doubts, conflicts and ambiguities. The way he carried on, you'd think he'd invented love after everyone had been satisfied with shoddy imitations for the preceding thousand years.

But what if Zen blundered in just as Iolanda or Libera – he could never remember which was which – was successfully putting the moves on this paragon of rectitude? That could ruin everything, and give Gesualdo the excuse he needed to bail out. Perhaps he should phone De Spino and check the lie of the land first. It might have been he who called him at Valeria's. No, that couldn't be right. De Spino didn't know that he was staying there. No one knew, in fact. Except that someone evidently did.

Another unsolved mystery, thought Zen, paying the bill and walking out into the honking, revving crush of vehicles in the piazza. How was it that everything became so complicated here? A week earlier, his life had been as he had always wanted it: calm, pleasant and predictable. And now even the smallest details seemed uncertain, as though subjected to the same bradyism as parts of the city itself, an imperceptible but continual seismic motion which undermined the strongest foundations and rendered every structure unstable.

He was lining up for a ticket in the dismal grotto which formed the lower terminus of the *Funicolare di Chiaia*, his transit pass having gone missing along with the other contents of his wallet, when an irritating electronic bleeping started somewhere close by. Very close. In fact, it seemed to be coming from *him*. He stared wildly down at his body, as though it might have turned into the steel limbs and greased joints of a robot.

'Eh, *signore*, do us all a favour!' said the elderly woman in front of him in the queue. 'If you aren't going to answer, kindly turn it off. In my opinion, those damn things have ruined civilized life. You can't go out to eat or even to the opera these days without hearing them. Once upon a time it was considered ill-bred even to answer the phone if you were talking to someone, but now . . .'

Zen apologized sheepishly while digging out the phone.

'Yes?' he barked aggressively, by way of over-compensation.

'Pasquale, *duttò*. Where are you?'

'On my way home. Well, what used to be . . .'

'Whereabouts exactly?'

'Piazza Amadeo.'

'All right, here's what you do. Take the train to Piazza Cavour. I'll be waiting right outside. At this time you'll get here far quicker than I can reach you with the traffic the way it is, plus we'll be at the right end of town, more or less.'

'No disrespect intended, Pasquale, but would you kindly tell me what the hell you're talking about?'

'Your missing American, *duttò*? He isn't missing any more.'

Questa è costanza

'It's fake, of course.'

'Has to be.'

'Odd name to choose. Doesn't even sound Italian.'

'Same initials, though.'

'They often give themselves away like that. Remember Vito Gentile? Constructed an entirely false personality for himself after he bust out of Procida. There were only two things he couldn't bring himself to change, the village where he was born and his mother's maiden name. And that's how they got him.'

The scene was a *Vini e Cucina* on a side-street just north of Via Tribunali: tiled walls, a cheap electric clock, large framed photograph of a dead relative, light filtering in from a net-curtained window high up on one end wall. Below, as in the depths of a drained swimming pool, a counter supported three wooden wine barrels with the price per litre chalked on the end. Beyond a serving hatch knocked through to the tiny kitchen area, plates were drying and tempers flaring.

Gesualdo and Sabatino sat at one of the two long tables, the remains of a snack between them. The only other customer was an elderly drunk with long greasy hair and huge sideburns, wearing a seemingly infinite number of clothing layers wrapped up in a luxurious and apparently new overcoat. Before him was a glass of white wine, an empty half-litre flask and a collection of cigarette butts from which he was removing and recycling the tobacco in a rolling paper.

'Pure mohair, *duttò!*' he called hoarsely, catching Gesualdo eyeing his coat. 'The new autumn line from Versace.'

'OK, so what have we got?' mused Sabatino rhetorically. 'Alfonso Zembla, supposedly some sort of civil servant, although we have no proof of that, is carrying fake identification enabling him to pass himself off as a high-ranking cop.'

'In the shops, a garment like this would cost at least two hundred thousand, maybe three,' said the drunk, finishing his glass of wine. 'And that's if you can get a discount.'

'Plus he went to a lot of time and trouble getting us to agree to stay at his house,' observed Gesualdo. 'We've assumed all along that he was telling the truth about that, and that he had no interest in us or any idea who we are. Maybe we were wrong about that. Maybe this whole thing is just a cover.'

'Certainly not, *duttò*!' said the drunk. 'Just a cover, indeed. You might as well say that a Bugatti is just a car. This is not a coat, it's a style statement!'

'A cover for what?' asked Sabatino with a look which was suddenly alert.

'It's warm but it's light, it's chic but sensible, a timeless classic that perfectly complements any ensemble which may grace your wardrobe now or in the future,' the drunk rhapsodized to the empty restaurant. 'And as for the price . . .'

'That's what worries me,' Gesualdo told Sabatino.

'I believe you, *duttò*! Two hundred thousand, you're thinking, maybe more. Brand new, never worn except by yours truly, which doesn't count because technically speaking I'm not wearing it but modelling it. Your worries are quite understandable, yet unfounded, because today only the price on this garment has been slashed to *ninety thousand lire*!'

'If he was aiming to pass himself off as a Vice-Questore, it must be something pretty serious,' Sabatino remarked.

Gesualdo nodded.

'And he must have connections, too. Whoever did that ID was a real pro. If we weren't in the business ourselves, I don't think I'd have spotted it for a fake.'

'A fake?' retorted the drunk indignantly. 'This is no fake, *duttò*. This is an authentic verified copy of a Versace original made right here in Naples by one of the best sweat-shops! It's no fake, but at eighty thousand there's no question that it's a steal.'

'In short,' said Gesualdo, 'I think we need to find out a little more about Don Alfonso Zembla, a.k.a. "Aurelio Zen".'

'We might start listening in to his phone calls for a start,' suggested Sabatino.

'Why not? I'll get Gioacchino on it right away. We'll need to get his number, but I can get that out of the Squillace woman by pretending to be someone else. Speaking of which, Orestina called me this afternoon. I told her I was thinking of going over.'

Sabatino frowned and shook his head.

'Going over where?'

'To London.'

'A waste of time, *duttò*, with all due respect,' the drunk declaimed, triumphantly lighting his completed cigarette. 'London, Tokyo, Paris, New York – there's nothing you can find there you can't get cheaper right here. But if you're thinking of an English look, I'll throw in a nice Burberry scarf, pure lambswool. Seventy thousand the package, and no packing, no language problems, no delays at the airport.'

Gesualdo leant forward across the table and looked into Sabatino's eyes.

'If I tell you something, will you swear never to tell another soul, on your mother's grave?'

'Make him swear by something else, *duttò*,' the drunk advised. 'Mothers don't have the clout they used to.'

Sabatino gazed wide-eyed at his partner.

'What is it, Gesuà?'

Gesualdo looked down at the tabletop.

'I'm in love,' he murmured. 'And not just with Orestina.'

'Guglielmo, more wine!' yelled the drunk. 'Oh, Gugliè!'

Sabatino's smile gained a little edge.

'You mean you've fallen for Iolanda?'

'I admit I'm attracted to her,' Gesualdo replied stiffly, as though already regretting this confidence. 'But that isn't going to change anything. I have a commitment to Orestina and I intend to honour it. This is more than a personal issue, it's a political decision. If there's to be any hope for this country, we've got to start accepting our responsibilities and keeping our promises. That's the only way to build a new Italy.'

'You sound like a spokesman for *Strade Pulite*,' Sabatino observed with a trace of malice.

'Personally I'm for the Fascists or whatever they're calling themselves these days,' the drunk interjected. 'But the main thing is to get someone in there who can get things done. To take a simple example, if you have the chance to pick up a fabulous Versace lookalike today at a knockdown sixty thousand lire, you don't want it next month at a hundred, am I right?'

'It's a question of principle,' Gesualdo replied primly. 'Whatever happens, I am not going to deceive Orestina. No matter how much I may be tempted, I'll always be able to control myself.'

'You won't be able to do a damn thing,' said Sabatino with a cynical smile. 'But what's the big deal, anyhow? I love Filomena just as much as you love Orestina, and I can't wait to see her when she gets back. But in the meantime I aim to enjoy myself.'

'Just be sure you inspect the merchandise carefully before taking delivery,' the drunk intoned. 'Not everything is what it seems at first sight, particularly here in Naples.'

'What do you mean by that?' demanded Gesualdo.

Sabatino shrugged.

'I gave Libera the key to my place in Mergellina. We're meeting there this evening.'

'What?'

'Why not? There's no way Filomena will ever find out. It's as if it never happened.'

Gesualdo looked at him for some time in silence, then sniffed loudly.

'Well, that's your business.'

The street door opened and a young man appeared. All conversation immediately ceased. The intruder walked to the centre of the room, looking about him in a pleasant, dopey way.

'*Vino?*' he said tentatively, waving a 50,000-lire note.

The drunk perked up at once.

'You want to drink?' he said in English. 'Maybe eat something? Sit down! Later I tell you of the war. Oh, Gugliè! *Addò cazzo staje? Puortace 'n'ato litro 'e chellu bbuono, pecchè ccà ce sta 'n'amico mije ca è arrivate mo' dall'America ca se sta murenne 'e sete!*'

Vi par, ma non è ver

Dario was at a loss. This was doubly disturbing for a man who prided himself on always knowing what was what and who was behind it, even on those rare occasions when he himself wasn't directly or indirectly involved. But now not only could he not get hold of either Gesualdo or Sabatino, but he was beginning to have an uneasy sense that everything that had been happening was merely a diversion designed to distract attention from the *real* action, which was taking place somewhere else entirely. In short he sensed that he, Dario De Spino, was in this case no better off than the hapless fauna on whom he was accustomed to prey, people dumb enough to think that they knew what was going on because they followed the news.

His two friends had not returned his calls, and the only person he had been able to trace who had any information on their whereabouts was Ciro Soglione, amateur of big bikes, busty blondes and other people's wallets. And even Ciro was conspicuously unhelpful, merely saying that he had met Gesualdo briefly in Forcella that afternoon and that the latter had 'tried to get heavy'.

'I soon put a stop to that,' Ciro continued airily. 'Gesualdo's a good guy, we all know that, but if you haven't got respect out here on the streets, you haven't got anything, right? I showed him he couldn't push me around, then when he backed off I eased up and told him not to worry so much. "Oh, Gesuà," I said, "you've got to learn to relax, kid!" But it was no good, he was too pissed off. What's the deal? Is his girl screwing around on him or something? Some guys come on so fucking tough, you know, but they let women push them around! I don't get it.'

In the time he had known them, Dario had learned that it was not unusual for Gesualdo and Sabatino to drop out of circulation

175

for hours or even days at a time. He had always assumed that this had to do with their work, into which he was careful not to pry. There were things you could discuss and others you couldn't. Dario respected their privacy and expected them to do the same in return. Plus he got the impression that the stuff they were working on was way out of his league. There were occasions when it was better even for Dario De Spino not to know what was going on, still less who was behind it.

But it was something the thief had said just before they parted which worried Dario most – or rather what he had *not* said. Swivelling around on the saddle of his motorbike, Ciro had smiled in a knowing way and called out, 'How about those *Strade Pulite* guys, eh?' Like it was a football team or something.

And that was all, except for the valedictory roar of the bike. Dario had walked away deep in thought. What was the purpose of that teasing reference to the 'Clean Streets' group? It must have something to do with Gesualdo, otherwise Ciro would have clarified it. Instead he had deliberately left it hanging there, vague but suggestive, right after their discussion about their mutual acquaintance. That could only mean one thing: he was implying that Gesualdo was linked in some way to the terrorists who had 'disappeared' three prominent local figures, with two of whom Dario had had professional dealings. And if Gesualdo was involved, then Sabatino must be too.

Once again Dario De Spino asked himself just how well he really knew these two young men. Not that there had ever seemed anything very much to know. They had always seemed absolutely typical young middle-management hoodlums, perhaps a trifle smarter and more reserved than some, but in no way exceptional. If they had been, Dario wouldn't have had anything to do with them. They were affable and efficient in exactly the sort of way you'd expect of people who knew the sort of people they said they knew and worked for the class of operation they let it be understood that they worked for.

Tough, it went without saying, and no doubt capable of ruthless viciousness if the circumstances called for it, but basically just a couple of average Neapolitan lads trying to get on in life and make a decent living. Certainly not *terrorists*! The whole idea was ridiculous. The South might have its problems, but ideological fanaticism had never been one of them. People down here were too smart to waste their time trying to change the world. They came to terms with life as best they could, each in his own way. History had taught them what happened to anyone who failed to do so.

Nevertheless it remained, this feeling which Dario couldn't explain but had learned to trust, an almost physical sense that all was not what it seemed. He plunged into the pullulating life of the Forcella market area, greeted friends and enemies alike, ate a pizza and drank a beer, made various deals on a cargo of microwave cookers and CD players due to fall overboard from a freighter shortly, scored three complimentary tickets for Sunday's big game, appreciated a variety of passing bums and biceps, picked up some cheap Gucci forgeries which would delight and impress the Albanians, and discussed some possibilities for their long-term placement in positions offering them security and assorted fringe benefits and Dario a reasonable consideration up-front plus a percentage of the resulting action.

All of this took several hours, at the end of which his feeling was still in place, a stabbing internal pain of the kind you initially dismiss as just a passing twinge but which ends up looking like a symptom of something more serious. Dario distractedly caressed the red horn-shaped amulet dangling from a gold chain around his neck, an antidote against the evil eye. In view of the proposals he had just discussed, he was understandably reluctant to give up on the two girls and the very lucrative returns, both immediate and deferred, which they represented.

On the other hand, he was well aware that *ragazze* and *ragazzi* were not to be separated, particularly in this case. And where the latter were concerned, everything he believed in and depended on for his everyday and long-term survival was telling him to get the hell out at the earliest possible opportunity without leaving a forwarding address. On yet another hand – how many hands you needed in this business! – he didn't have a single scrap of evidence to suggest that anything whatever was wrong.

In short, Dario was facing a dilemma familiar to every Neapolitan: reason was telling him one thing, instinct another.

The resulting struggle was short, painful and – despite a life-time's training and the tradition of centuries – obscurely humili-ating, but the outcome was never in any real doubt.

Bisogna pigliarlo

Like so many things in Naples, the so-called *Metropolitana* wasn't quite what its name suggested. True, a purpose-built underground railway was now under construction – and had been for as long as most people could remember. One fine day it might even open, but meanwhile the name was attached, like a fake designer label, to a stretch of the national railway network which happened to run between the western and eastern suburbs of the city through one of the more recent portions of the complex and only partly charted system of tunnels, reservoirs and subterranean quarries which underlay the city.

And Zen was not entirely surprised to discover, when he finally made contact with Pasquale outside the station in Piazza Cavour, that the news that John Viviani 'isn't missing any more' also contained an element of euphemism.

'I got the call when I was on my way in from the airport with a couple of tourists,' Pasquale told him. 'Normally I'd have given them the scenic route via Pozzuoli plus the statutory one hundred per cent surcharge, excess baggage fees, motorway tolls with handling charges and twenty per cent tip, all rounded up to the nearest hundred thou. But seeing as it was you, *duttò*, I let them off lightly.'

'Remind me to reimburse you, Pasquale. At the rate things are going, I may need to use that line of credit you mentioned after all.'

Pasquale gestured casually to show that it was unnecessary if not slightly vulgar even to mention such matters.

'"I'm sure it was him," Fortunato told me. "I remember the face. And he was definitely a foreigner, didn't speak a word of Italian." He'd got the poster from Decio at the rank in Piazza Dante, and the moment he saw it he recognized the fare he'd just

179

dropped off in Via Tribunali. Of course there's no knowing where the guy is by now, but sooner or later he'll have to pick up another ride, and this time we'll be ready.'

'That's if he's still alive,' his passenger remarked morosely.

'Why wouldn't he be alive? Unless he drinks himself to death. Fortunà said he was pretty far gone even then.'

'Great. So he's drunk, lost, doesn't speak the language, and is probably waving a wad of banknotes around in one of the roughest parts of town. Plus there's a fairly good chance that the mob is after his blood.'

Pasquale's eyes narrowed in the rear-view mirror.

'Wait a minute, *duttò*! I thought this job was strictly private enterprise. If there's a corporate interest in this guy, then I don't want any part of it.'

'I'm not sure there is. But I just found out that a certain item of merchandise for which Viviani may have acted as courier has inadvertently been switched for another. As a result, it's just possible that the interested parties may believe – wrongly, as it happens – that Viviani double-crossed them.'

A complex counterpoint of electronic chirping filled the air. Both men reached for their mobile phones and started talking at once.

'Good evening, Don Orlando,' said Zen's caller.

'I'm afraid you have a wrong number.'

'No, no. I obtained it personally from Signora Squillace, with whom I believe you are staying. I also understand that you are currently using another name. I will of course respect your wishes in that regard.'

The male voice was mature, urbane and intimate, that of an old friend or relative.

'Who is this?' Zen demanded.

'Under the circumstances, I would prefer not to identify myself on a channel of communication which is notoriously insecure. Let's just say that I have information regarding a matter of mutual interest, and wanted to establish contact. I'll call you with more details later tonight.'

'I'm going to the opera,' Zen replied automatically.

'Really? I hear the production's a mess, but a couple of the voices are quite tolerable, particularly the bass. *Buon divertimento.*'

'I still think there's some mistake. My name is not . . .'

But the line was dead.

'Got him!' exclaimed Pasquale, starting the engine.

'Don Orlando?' murmured Zen.

'Immacolata picked him up five minutes ago. It couldn't have worked out better. I told her to take him down east and keep him in a holding pattern until we get there. She's perfect for a job like this. If it was a man, he might try to cut up rough, but *'a signora Igginz*? Never!'

They drove off along a wide boulevard, cutting and running through the traffic.

'Who?' Zen demanded distractedly. Not only was the plot slipping from his grasp, even the names of the cast appeared unfamiliar.

'That was her late husband's name,' Pasquale explained. 'A foreign soldier. She still uses the name to add a bit of chic, but no one teases her about it. You don't mess with Immacolata.'

They veered off to the right through the dismal back streets where Zen had recruited the two 'Albanians'. Already fires were flickering at every corner and figures loomed out of the shadows as they approached. Pasquale picked up the phone and dialled.

'So how's the grand tour of Naples by night? Really? Great. Just crossing Piazza Nazionale. How about you? OK, let's rendezvous in Via Laura. You pull over, pretend the engine's playing up. I'll pull over and offer help to a fellow cabby, discover there's nothing to be done, then we transfer the guy to my car and take off. What? *'Mmaculà mia*, let's not talk about money! No, but . . . I've given you my word that . . . We're talking about . . .'

He switched off his phone with a sigh.

'Women! *La Igginz* may have more balls than most men I know, but when all's said and done even she owes allegiance to San Gennaro.'

'How's that?' Zen murmured abstractedly. A problem had just occurred to him which he should have foreseen long before, one which made a mockery of the whole enterprise.

'The blood, *duttò*!' exclaimed Pasquale. 'Every time it liquefies, you're in trouble. And if it doesn't, then you're really screwed.'

'Pascà.'

'*Duttò*'.

'I don't speak English.'

'Me neither.'

'And despite his name, this American doesn't speak Italian.'

'My cousin's family in New York, the kids don't even speak dialect any more, never mind Italian.'

'So how are we going to communicate?'

Pasquale made an expansive gesture which necessitated taking both hands off the steering wheel.

'You never told me you wanted to *talk* to him!' he protested.

'Look out!'

Pasquale swerved violently to avoid two men in police uniform standing in the darkened street.

'Eh, eh, the old trick! They get you to stop, then mug you and take the car. But you won't catch Pascà that way, lads!'

'Good work, Pasquale. Those caps are no longer standard issue. Also they were using an unmarked car, which uniformed officers never do.'

'I didn't notice that,' Pasquale admitted. 'But this street is a dead-end loop. The only thing that ever comes along here is courting couples and garbage trucks on their way back to the depot. That's why I chose it for the hand-over. It's nice and private, and if the American tries to make a run for it, there's nowhere for him to go. And if you need to work him over, I know just the place. You want to make him talk, right?'

Zen sighed.

'Yes, except that I won't be able to understand him. This has all been a waste of time.'

'If you could waste time, *duttò*, life would be nothing but a rubbish dump,' Pasquale replied.

Zen gave a contemptuous snort.

'Isn't it?'

Pasquale jerked his thumb across the road at a group of low concrete buildings surrounded by a barbed-wire fence. Orange garbage trucks stood parked outside in rows.

'You mean we're not waiting for the grim reaper but for those guys?'

He burst into laughter.

'In that case, we'd live for ever, *duttò*! But that's impossible. Time's like wine and love. You can have it or lack it, lose it or abuse it, but you can't waste it.'

'Thanks for the words of wisdom,' retorted Zen. 'The fact remains that I still don't have an interpreter. Unless you're going to tell me that this precious Immacolata of yours is bilingual into the bargain.'

Once again leaving the taxi to look after itself, like a well-trained horse, Pasquale turned to his passenger with an expression of astonishment.

'Now how in the world did you know that, *duttò*?'

Mi confondo, mi vergogno

He should never have had that second litre of wine, but the guy was so persuasive, he didn't want to hurt his feelings. In fact, face it, he should never have had the *first* litre. Not the one before the second, but the very first of the series, dating back . . . well, that's a little tough . . . a heck of a long way, anyways . . . maybe even to sometime back in the Plasticine Age when giant monsters such as Bronta (large, warm, vegetarian, kind, sweet, loving, maternal) and Tranno (small but vicious, cold, flesh-tearing, sarcastic, totally evil step-father from hell) roamed the house . . .

Whoa! Let's have a statute of limitations here. Nothing that happened before the ship docked counts, right? Check. It's since then that things have gone down the tubes at such an alarming rate. Particularly after he got his hands on the actual dosh, the fat pack of banknotes, crinkly, sweated, smelly, tough, ageless, totally corrupt and corrupting. He hadn't foreseen that at all. In his mind, the whole transaction was as abstract and unreal as those in the merchandise itself, where you could kill and die many times, rack up lives and points, find the hidden stash of treasure, then switch off the game and get on with your real life . . .

Right from the start, this deal had felt like a game, something you made up as you went along. If Pete hadn't starting bitching at Christmas about getting canned, or if Larry's uncle hadn't been on an extended visit because of some tax problem or something he was having back in the old country . . . Above all, if the ship hadn't been posted to the Mediterranean because of the Bosnia crisis . . . But one thing had led to another, from Pete sneaking a prototype of the new game out of the factory just days before he had to clear his desk, to the Pagan – as *zio*

Orlando was known – setting up a surprisingly sweet deal over the phone.

That just left the question of delivery. The original idea had been for Pete to hop on a plane and drop it off in person, but that had to be ditched when the company found out about the missing game and, by a process of elimination, tied it to one of the most recent and bitter casualties of corporate down-sizing, Peter Viviani. The software developers might all be American, but the executives and the funding was Japanese, and those guys didn't fuck around. The original game of which this was an enhanced sequel – same characters, more levels, upgraded graphics, plus a bunch of other cool stuff – had sold something in the region of two million copies world-wide at around thirty bucks a pop. This one was expected to do even better. You didn't need a math degree to figure out why the samurai didn't want anyone cutting themselves a slice of that market by pirating a virtually identical product at half the price three months before the official release date.

So it was too risky for Pete himself, or any other member of the extended Viviani clan, to act as personal courier. The company knew that there was no risk of the game being duplicated in the States. To cash in, they had to get the stolen prototype out of the country, and as soon as possible, to maximize profits before the game became legally available. But wherever any member of the extended Viviani clan went, the local customs would have been alerted – and, if necessary, heavily bribed. As Zi'Orlando put it, they wouldn't be able to smuggle in a gnat's turd, never mind a chunk of pilfered intellectual property the size of a brick. The same went for anyone from Naples he might have sent over to pick it up.

So when John Viviani got his sailing orders, it seemed a heaven-sent solution. As one of hundreds of crew members aboard the aircraft carrier, he could easily slip ashore, rendezvous with the purchaser's representative and make the delivery in person. It was a clean deal, cash for merchandise, with no risk and no loose ends. Above all, it kept the whole transaction in the family. What could go wrong?

Sure enough, the hand-over had proceeded without incident.

The only problem was that the courier had been late arriving at the little bar where they were to meet, and to wile away the time John had ordered a couple – OK, maybe more like half a dozen – garishly coloured liqueurs from the extensive selection displayed on glass shelves behind the bar. This was the first time he had ever set foot in the city from which his paternal grandfather's family had emigrated at the turn of the century, and he was naturally excited. Every sound and smell and flavour, each overheard snatch of raucous dialect, seemed at once colourfully exotic and insidiously familiar.

The instructions he had received from Zi'Orlando were simple and precise. When he took possession of the money, he was to return immediately to the ship and stash it away in his locker. He was not to go ashore again, and under no circumstances to leave the port area. The city, he had been warned, was a den of thieves, con men and worse who would gobble up a young innocent such as himself and spit out the remains.

But by the time the courier finally showed, got up in a fake Navy uniform like some outsized organ-grinder's monkey, these orders had come to seem remote and ridiculous. He wasn't a child, after all! To make matters worse, there was the cash itself, fat bundles of it, packed with power and possibility. US currency had always seemed solid, staid and stuffy. It was what you got for doing dead-end jobs and spent on rent and food and dental work. This Italian stuff was quite different. It looked sleazy and enticing, racy and unreal, like the token fortunes made and lost with fabulous ease in a board game. Once the game stopped, it was worthless, but until then there were no limits to what you could do.

So instead of going back to his ship, John had a couple more drinks and then headed off the other way, out of the port and into the pulsating streets of the city beyond. He was rather vague about what had happened after that. In fact he wasn't even sure exactly how much time had passed. He remembered waking up in a hotel bedroom, very much the worse for wear, and realising that he had failed to show up for muster and would therefore have been posted AWOL. This thought had plunged him into a state of panic which had required the best part of a bottle of

Scotch to assuage. The great thing about Italian bars was that they would serve you hard liquor at any time of the day or night – even, as in this case, seven in the morning.

After that things went kind of hazy again. At some point he had decided that enough was enough and headed down to the port to rejoin his ship, only to discover that it had already sailed. This discovery had plunged him into a state of panic which had required the best part of another bottle of Scotch to assuage. The lousy thing about Italian bars was that they would serve you hard liquor at any time of the day or night – even, as in this case, three in the morning. After that, one thing had led to another, and by now he had nothing left to lose, except of course the remaining wad of the fascinating currency which he had been handed, however many days ago it was, in trust for the Viviani clan back Stateside.

The bundle of notes seemed quite a bit thinner than it had originally been, but at least he had something to show for it. This fabulous coat, for example. Whatever exception the family might take to other aspects of his spree – something he was almost as worried about as the problems arising from his failure to report for duty, all present and correct, *sir*! – they'd have to admit that he knew a bargain when he saw one. A genuine Versace, pure mohair, the latest autumn line, and all for a mere 300,000 lire! In dollars that's just . . . say 2,000 lire to the dollar, so you divide by . . . knock off the zeroes and then it's . . .

But the zeroes refused to stay knocked off. They not only came back, but brought their friends with them, a mob of plump little manikins running around in threes, arms linked, singing that number the old man who'd sold him the coat had taught him, some marching song. He hadn't understood the words, of course, but it had a great tune. A great tune, great wine, great company, a great deal on the coat . . . But now it was definitely time to get back to his hotel and sort things out.

Speaking of which, where the hell were they? He'd told the woman driving the cab to take him to that place on the seafront, the best hotel in town, what's its name, the one where Clinton stayed when he was here for that conference. It cost the earth, probably, but what the hell? It would be comfortable, familiar and safe, all sensations he was rapidly losing contact with amid the splendours and miseries of the last however-many-it-was hours on the town . . . *'Il meglio!'* he had told the cabby impatiently. 'Take me to the best place!' She'd know which the best was. Cabbies always knew that. But wherever the best was to be found, it didn't seem likely to be anywhere near where they were now, and had been for . . . however long they had been there, going round and round what looked like the same broad, empty streets, lit with a cold, menacing glare, and quite deserted.

It was only now that he realized what should have been obvious long before, even to someone as innocent and – let's face it – frankly *dumb* as John Viviani now realized he had been. Clearly he was being set up to be robbed, maybe even murdered! The tough-looking broad up front was keeping him on ice until the heavies arrived. She'd looked at him in a kind of weird way when she picked him up, almost like she recognized him, then made some sort of call on her mobile phone right away. The drunk back there at the fast food place must have set the whole thing up. Maybe it hadn't been such a smart idea to bring his whole wad of cash out when he paid for the coat. And there wasn't a damn thing he could do about it now. The taxi was going too fast for him to jump out, and, even if he did, there was nowhere to hide in these inhospitable, brutally utilitarian streets. To the left, the modernistic monolith they were circling, as empty as an architect's sketch. To the right, the ambient wastelands, partly developed, partly cleared, old industrial sites, factories whose products no one wanted, stockyards, a fenced-off area where ranks of orange trucks were drawn up like mothballed tanks . . .

And then, as if in answer to his prayers, he saw a couple of policemen up ahead, holding those lighted red wands they used to stop traffic. They must be doing one of those routine searches that Zi'Orlando mentioned, ostensibly to check that everyone's papers are in order, but actually to pick up some easy money because they knew damn well that they weren't. He didn't care. If they wanted bribes, he would be happy to bribe them. Whatever it took.

But to John Viviani's disappointment, the two men in police uniform made no attempt to stop the taxi. On the contrary, they waved it past with vigorous gestures, as though impatient to have the street to themselves once more. But they compensated for this apparent negligence as soon as the next vehicle appeared, a few minutes later. Its hump-backed form and orange colour indicated that it was one of the municipal rubbish trucks returning to the depot, and as such might reasonably have been expected to be waved through the road-block just as the taxis had. But this time the red wand was raised, the official hand held out, the service revolver drawn, and the crew obliged to descend.

Un disperato affetto

On the Scalini del Petraio, it was already night. The steps scuttled away, a gutter between high crumbling walls overhung by gauds of greenery, sparsely lit by isolated lamps whose patches of yellowing light merely served to emphasize the topographical complexities concealed in the darkness all around and the twilit immensity above, defined by the conflictual paths of swifts and bats. The former swarmed, scooped, coiled and collided in a turbulence as continual and serene as that of electrons; the latter tirelessly maintained their preordained courses to and fro, like mechanisms in some early industrial process superseded elsewhere by more up-to-date technology but surviving here, like so much else, for want of capital investment.

Seemingly unaware of any of this, a young man made his way down the steps with a rapid, impatient stride. From a window in the little *piazzetta* where the alley briefly levelled out before flowing into its final and even more precipitous plunge towards the depths below, an old man sat on a balcony looking out at the night, the moon rising behind Vesuvius, the sketchy indications of the peninsula and islands out in the bay. He leant forward as the footsteps clattered across the pitted black paving stones beneath, a look of wonderment on his face.

'*Arcangelo*!' he murmured. '*Si tu?*'

But it wasn't, of course. Arcangelo had been killed in 1944, aged two, buried alive when a bomb collapsed a six-storey building down by the port. The person speeding across the paving and down the second series of steps was Gesualdo, on his way to gather up the few belongings he had left at Don Alfonso's house, to erase this entire episode from his life as though it had never occurred.

That's all I need to do, he thought, just clear out and forget everything that's happened, and still more what hasn't. Then, just as soon as he could get a few days off, he would find out the name of the hotel where the girls were staying and hop on a plane. A couple of hours later he would be in London, knocking at their door. Orestina would come to open it, thinking maybe it was the maid come to turn down the beds, and instead . . .

That's what he was thinking as he slipped the key Don Alfonso had given him into the lock and twisted it masterfully. Like the cheap copy it was – three for the price of two at a stall in the Forcella market – it snapped off, leaving a jagged remnant in the lock. Filled with frustrated rage, he punched the bell button repeatedly. At length a light came on and feet descended the staircase.

'Who is it?'

A man's voice, one he doesn't recognize.

'Police! Open up!' yelled Gesualdo.

A pause, a click, and the door slid open. Iolanda stood revealed in a full-length gown buttoned decorously tight about the throat.

'Ah, it's you,' she said.

Gesualdo pushed past her and hurried upstairs. The apartment on the top floor was as he left it that morning. He speedily gathered together his belongings and packed them into the canvas bag in which he brought them. Then he turned, to find Iolanda gazing at him.

'You're going,' she said.

Gesualdo zipped up the canvas bag and looked around to see if he had overlooked anything. With chilling precision, Iolanda spat on the tiled floor at his feet.

'Coward!'

She turned and walked out. Fine, he thought, what do I care? Better that she despises me, that way she won't come muling and whining after me. All the same, calling him a coward! What a fucking nerve! What did she know about cowardice or courage or anything else? What did she care about what he had been going through, about how tough it was for a man to do the right thing? His last remaining doubts were swept away. Bitch!

Bag in hand, he strode downstairs. Outside the door to the

lower apartment, Iolanda was waiting for him. He ignored her, but she stepped in front of him, blocking his way. Once again Gesualdo tried to push past, but this time he was repulsed with disconcerting strength.

'Listen to what I have to say,' she told him, 'then leave, if you want to. You may think you know me, but you don't. Don't think I'll come running after you like your other women. I am not like other women.'

Gesualdo stood there, mesmerized by her intense, brilliant stare. It was only once she started talking again that he realized that she was not speaking broken Italian any more, but his own harsh, musky dialect.

'This is all a farce. I am not Albanian. I am not a virgin. I am not looking for work. The man who owns this house set this up to trick you. But I'm the one who's been tricked. I've fallen in love. I know it's hopeless, but I don't care. Even though you're leaving, and I'll never see you again, I need to humiliate myself by telling you that I love you, and that I always will.'

She stepped back, leaving his way clear. For a moment neither of them moved. Then Iolanda came up to him and grazed his cheek lightly with the fingers of her left hand.

'I will be whatever you want,' she said. 'Your friend, your lover, even your wife.'

Gesualdo looked at her, his breath coming in rapid, shallow spurts.

'I don't know,' he said. 'I don't know what to do.'

'Just take me.'

He let his bag fall to the floor and covered his face with his hands.

'What's the use?' he demanded in a tone of despair. 'You know you can do anything you like with me. We men are all the same.'

Iolanda gripped his wrists, pulled his hands apart and kissed his mouth briefly.

'Not *quite* all,' she said.

Tanti linguaggi

'What part?'
  '*Come?*'
'Hackney.'
'What means "acne"?'
'Commonplace. Trite. Done to death.'
  '*Cosa dice?*'
'No, he died in his bed, although I have to admit as how the Krays had put the word about. Only as luck would have it, they got nicked before anything came of it, know what I mean?'

It was clear from the expressions of the other three people at the table that the answer to this question was 'no'.

'His 'art did for 'im!' exclaimed Immacolata Higgins impatiently, clasping the imposing sculptural massif of her left breast.

'Like Rimbaud,' John Viviani murmured, drunkenly moved. 'When I was young, I wanted to die for my art too. Only it turned out I didn't have any.'

'Rambo?' queried Aurelio Zen in a tone of desperation. '*Cioè i film di quell'italo-americano, come si chiama . . .?*'

'Stallone, Silvestro,' replied Pasquale complacently. "*'O cunuscevo 'a guaglione. 'A famiglia soja steve 'e casa propio 'e rimpetto a nuje.*'

'"I knew him when he was knee-high to a grasshopper",' Immacolata translated for the benefit of the American. '"His mob lived just down the terrace, number twenty-four. Vesty – that's what we used to call him – was a skinny little runt. I remember I used to sneak him out some of my bangers with bubble and squeak, try and feed the blighter up a bit. That's how he came to have those big muscles, but needless to say I never got so much as a simple 'Thank you' when he became a big noise up there at your actual Cinecittà . . . "'

  '*Per l'amor di dio!*'

Silence fell. Zen looked around the gathering.

'Well, this meeting has certainly been a huge success so far,' he began.

'Absolutely!'

'No kidding!'

'Your glass is empty, *duttò*. Waiter!'

Zen glowered at them.

'Signora Higgins has been kind enough to regale us with the complete story of her interesting life, from those difficult early days in the village near Aversa to her memorable and fateful encounter with a young British soldier in 1944, leading us with tireless energy through every detail of the years of exile in London, where she acquired her excellent command of the native dialect, to her eventual return home following her husband's untimely death.'

'I just love listening to Italian,' John Viviani enthused. 'It's kind of like going to the opera. You don't understand what the hell's going on, but it all sounds really cool.'

'Great coat!' commented Pasquale.

La Igginz translated.

'Guy I met this evening in a wine shop sold it to me,' Viviani replied. 'It's a genuine Versace, and guess how much it cost me? Only thr . . . two hundred thousand!'

'You were robbed! I could have got you two like that for . . .'

'*Basta, altrimenti impazzisco!*'

They all stared at Zen, who had risen to his feet.

'Who is this guy, anyway?' demanded John Viviani.

'Filth,' Immacolata Higgins replied with a dismissive gesture.

'Say what?'

'A rozzer! Old Bill.'

She looked at him with irritation. Didn't this Yank understand his own language? Pasquale stepped into the breach with a vivid mime showing someone being arrested, handcuffed and led away, protesting vigorously but in vain.

'He's a cop?' asked Viviani incredulously.

'Too right,' Aurelio Zen replied, speaking through the medium of the British Tommy's widow. 'And you, my son, are in dead lumber.'

Viviani shook his head.

'This is like just too weird.'

'According to the official record, you are listed as a disgrace to the regiment and rotten to the core, a deserter to be shot on sight, no questions asked.'

'I don't believe this!' Viviani exclaimed. 'The guy's an imposter! Tell him to show me some ID.'

Unfortunately Immacolata had just swallowed some pizza the wrong way and was temporarily indisposed, although she recovered in time to deliver Aurelio Zen's concluding remarks.

'However, seeing as how your granddad was from Naples and therefore you're one of the family, so to speak, I'm prepared to bend the rules, turn a blind eye and look the other way as long as you keep your end up and do your part. In short, you scratch mine and I'll scratch yours.'

'Is this guy some kind of pervert?' whispered Viviani.

Zen produced the mug-shot of the escaped prisoner and handed it to the American with a sense of growing futility. It was by no means clear what, if anything, John Viviani had made of the proceedings so far. His grasp of Italian appeared to consist of a few words such as *vino* and *grazie*, and Immacolata Higgins' English was apparently not much less foreign to him. On the other hand, after an initial moment of panic when he seemed to think he was about to be robbed, he had not made any objection to being brought to this suburban *pizzeria* and subjected to an informal interrogation across the red-and-white checked table-cloth.

'I get it!' he said at one point. 'Living here is kind of a West Coast thing, like surfing. You either ride the waves or you get crushed by them.'

But now, suddenly, that fluid ease had gone. As Viviani gazed at the photograph of Giosuè Marotta, he seemed to awaken from a long and restless sleep, the dream fled and his worst fears were confirmed. He began babbling in English, ragged, incomplete phrases that seemed to make no sense even to himself. His translator, however, had no difficulty in identifying and articulating the gist of Viviani's incoherent diatribe.

'It weren't 'im!' shouted Immacolata Higgins, clasping the

American to her formidable bosom. 'He didn't do it! He's got friends who saw 'im not do it! For Gawd's sake, sir, don't break the 'art of 'is poor old white-'aired mum by sending my only boy to the Scrubs! He'll go straight in future, as San Gennaro's my witness. And if there's anything you need in a dry goods or bespoke line, yer 'onour, a nod's as good as a wink, know what I mean?'

When she finally fell silent, Viviani wrestled free of her surrogate maternal grip and turned to confront Aurelio Zen.

'OK, what's the deal?' he asked stonily.

'The deal,' Zen replied, 'is that you tell me everything you know about this affair – what, when, how, why and with whom – unabridged and unedited, from start to finish. In return, I shall contact the US Navy with the news that you have been safely recovered following a tip-off, although the kidnappers who had been holding you unfortunately escaped.'

This was filtered through *la Igginz* a few times before comprehension, followed by incredulity and then immense relief, finally dawned on the American's face.

'Sounds good to me,' he said.

Siete d'ossa e di carne, o cosa siete?

The last lingering trace of light, a greenish glimmer above the bank of thick haze out to the west, had faded from the sky. Night settled on the town, muffled and dense, smothering sounds, it seemed, as much as sight. Certainly the three figures descending the steps of the Salita del Petraio made so little noise that they startled Don Castrese's cat which was out on the prowl, having detected the faint but unmistakable odour of fellow creatures in heat. It was only at the last moment that some sixth sense alerted the beast to the presence of the advancing trio, masked by silence and cloaked in darkness. It leapt nimbly on to a window ledge and immersed itself in an exacting ritual of washing and grooming, as though to exorcize the malignant power of this encounter.

The three strangers who had crossed the cat's path came to a stop outside the house opposite. The shutters of the first floor windows were closed, but a faint light filtered out through the slats and occasional outbreaks of laughter punctuated the muted hush of the night. The top floor, by contrast, was perfectly dark and silent, the windows standing open to let the air flow in.

'This is the place.'

The cat paused in its obsessional laving as the speaker, a shorter, bulkier, older figure than the other two, stepped up to the door and pushed each of the two buttons mounted on the frame, the superscribed names illegible in the dark. A bell and a buzzer sounded distantly, cutting off a further burst of laughter inside. For a moment nothing happened, except perhaps some quiet, hair-raising modulation perceptible only to cats. Then the windows on the first floor were flung open and a man's head appeared.

'Yes?' he barked.

'We're looking for Aurelio Zen,' said a female voice from the darkness below.

'Who?'

The name was repeated by the other two in chorus. Another head appeared at the window, a girl in her twenties with long hair and sharp, lively features.

'What's going on?' she asked her companion.

'There's no one here by that name,' he called down.

The three figures below consulted briefly in an inaudible mutter. Then the one who spoke first looked up at the window.

'ZEN, AURELIO,' she said, pronouncing every syllable with exaggerated distinctness.

'You've got the wrong opera, grandma!' the girl above jeered.

'I am Aurelio Zen,' said a new voice.

Everyone looked up at the top floor of the house, where another young man, naked to the waist, had appeared at the window.

'That's not him!' exclaimed one of the women indignantly.

'If only!' added another.

'He was never that good-looking,' commented the third, 'even at that age.'

The man at the lower window leant out as far as he could, craning up towards the upper storey.

'Oh, Gesuà, what the hell are you playing at?'

The three figures below again consulted briefly.

'We're going now,' the one on the left announced.

'But we'll be back,' added her companion.

'What's that man doing in Aurelio's house?' asked the shorter one in the middle.

They moved away down the hill, still conferring in an undertone, and were soon lost to sight.

'Maybe we should have told them he's at the opera,' said Sabatino.

'How do you know where he is?' Libera asked.

Sabatino smiled in a superior way.

'Because a friend of ours is currently listening in to all his phone calls, my dear. There are already quite a few little mysteries about our Don Alfonsetto. This just makes one more.'

Gesualdo's voice drifted down from the upstairs window.

'Maybe we should have followed them, found out who they are . . .'

'Well, if you've got nothing better to do, Gesuà . . .'

'What's that supposed to mean?'

'Are you alone up there?'

There was a pause. Sabatino and Libera exchanged glances.

'Iolanda's here too,' Gesualdo finally replied, as though making an official declaration.

'Well, in that case,' said Sabatino languidly, 'I'd suggest you forget about volunteering for overtime work and take advantage of that fact, just as I'm about to with my companion.'

With another of her rippling laughs, Libera pulled him inside and closed the window.

Eccoci alla gran crisi

Higher up the Vomero, on Via Cimarosa, the streets were more brightly lit and there were still a few people about. Nevertheless, Pasquale circled the lugubrious *palazzo* which was his passengers' destination for so long that they finally grew restless.

'There's no point in trying to bump up the fare, since the meter's not even running,' Valeria Squillace remarked tartly. She had not taken to Pasquale, whom she regarded as low class and over-familiar.

'Pascà and I have an informal arrangement,' Aurelio Zen intervened in a diplomatic tone. 'The fare is calculated on a sliding scale agreed in advance and payable within a mutually acceptable period subject to financing and handling costs where applicable, right Pascà? So why the hell don't you take us straight home?'

'And those thugs, *duttò*?' demanded Pasquale. 'The two we had to shake this afternoon?'

Zen frowned. He had already forgotten them.

'They followed us from outside this very building,' the cabby reminded him. 'Once they lost us at the hotel, they'll most likely have come back to wait. They must have found out you're staying here.'

'You've been watching too many movies, Pascà.'

'Never, *duttò*! My wife took me to the cinema once, back in the fifties. I couldn't sleep for weeks afterwards. Even now I have nightmares about it.'

He continued to weave his way down side-streets and alleys, peering attentively into the cars parked higgledy-piggledy to either side. Unable to find any excuse for further delay, he finally drew up outside the door. Zen got out and held the door open for Valeria.

'Goodnight, Pascà.'

The driver rooted around in his pocket and handed Zen a small battered oval box of what appeared to be silver.

'What's this?' asked Zen.

Pasquale shrugged.

'Keep it on you at all times. Don't even go to bed without it, understand? As long as you have it with you, you'll be all right.'

Zen smiled broadly, but there was no question that Pasquale was absolutely serious.

'Are you coming, Alfonso?' Valeria demanded pointedly.

Zen put the box in his pocket.

'Thanks,' he said.

The taxi pulled away, leaving Zen standing on the kerb with a sense of dread which had nothing to do with Pasquale's imaginary assassins. The feeling was accentuated when he turned to find Valeria Squillace smiling at him in a way that needed no translation. But there was nothing for it but to follow her inside. In the cavernous entrance hall, a host of plaster statuary he had not noticed before leered down at him: prancing *putti*, writhing Hercules, ample Junos whose last scrap of drapery was about to slip off their heavily engorged nipples.

'What a fabulous evening!' Valeria enthused. 'And those seats, Alfonso! They must have cost a fortune.'

The tickets provided *gratis* by Giovan Battista Caputo had proved to be the best in the house, right in the centre of the dress circle. Zen smiled and shrugged.

'An experience like that is priceless,' he replied, even though he had personally found the opera to be poor stuff, thin and old-fashioned, with weak orchestration and no big tunes.

The elevator clacked to a halt behind them. Zen opened the metal concertina gate and the glass-plated doors, ushered Valeria inside and activated the machinery into jerky life by dropping a fifty-lire coin in the slot. While the elevator rose in its wrought-iron cage, like a vertical coffin, towards the ceiling bedecked with writhing nudes, Zen took out the silver box Pasquale had given him and examined it in the yellowing light of the ceiling bulb. He pressed a catch on the side and the lid yawned open. Inside was a wad of cotton wool stained with some dark brown substance. It smelt musty and vaguely sweet, like rotten meat.

'What's that?' demanded Valeria, wrinkling her nose. 'Some fake saint's relic, I suppose. Your new acquaintance is just the type to believe in nonsense like that.'

Zen shrugged and put the box away as the elevator came to a stop at the fourth floor.

'Are you hungry?' asked Valeria, unlocking the front door. 'There's some *parmigiana di melanzane* I can heat up.'

Zen shook his head.

'I had some pizza earlier, thanks. I wouldn't mind a glass of something, though . . .'

Valeria opened a hatch in the fitted unit which covered the end wall, revealing a selection of bottles.

'Help yourself. This one is particularly good. One of my cousins makes it with fruit from his country estate. If you'll excuse me for a moment, I want to call the girls.'

Zen opened the elegantly asymmetrical decanter she indicated. The contents were as clear as the container, and keenly perfumed with cherries. He poured a small quantity into one of the hollowed knobs of crystal on the shelf above.

'Signorina Orestina Squillace, please,' Valeria said into the phone in heavily accented English. '*Squillace*. I don't understand. Room 302. What? That's impossible! Please check again. Really? Are you sure?'

She hung up and turned to Zen.

'The hotel says they've checked out.'

'What? Where have they gone?'

Valeria massaged her fingers nervously.

'They didn't say. Of course they may just have moved to another hotel, or maybe taken off on a trip somewhere, but it's strange they didn't phone and tell me. My God, I hope they're all right! Maybe we should never have sent them off in the first place. If anything happens to them, I'll never forgive myself.'

His earlier scruples forgotten, Zen came over and took her hand comfortingly.

'They may have phoned while we were at the opera. Try not to worry. I'm sure they'll be all right.'

She sighed and squeezed his hand. Their eyes met. Zen swiftly knocked back the rest of the cherry liqueur.

'Superb!' he said, disengaging his hand from hers.

'Have some more.'

'I will.'

'And then come and sit down with me.'

She dimmed the lights and put on some music.

'Recognize this?' she asked with a flirtatious glance.

'Verdi?'

Valeria laughed girlishly.

'It's what we heard this evening, silly! The seduction scene in the second act.'

Zen filled the liqueur glass right to the brink, drank half of it and topped it up again. Glass in hand, he began circling the room as though searching for the exit.

'Come and sit down,' Valeria told him. 'You're making me nervous, prowling about like that. Besides, I'm still worried about the girls. Do something to distract me.'

With a sense of impending but inevitable doom, Zen went to sit beside her on the sofa, his own sensation one of panic. Despite his age and experience, there were some situations he had never been able to handle gracefully. Turning down an offer like this was one.

'You've been smoking,' Valeria remarked, drawing closer to him.

'Just the odd one.'

'Have you got some on you?'

'You want me to throw them away?'

'I want you to give me one.'

He looked at her in amazement.

'But you told me you didn't smoke! You told me . . .'

She smiled charmingly.

'That was just a test, to see if I had any power over you. As a matter of fact I used to smoke like a chimney. It was Manlio who made me give it up. He said it was unattractive in a woman. But Manlio's dead, and I'm in a mood to do something silly.'

Zen passed her his packet of *Nazionali*.

'Nothing fancy, I'm afraid,' he said apologetically.

'I don't need anything fancy. Just plain, simple pleasures. If it's a little rough, that's fine too.'

When Zen held out his lighter she grasped his hand, although the flame was perfectly steady. Replacing the lighter in his pocket, his fingers touched the mysterious silver box which Pasquale had insisted on lending him. Zen rubbed the smooth metal fervently. It was going to take a miracle to get him out of this one.

Valeria leant forward so that her left breast pushed negligently against Zen's jacket, which immediately began to emit the rising sequence of electronic chirps whose origin and meaning he had by now learned to recognize.

Che sembianze! Che vestiti!

The disturbing effect of midsummer night, to say nothing of the full moon, may have caused confusion to humans and even cats, but out at Capodichino the planes, thanks to their more advanced equipment, kept right on landing and taking off. Which was good news for Concetta Biancarosa Ausilia Olimpia Immacolata Scarlatti *in* Higgins, who had picked up a fare to the airport shortly after the conference at the pizzeria broke up.

Now she was cruising the arrivals hall, watching for likely prospects among the passengers on an international flight which, according to the board, had just landed. If she had taken her turn in the rank outside, it would have made more sense to drive straight back into town without a fare, but Immacolata was not born yesterday nor yet the day before, and knew how to take care of herself in more ways than one, to say nothing of putting her linguistic talents to good use.

Taking up a position near the automatic doors through which incoming passengers re-enter the real world, she assumed the long-suffering aspect of a Neapolitan matriarch awaiting the arrival of relatives on a flight already delayed for hours if not days. Her hunched stance, grimly stolid expression and air of defiant endurance made her as invisible as the official notices on the wall which no one ever read. 'Eh, 'a nonna,' everyone thought, and looked away. Which was just as well, because if she had been spotted touting and reported to the Camorra clan which regulated cab traffic at the airport, and took a cut of the resulting trade, the consequences were likely to have been extremely limiting both socially and professionally. Naples was a challenging city for those confined to a wheelchair.

Passengers from the flight she had noticed had started emerging in dribs and drabs, but so far none of them looked suitable for her purposes, and Immacolata had learned to wait for exactly the right client before moving in. She couldn't risk making her pitch more than once, so it had to stick. Her patience was rewarded in the form of two young women pushing a trolley laden with expensive suitcases and looking about them with an air of slight trepidation. One of them was more or less conventionally dressed, although with that fatal lack of focus of which the English seemed to make a virtue. Her companion's appearance represented another aspect of those alien cultural codes which, even after almost ten years, Immacolata had been forced to admit that she would never crack. Taller and sparer, she had cropped black hair, with two silver rings in her pierced nostril and a tattoo of some fabulous reptile on her throat. Her jeans had holes torn or cut at the knees, above which she wore a man's shirt left open to her evidently unsupported breasts and a black leather jacket sporting an aggressive quantity of zippering and other metal accoutrements.

Not, at first sight, what Immacolata was looking for. But a quick check of the women's shoes – always the key – revealed that between them the couple were carrying upwards of three quarters of a million lire underfoot. Their hesitant demeanour made it equally obvious that they were not expecting anyone to meet them. Perfect. Immacolata fell in behind them and then casually drew alongside, as though she were just another weary traveller heading for the exit.

'Excuse me, ladies!' she whispered in the tones of one born well within hearing of Bow Bells. The two women stopped and looked at her in astonishment.

'You'll be wanting a ride into town, I dare say,' Immacolata continued rapidly, urging them on towards the door. 'Perhaps somewhere to stay, too. A nice cosy residential hotel, safe and clean but not too pricey, know what I mean? I know just the place. Put yourself in Auntie Imma's hands, my dears. I'll see you right!'

The women consulted briefly in a silent glance. Then the taller one turned back to Immacolata with an amused smile.

'That's good. These is our baggages.'

Oh bella improvvisata!

And when they finally made it to the top of the steps, guess what? The car was gone.

Of course, everyone knew that parking your car on the street in Naples was just asking for trouble, to such an extent that some insurance companies refused to offer coverage at any price. This was all the more true in the case of a luxury import, which was no doubt why Don Ermanno had had his Jaguar equipped with a variety of anti-theft devices, including special locks and two alarm systems.

Nevertheless, it was gone. This was particularly galling for Gesualdo and Sabatino, who were used to getting a measure of respect from the trash who pulled these kind of jobs, and even more because this unexpected lack of mobility was going to make it difficult if not impossible to carry out the assignment for which they had reluctantly torn themselves away from the embraces of their respective conquests and rushed at full speed up the darkened alleyway of the Scalini del Petraio as though through infinitely thin, tenuous layers of black satin.

It was Gesualdo who had taken the call, rolling naked out of bed and fumbling amongst his clothes until he located the phone.

'We just had a hit,' a voice said.

'Which line?'

'Zembla.'

'Give me play-back.'

A scratchy silence intervened, then a new set of voices came on the line.

'. . . remember that we spoke earlier today. I'm now in a position to offer you the information I mentioned then.'

'Regarding what?'

'Regarding the present whereabouts of Attilio Abate, Luca Della Ragione and Ermanno Vallifuoco.'

There was a long silence.

'Why should I care about that?'

A faint laugh, like an exhalation of air bellying out the curtains and making the candles flicker.

'I think we both know the answer to that, Don Orlando. Excuse me. Signor Zembla, I mean.'

Another silence.

'Well, I'm listening.'

'As I have already had occasion to remark, these phones are notoriously insecure. In the circumstances, I hope you will not object to a personal meeting. If you will leave the building in which Signor Squillace's apartment is situated and proceed north on foot towards Piazza degli Artisti, I will make contact at some suitable point.'

'It's very late . . .'

'Later than you think, perhaps. That's why this information is so vital and so sensitive.'

The recording dissolved in a haze of crackles, then Gesualdo's caller came back on the line.

'That's it,' he said.

'Caller's number?'

'Phone box at a service station on the motorway.'

'Time?'

'Six and a half minutes ago. You'd better get moving.'

And so they had, although Sabatino had been decidedly reluctant. He had been having a very pleasant time with Libera, who was both compliant and inventive, with some interesting moves he hadn't come across before. Just because Gesualdo's partner had proved to be less forthcoming seemed at first no reason to drag him, Sabatino, out on a wild goose chase at that time at night.

But Gesualdo rapidly made it clear that they had no choice. Not only was Alfonso Zembla not what he seemed, but it now appeared that his alternative identity as 'Aurelio Zen' was, as they had suspected, also a fake. It was only on hearing the anonymous caller address him as Don Orlando that Gesualdo realized that the avuncular, mild-mannered, slightly ineffectual individual who had insinuated himself into their lives bore a striking resemblance to Don Orlando Pagano, head of one of the leading clans in the city, who had recently disappeared from circulation. His voice was all wrong for a Neapolitan, but Don Orlando had spent several years in exile near Verona as a guest of the government, and could probably fake a creditable Northern accent.

As if this was not enough, the caller had explicitly promised 'vital and sensitive' information concerning the present whereabouts of the three supposed victims of the *Strade Pulite* group. If there were a grain of truth in this, it might represent a potentially fatal breach of security within this mysterious organization. And the whole conversation was preserved on tape, along with Gioacchino's injunction to 'get going'. They would not be forgiven if they let such a chance slip.

The first stage had been bad enough: the hurried dressing, the garbled explanations, the mad dash up those steps through the black drapery of the night. Even with all the time they put in at the gym, Gesualdo and Sabatino were soon gasping for breath. And then the discovery that some son of a whore – some half-smart low-life with no connections, some small-time self-starter who couldn't even get a job with a recognized team – had ripped off their car, reducing them to the expedient of walking, running, stumbling and crawling up another half-mile or more of this terrible Via Crucis, tormented not only by the physical stress but even more by the fear that it was all in vain, that by the time they got there it would be too late.

At length they emerged, panting and sweating, on the blessedly straight and flat expanses of Via Cimarosa. There was no one in sight, no unusual activity, no sign of anything of interest. They walked down the street past a succession of turn-of-the-century apartment blocks, the street doors securely locked, the shuttered windows above dark. Somewhere in the distance a deep, businesslike motor roared along a street lower down the hill. Then Sabatino pulled Gesualdo sharply into an adjacent doorway. A figure, tall, dark and spare, had appeared in the entrance of a building some distance ahead. The man paused briefly, looking about, then stepped out on to the pavement and walked off at a steady pace, heading north.

Al concertato loco

By contrast, Aurelio Zen was in the best of humours. The phone call he had just received effectively killed two birds with one stone. Not only had it got him off the hook with Valeria Squillace, romantically speaking, but if his anonymous informant was telling anything like the truth – and what interest could he have in doing otherwise? – Zen might well be in a position to hand the Questura not only the information he had extracted from John Viviani concerning the Marotta stabbing, but also a substantial bonus in the form of a major breakthrough in the terrorist case currently occupying national attention. After a coup like that, he could return to his former state of absentee indolence without the slightest risk of any reprisals.

He proceeded briskly along the deserted street, dodging the prows of the cars parked at all angles across the pavement. One of these was wedged so tightly against the wall of the adjacent building that he was forced to turn back and go around the other end. It was then that he noticed the two men fifty feet or so farther back. He paused for a moment, then continued on his way with a little more urgency in his stride. At the next corner he turned left and crossed the block half-way down, glancing casually behind him as though checking for traffic. The men were still there.

He remembered Pasquale's warning, which he had so thoughtlessly dismissed, his mind on other problems. This pair looked very much like the ones who had followed the taxi from the house that morning, young and trim, wearing the casually tough uniform of their type. Reaching the corner, he turned right and started to run, making as little noise as possible. The streets were empty, the windows dark, and his pursuers had cut off his route back to the only door open to him.

At the next corner he looked round again. One of the men was in sight, but the other had disappeared, having probably circled back around the block to cut off his escape in that direction. The fact that they were no longer making any attempt to disguise their intentions made it chillingly clear what these must be.

But then, just when all seemed lost, fate lent a hand in the form of a garbage truck on its nightly rounds. The moment he saw it, Zen realized that the deep growl of its motor had been audible for some time. Several of the crew, dressed in blue overalls, were walking alongside their vehicle. What a stroke of luck! Even the most ruthless of killers would hardly dare attempt anything before so many witnesses. Zen walked confidently towards the oncoming truck, his arm raised in greeting.

Cose note, cose note!

If there had been anyone about in Via Bernini on the night in question, this was what they would have seen.

As the man in the overcoat and hat approached, his arm raised in greeting, the orange truck slowed down and its crew surrounded him. He turned and pointed back the way he had come, as though indicating the presence of something or someone, although there was no one in sight. At the same moment, the workman standing behind him took something from one of the many pockets of his overalls and swept it through the air as though swatting a fly.

Simultaneously, although without any obvious sense of cause and effect, the man in the overcoat tumbled forward, very much as though he had tripped on the raised edge of one of the black paving slabs – always a hazard, even in this relatively well-to-do area of the city. Luckily the other workman, now level with the rear of the still moving truck, managed to catch the falling man, thus preventing him from doing himself any serious injury.

The other workman now tossed aside his implement, which struck the paving stones with a sharp metallic ring, and bent to grasp the victim's feet. Without a word, the two men lifted him clear of the ground, holding him suspended limply in mid-air by his shoulders and calves. By now the truck, in its inexorable progress, had passed them. With a preliminary swing they heaved the inert body up and over the tail-gate, where it disappeared from view.

While the first workman retrieved his discarded wrench, the second pressed a green button protruding from a box mounted on the rear of the truck. With a loud roaring noise, the massive ram began to descend. The top and sides were dirty and dull, but the curved blade had been polished by constant abrasion to an attractive silvery sheen. The ram moved steadily down into the body of the truck, the racket of its powerful machinery completely obliterating any sounds which might otherwise have been audible.

At this point there was an unexpected touch. Two young men appeared in the street ahead of the garbage truck, one waving a pistol, the other talking urgently into a mobile phone. The gunman fired twice, bringing down two of the blue-overalled crew, then sprinted forward and blasted another shot into the control console, disabling the ram. He then clambered aboard the orange truck, which was by now accelerating away.

His companion had meanwhile also drawn a pistol and forced the remaining members of the crew to lie on the ground. Far below, in the dense jumble of the old city, sirens started to wail and whine. The garbage truck spun around in a tight turn, almost spilling the first gunman from its roof, but he managed to cling on to a metal reinforcing ridge until the manoeuvre was complete, then inched his way forward along the roof as the truck bore down at speed on the crew members being held at gunpoint by his companion.

Three more shots sounded out, fired directly down through the roof of the cab. Like a stricken fish, the truck went wild, veering all over the street and smashing into a succession of parked cars which gradually broke its headlong progress, albeit at considerable expense to the owners, few of whom have been able to get insurance for their vehicles from those tight-arsed sons of bitches in Milan who seem to regard Naples as some sort of war zone. The resulting series of violent impacts finally dislodged the gunman whose shots were responsible for all this damage. He landed on the roof of a pale blue Lancia, which buckled beneath his weight like silk sheets as the garbage truck roared away into the night.

If there had been anyone about in Via Bernini on the night in question, this is what they would have seen. And in fact lots of people were about. The only thing stronger than *omertà* was curiosity, and the combination of shots, crashes, screams and sirens had been simply too much to resist. They craned out of windows and peered down from balconies and roofs. A few hardy souls even ventured tentatively forth from their door-ways.

Catching sight of a man in uniform – a fireman visiting one of his mistresses, it emerged later – the gunman who had been covering the garbage crew pressed the pistol into his hands and told him to keep them covered until the police got there. The shrieks of the converging emergency vehicles were much closer now. The man ran across the street to his partner, who was sitting up on the roof of the Lancia like someone awakening after a heavy night.

'Oh, Gesuà!' he shouted. 'The cops are almost here! Let's go, for Christ's sake.'

La porta dell'inferno

His first conscious thought was that this was definitely the worst hangover he had ever had, on a scale and of an intensity that he had not previously believed possible.

The smell, to take just one aspect of the prevailing vileness, was such as he had not experienced since the age of seven, when a combination of freak flood tides in the Venetian lagoon and a collapsed sewer had transformed the toilet in the Zen household into a seething cornucopia of filth, spewing forth the accumulated faecal products of the neighbourhood which cascaded down the staircase and into every corner of the living area. But even that memorable event was no more than a dress rehearsal in a provincial theatre compared with the world-class, state-of-the-art, no-expense-spared, cast-of-thousands-in-a-football-stadium production currently being visited upon his nostrils.

Nor were the other senses neglected. His ears, in particular, were taking a battering on an unprecedented scale, rather as if he were trapped inside the electronically enhanced bass drum during the Grand Triumphal March from the aforementioned spectacular. This hypothesis would also have accounted for the darkness, which was total except for brief, jagged, laser-like beams which traversed his surroundings without illuminating them, as in some high-tech light show designed to keep the crowd amused until the star tenor finally came on to do *'Nessun dorma'*. Was this another clue? Sleep, although devoutly to be wished, was certainly out of the question.

But none of this began to explain the agony in his skull, external as well as internal, or the smell of blood on his fingers when he worked them around, squirming in the glutinous mess pressing in on him from every side, to explore the sticky patch on the back of his head, still less the fact that everything was so violently jolting and swaying, or the acrid aftertaste of vomit which coated the membranes of his mouth.

The last thing he could remember was leaving Valeria's apartment after drinking a glass and a half of her cousin's cherry brandy made 'with fruit from his country estate'. Christ almighty, what did he use for crop-spray? Cyanide? Or was the problem with illegal additives in the alcohol, as with the tainted wine scandals that were such a regular feature of Italian life?

Or was the problem with *him*? Was he blocking out some truth too horrible for remembrance, some news unfit to be imprinted? Only a glass and a half! A likely story. He must have drained the entire bottle, and then raided the remaining stocks in the cupboard like those American sailors who had gone to MIX DRINKS, pouring the stuff down his throat as though there were no tomorrow, or rather to obliterate the possibility of one.

Nevertheless, it had arrived, his tomorrow. And just when he had consoled himself in the traditional way that things could not get any worse, in the traditional way they did. Back in the distant past, maybe a couple of seconds earlier, it had seemed absolutely impossible to improve on what had gone before, yet it now turned out that there wasn't the slightest problem about this.

As with all good dramatic effects, things got better before they got worse. The appalling noise died away to almost nothing, the flashing slivers of light ceased, the terrifying shudders subsided to a mild and constant vibration. Only the stink and foul taste remained, and even they were by now coming to seem familiar and tolerable. And of course it was then, when his defences were down and he was starting to think that maybe things weren't so bad after all, that all hell broke loose.

Broke in, rather – not that finicky distinctions of this kind were uppermost in his mind as the surface beneath him suddenly reared up with astonishing rapidity, tilting at an alarming and apparently impossible angle which nevertheless turned out to make perfectly good sense as he started to roll back, hands helplessly outstretched. His cramped confinement receded as the darkness opened up to receive him, one item among many falling in purposeful disorder. Even the terminal impact, when it finally came, was mercifully soft.

Dove son?

'*Pronto?*'

'*Dottore*, is that you?'

'Is what me?'

'You're alive?'

'I am?'

Pause.

'Am I speaking to Vice-Questore Aurelio Zen of the *Polizia dello Stato*, serial number 4723 stroke vz stroke 798?'

'Present and correct, sir!'

'Identify your present whereabouts.'

'Unknown.'

'Describe same.'

'A pit of some kind. Dark, silent. Abundance of foul-smelling and slimy materials all around.'

He took out his cigarette lighter, producing a feeble, flickering flame.

'Proximity of one, possibly more, human corpses.'

'Do not break this connection! Repeat, do not break this connection. How long will your mobile phone go on functioning?'

'The battery indicator light is flashing. Five, possibly ten minutes operational time remaining.'

'Jesus Christ! I don't think we can trace you in time. Can you get out yourself?'

'Negative.'

'Is there anything you can do or tell me to indicate your position?'

'Negative. But don't worry, I still have Pasquale's box.'

'Sorry?'

'It got a bit dented, but I suppose the miracles work anyway. Oh, and listen, if you have time to drop by Valeria's and pick up some of that cherry brandy . . . The hair of the dog, you know.'

Non mi fate più fare triste figura!

It was almost four in the morning when they finally found him. By then the power pack of his mobile phone had long since failed, but one of the bullets fired by Gesualdo into the cab of the stolen garbage truck had pierced the oil line and the resulting trail of drops led the investigators step by step into the heart of the labyrinth to the deep pit where Aurelio Zen was lying on a mound of garbage next to a hideously mutilated cadaver, as peaceful as a child in bed with his bear. He looked up, blinking in the glare of torches and spotlights.

'There he is!' yelled a voice.

'And isn't that Attilio Abate?'

'No, there's Abate over there. That's one of Vallifuoco's henchmen, what's his name . . .?'

'Marotta. And there's Don Ermanno himself!'

'Get the chief over here! This is going to be huge.'

Rope ladders were lowered and men clambered down. Zen sat up, feeling distinctly under-dressed for the occasion. Almost everyone else seemed to be wearing uniform and carrying guns. Not only was he unarmed and in civilian clothes, but he seemed to have a large pool of dried vomit on his shirt and trousers.

Much to his surprise, the intruders seemed solicitous rather than critical. Two hefty types in battledress lifted him on to a stretcher which was then hoisted to the rim of the pit in a series of fits and starts reminiscent of the elevator at the Squillace apartment building. One of the few persons in plain clothes, apparently a doctor, examined him physically and then gave him a little quiz. This was quite fun, involving questions about his name, address, age, background, as well as a few general-knowledge teasers: what year it was, the name of the current prime minister, the capital of Emilia-Romagna, the numbers and playing positions of the Juventus team, Moana Pozzi's vital statistics, the percentage of Trebbiano grapes permissible in *Chianti Classico*, and so on. He was able to answer all of these correctly – except of course for the second, which had been deliberately inserted as a trick question to trap malingerers.

Once Zen's mental competence had been established, he was hurried into the presence of a compact, sturdily suited man wearing dark glasses and a lethal smile who appeared to be directing the proceedings.

'This whole operation must be planned down to the last detail!' he was telling his clustered subordinates. 'Nothing must be left to chance. This is our great chance to smash these people once and for all. I want everything to go like clockwork. Understand?'

A chorus of dedicated assent greeted this rhetorical question.

'Piero? You handle the TV people. We're talking all three RAI channels, naturally, but also the leading independents and cable providers. Pack the room, lots of confusion, a sense of breaking news. I want jagged conflictual lighting, a mass of urgent but chaotic motion, then a segue into the strong, firm presentation from the podium restoring a sense of order and control. Mario, you handle the print media. Pack them in as extras for the TV coverage, get that quality of grainy actuality. Then line up the *Corriere*, *Stampa* and *Repubblica* for the off-air, in-depth, back-story pitch.'

'What about the *Mattino*, *dottore*?'

Even through his shades, the suited man's stare was perceptibly cutting.

'Mario, I assumed it was clear that we were talking *national* here.'

'Right, chief. Of course.'

'Keep the locals in the picture, but at a distance. They'll be only too glad to pick up the scraps from the table. These are not some small-time provincial gangsters we're talking about here. This is a world-class event of national and even international proportions, and I want it treated with the proper respect, God damn it!'

'You've got it, chief.'

'All right, get to work.'

The suited man turned his blank regard towards Zen.

'Now then, *dottore*, let's discuss what we're going to tell them. After that we'll get you showered, shaved and suited up. Or maybe we should go for the haggard, back-from-the-brink look. What do you think? There's a lot riding on this, for both of us. Let's not screw it up.'

Forme giudiziarie

'Are you saying that this operation began even before the communication from the group calling itself *Strade Pulite* was made public?'

The question came from a man in the first row, identified on his name tag as a reporter for the *International Herald Tribune*, but in fact an aide who had been planted among the audience to 'facilitate efficient and expeditious coverage of this historically significant event'.

The Questore, whose eyes were no less dark and obscure than the glasses he had worn earlier, nodded briefly.

'My officers have been aware of the existence of these terrorists for several months. Indeed, it was for this very reason that I arranged for the transfer of a noted specialist from the Criminalpol squad in Rome . . .'

He turned to Aurelio Zen, who was standing slightly behind and to one side of him, facing the mêlée of reporters, cameras, microphones and lights.

'To preserve the secrecy of our operation, Dottor Zen was nominally appointed to an administrative post in the Port of Naples. It was there that we had our first breakthrough, with the arrest of one of the men whose bodies were discovered today, Giosuè Marotta.'

'But surely he was charged with stabbing a Greek sailor?' a TV reporter asked with a puzzled frown.

'Exactly! Marotta, a noted hothead, was injudicious enough to get involved in a scuffle with some foreign naval personnel while acting as courier in a low-level smuggling operation of no relevance to the present case. This gave us a convenient pretext to arrest him without revealing our hand and thereby losing the initiative. But his connection to the *Strade Pulite* terrorists was

proved in tragic and dramatic fashion when one of their com-
mandos attacked a police car in which he was being transferred
to hospital and cold-bloodedly gunned down one of our most
promising younger officers, Ispettore Armando Bertolini.'

There was a moment of respectful silence.

'But if you knew about *Strade Pulite* from the first, why
couldn't you protect the other three victims?' another voice
demanded.

The Questore raised one finger.

'It is essential to distinguish here between knowledge of the
group's existence and precise intelligence as to its goals or targets. Thanks to our extensive intelligence efforts, we have been
aware of these fanatical throwbacks to the *anni di piombo* for
some considerable time, but it is only within the last few days
that we have been in a position to predict where they would
strike next.'

'What can you tell us about the method of assassination they
employed?' asked the plant, helpfully changing the subject.

'It was the same in every case,' the Questore replied, as though
reading from a tele-prompt. 'A truck belonging to the municipal
cleaning department would be stolen at gunpoint. In the present
case, the attackers disguised themselves as policemen perform-
ing a routine traffic control. Meanwhile the prospective victim
had been followed, his movements noted, and a suitable time
and venue selected. He would then be knocked unconscious and
thrown into the truck, there to be crushed to death by the com-
pacting machinery. The whole thing took only a few seconds.
Afterwards the truck was driven to an abandoned factory site in
the Pendino area, where there was vehicular access to a series of
underground quarries. The contents were then deposited in the
disused cistern where we discovered them today.'

A female reporter held up her hand and received the
Questore's nod.

'Three of the victims – Attilio Abate, Luca Della Ragione and
Ermanno Vallifuoco – were all under judicial investigation for
alleged offences ranging from bribery and tax evasion to association with organized crime,' she noted. 'The other, Giosuè
Marotta, was a known confederate of Vallifuoco. How do you

explain this choice of targets? What were the terrorists' long-term aims?'

The Questore assumed an air of intense gravity.

'The men arrested this morning are still under interrogation, and we hope to have more precise answers to your questions soon. However, the overall object seems quite clear. It is true that the victims had been accused of various offences, but we must not forget that these allegations had not been tested in a court of law. Without wishing to prejudge the findings of the investigating magistrates, I suggest that the aim of these terrorists was to ensure that they never were.'

'You mean that these were political acts?' prompted the plant.

'Without doubt. This was a classic campaign of destabilization, such as we have seen so many times before in recent years. In short, it was the work of ideologically motivated extremists determined to demonstrate that the rule of law had broken down and that only direct vigilante action could "clean the streets" of our cities. And unfortunately there were many ready to believe them, to call for a suspension of due legal procedure and the implementation of new, so-called "élite" law-enforcement agencies, operating independently of the police and unaccountable to our democratically elected representatives in Rome.'

He smiled.

'Not the least of the triumphs we have achieved here today is to prove beyond a shadow of a doubt that good old-fashioned policing, using tried and true methods, is capable of obtaining the desired results without any recourse to such new and potentially risky experiments.'

'So how did you trap them in the end, *dottore*?' asked a reporter from RAI Uno.

'Thanks to a combination of diligent and tireless work by the staff of this service, and the exceptional heroism of the operative whom I personally seconded from Criminalpol.'

Another nod in Zen's direction.

'Despite all our stringent security measures, we learned a few days ago that our targets had identified him, that they were aware of the threat which his presence in Naples posed, and that they were preparing to eliminate it. I personally communicated these facts to Dottor Zen in a conference late last night. I told him that I was not prepared to order him to proceed with an operation which put his life in imminent danger, but that if he agreed to volunteer, then we might draw the terrorists into a trap and smash the whole operation once and for all. I am proud to say that, faced with such a terrible choice, he did not hesitate for a single moment.'

The serried faces all turned towards Zen with expressions of awe and admiration. Flash bulbs exploded, cameras whirred, microphones were pushed forward.

'The Questore is too generous,' Zen said with an embarrassed shrug. 'I only did my duty, as I hope and believe that any other member of the force to which I am proud to belong would have done in the same circumstances. But let us not exaggerate the contribution of any one individual. A coup such as this is dependent not on the exploits of one person, but rather on team-work, dedication, discipline and efficiency. I would like to add that I have never seen these qualities more abundantly or effectively employed than here in Naples, under the inspirational leadership of my esteemed superior and colleague.'

'What about the identity of the terrorists?' someone called out. 'Have they any links to other organizations, domestic or foreign?'

The Questore shook his head and held up his hands.

'That's all we have time for now,' he declared firmly. 'I and my men have pressing work to do to clear up the remaining questions surrounding this case. As for Dottor Zen, as I am sure you will appreciate, he is in need of rest and recuperation after his heroic ordeal.'

The Questore sweeps out with his retinue, the reporters hasten away to break the news he has given them to a waiting world, and the various soldiers, servants, sailors, wedding guests, street people and hangers-on who have somehow squeezed in all withdraw, leaving Aurelio Zen alone upon the bare, brilliantly lit stage.

Finale

Not for long, however, for almost at once the doorbell sounds, unleashing a bustle and scurry of activity. First the food arrives, carried upstairs in deep trays balanced on the shoulders of two strapping lads who proceed to lay it out on silver platters under the direction of an elderly retainer distinguished both by his uniform – significantly more pleated and layered than theirs – and by the expression of transcendental dignity which he retains throughout these proceedings, contrasting pointedly with the air of barely controlled panic with which his underlings go about their business.

Before long, bottles of *spumante* make their appearance, arrayed in beds of cracked ice, together with yards of snowy starched linen to cover the trestles hastily erected at one end of the terrace to accommodate all these goodies. And not a minute too soon, for the guests are already starting to roll up. The first to arrive is Valeria, who has only with difficulty been dissuaded from bringing a selection of snacks and appetizers of her own devising in a well-meaning attempt to bail out the helpless bachelor who has impulsively decided to throw a party for the entire cast, and now appears awed and slightly resentful at having so misjudged both the competence of the host and the scale of the hospitality which he has laid on.

But this mood does not last. As she tells Zen, her daughters have been in touch and assured her that all is well, and with that anxiety dispelled she is in a mood to celebrate. Pasquale and Immacolata Higgins are the next to appear, the former almost unrecognisably elegant thanks to a very nice near-Armani suit and all the accoutrements. *La Igginz* has just spent all day, not to mention a lucrative part of the night, behind the wheel and is wearing a rather less fetching ensemble designed with a view to comfort rather than style, terminating in a pair of garish yellow plastic sandals. Valeria Squillace starts to feel even better.

Zen returns the silver box which Pasquale gave him, slightly battered by the experiences he went through, and explains how it saved his life.

'So what's the secret?' he asks.

Pasquale shrugs.

'It's not something to speak about at an event like this, *duttò*. A bit of respect is called for. Let's just say that every year the corpse of a certain saint, preserved here in Naples, exudes a liquor which the priests soak up with cotton wool and make available to a few select people who . . .'

Aurelio Zen is already beginning to look as though he was sorry he asked, but luckily for him Dario De Spino now emerges from the interior of the house, whose front door downstairs has been left open to save the host from having to run up and downstairs every time someone rings. Dario, it must be said, thought long and hard before agreeing to show up at all. His sixth sense still told him that it would be better to lie low for a while, particularly at any function to which Gesualdo and Sabatino will inevitably have been invited.

Nevertheless, the promise of a lavish party with lots of free eats and booze was a powerful inducement, and the flattering pleas of the two Albanians, who phoned him personally and practically burst into tears when he hesitated, was just enough to swing the balance, albeit against his better judgement. He does not want to lose contact with Iolanda and Libera, for whom he still has plans whose scope is validated by the spectacle they offer, entering with a studied air of confidence and sophistication, resplendent in the outfits which Dario has had knocked up for them through a friend of a brother-in-law's friend's cousin's business associate.

'Quite the party, Don Alfonso!' he exclaims, voicing the thoughts of the other guests, none of whom, however, has been vulgar enough to express them.

Zen shrugs modestly.

'It's not every day one survives a murder attempt.'

'Murder?'

'How?'

'When?'

'Where?'

'Why?'

The guests, including Professor Esposito, who has just joined the gathering, crowd eagerly around Zen.

'Shortly after midnight this morning,' he begins, sending Valeria a meaningful glance, 'I was on my way home when I encountered a team of garbage collectors at work.'

The newcomer laughs.

'Impossible! I'm sorry, *dottore*, but you'll have to do better than that. City employees at work at such an hour here in Naples? Unheard of!'

Zen smiles and nods.

'Exactly, Professor. They weren't garbage collectors at all, but a team of killers from the terrorist organization known as *Strade Pulite*.'

'Wait a minute!' objects Dario De Spino. 'I saw the TV news story about that. It happened all right, but not to you. It was some policeman from Rome, a certain Aurelio . . . I don't recall . . . Aurelio . . .'

'Zen,' says Gesualdo, coming out on to the terrace with Sabatino. 'His name's Aurelio Zen, and he's a policeman.'

'Don't be ridiculous!' Valeria exclaims. 'He's called Zembla. Aren't you, Alfonso?'

She is furious at the unexpected appearance of her daughters' unsuitable suitors, even though Zen has explained that that's all over now that they've fallen head over heels for the fascinating Albanian immigrants installed in the lower apartment and have completely forgotten the Squillace girls, far away in a foreign land, thank heavens, blissfully ignorant of how quickly and with what little trouble they have been displaced in their lovers' affections.

'Why would terrorists want to kill someone like you?' demands Iolanda. 'They only go for big shots, people of real importance.'

The majestic majordomo advances, holding a telephone on a long extension cord.

'For you, *cummendatò*,' he says, handing the instrument to Zen. 'Hello?'

227

'Aurelio?'

'Is that you, Gilberto?'

'I just . . . check you're . . . after the . . . congratulations on . . .'

'Speak up, can you? It sounds like you're calling from Russia!'

'I am.'

'What?'

'That's how I was able to get the passport so quickly, courtesy of my partners here. If you know the right people, Moscow's even better than Naples these days. Anyway, I was watching CNN here at the hotel and who should I see but you!'

'They ran that in Russia?'

'You're world-famous, Aurelio! And after smashing those terrorists they'll have to give you your old job back, maybe even with some promotion.'

'Well, I don't know about . . .'

'So it seemed a good moment to make a small confession.'

Zen wiggles his empty glass at a passing waiter, who fills it with scintillating wine.

'When you brought me that video-game cassette,' Nieddu says faintly, 'I was at a very low ebb, as you know. Times were difficult, not just for me but for Rosa and the kids . . .'

'Yes?'

'Well, like I told you, the cassette I returned to you was not the same as the one you brought me. What I didn't tell you was that it wasn't an accident.'

'It wasn't?'

'I'm only human, Aurelio. The temptation was too strong. Anyone would have done the same. It was just too good a chance to pass up. The first version of this particular game sold millions, billions! And now I had my hands on a usable prototype of the sequel, months before it was scheduled to hit the shops anywhere! Can you imagine the possibilities? Of course I wasn't in a position to manufacture and market it myself, but I'd heard that they had the facilities here in the former Eastern bloc, plus a progressive, libertarian approach to things like copyright laws. So . . .'

Zen hangs up and hands the phone back to the grave retainer.

'I am not taking any further calls,' he says.

The paid functionary bows silently and withdraws as though he has been in the service of the family his whole life.

Meanwhile Gesualdo and Sabatino have paired off with their respective mates, and the rest of the party are disputing vociferously about their host's identity. The exchange on this subject between Pasquale and Professor Esposito is characterized by a particularly colourful and inventive display of rhetoric, which is unfortunately lost on the subject himself since it is conducted not merely in dialect, nor yet that variant common to the Borgo San Antonio Abate neighbourhood, but a sub-species of the latter, a sort of family jargon spoken only by persons of a certain age and social class from a particular couple of streets in the shadow of the eponymous church – and only then in moments of great emotion.

The resulting encounter is both competitive and cohesive, at once an affirmation of a common heritage incomprehensible to outsiders and a struggle for dominance in terms of criteria which only the other is capable of judging. It is also incredibly loud and animated, suggestive of imminent bloodshed to ears untuned to its finer nuances. Zen makes the mistake of going over to calm them down, and immediately becomes the centre of attention once again, deflecting questions and fielding comments, gesturing hugely and maintaining a confident, unproblematic smile while he tries to work out who knows what about which aspect of whatever it is that has happened to whom.

Meanwhile the young people, left to their own devices, gravitate by unspoken agreement towards an outlying area of the terrace overlooking the cascade of steps far below, the tiled roofs of the house opposite and the seeming avalanche of the whole city petrified whilst scurrying down the hill towards the level expanse of the bay. The exhausted evening air, laden with an intimate, insinuating heat, coils and swirls around the quartet as they stand together, chatting and nodding, ignoring the stunning vista in a grand, proprietorial way.

Although their words are inaudible, the thoughts which they convey and conceal in equal measure are fairly clear to any casual onlooker. Gesualdo is in love with Iolanda. Look how he leans forward and brushes his lips against the nimbus of her long hair, how his eyes always seek hers out and then focus afresh when they meet, how the motions of his hands seem at once to respect and caress the contours of an emanation which surrounds her body, perceptible only to him.

His beloved, on the other hand, is more problematic. The open stance and glowing, shocked expression convey a message which that muscular tautness and those convulsive gestures appear to call in question, if not contradict. This ambiguity might be explained in various ways, from the banal 'Does he really love me?' to the rather more suggestive 'Would he still love me if he knew . . .?' But the exact nature of the revelation Iolanda so obviously fears, but also desires, remains for the moment unclear.

The young buck to her left, on the other hand, leaning over the edge of the terrace with breathtaking *disinvoltura*, presents no such problem. He eyes up Libera with a disconcertingly frank appreciation which is neither tainted nor redeemed by any ambiguity. 'I've had this,' his eyes say, 'and if it came my way again, and there was nothing better on offer, I'd have it again.' Unappealing as this may sound, it must be said that Sabatino is easily the least constrained and most charming of the four. If you were there, scanning the company, glass in hand, he's the one you'd head for.

It is when we come to the object of his salacious homage that the whole thing threatens to fall apart. The other three are each, in their varied ways, paying tribute to the object of their desires, with whatever unspoken and perhaps unspeakable reservations. But Libera . . . She isn't even looking at Sabatino, for a start-off, but at Iolanda, and her gimlet stare expresses no love for anyone, with whatever qualifications or reservations, only the purest, crassest . . . well, frankly, *bitchery*. It's as though Iolanda had done her some wrong, scored a point over her in some way. But how can this be? Libera certainly isn't in love with Gesualdo. Why should she care? What's going on?

'*Mannaggia 'a Madonna!*'

This cry comes from Sabatino. Having told everyone what he wants them to know in a shameless survey of his conquest's charms, he is now gazing down at the alley below on the lookout for fresh game. And here it comes, in the form of two young women making their way down the steps through the hushed, expectant dusk. Sabatino stares at them fixedly for a long moment, his face a collapsed parody of the complacent mask he was wearing a moment earlier. He whirls around, staring wildly at Gesualdo, who is lost in the mists of love's young dream. Sabatino runs up to the other end of the terrace, where Aurelio Zen is holding forth to a confused but still attentive audience. The young man whispers urgently into his ear.

'Impossible,' replies Zen in the confident tone he has been using for his explanatory discourse.

'They're right outside the house!' Sabatino shouts, unable to modulate his emotions any longer. 'They'll be here at any moment!'

'What is it?' demands Valeria.

Zen turns to her.

'It seems that your daughters have returned.'

'Nonsense! I spoke to them on the telephone just before I left to come here.'

'What are we going to do?' wails Sabatino. 'They'll be here any moment! If they find those Albanians here . . .'

'I wouldn't worry about that,' Valeria comments in a tone of unctuous malice. 'I'm sure they'll be *very* understanding. Women always are about these matters.'

'What women?' demands Libera, joining the group.

Zen grasps her by the arm.

'Get your companion, go down to my bedroom, close the door and don't come out until I tell you. First, though, give me one of your shoes.'

Libera frowns.

'My shoe? Why?'

'Because that's what I'm paying you to do, *carina*,' Zen replies sweetly.

Libera slips off one of her shoes and hands it to him.

'Fetishist.'

She turns to Iolanda and gives a piercing whistle.

'Pay-off time!' she trills mockingly.

Her companion is clearly none too happy about having her rapturously fraught unspoken dialogue with Gesualdo interrupted, but after a few barked phrases in dialect from Sabatino he relinquishes her to Libera, who hustles her back into the house.

'What are you playing at?' Valeria hisses to Zen. 'I *want* my girls to catch them together!'

'Catch them doing what? Attending the same party? What does that prove? The whole idea was to arrange for them to be caught *in flagrante*, but since your daughters have shown up without any warning, we'll have to improvise.'

'I still don't believe they're really here. That young delinquent must be imagining things. He's probably on drugs. There's no way my girls would come back to Naples without letting me know.'

Here they are, nevertheless, stepping out on to the terrace and looking uncertainly around.

'Stap me!' exclaims Immacolata Higgins. 'If it isn't my two young ladies of last night. Well, well, it's a small world, to be sure.'

Valeria Squillace inspects the pierced and tattooed apparition in black leather.

'Is that you, Orestina?' she demands in a tone of mingled anxiety and menace.

'We were robbed, mamma!' cries Filomena, rushing forward with outstretched arms. 'They threatened us with a knife and took our money, credit cards, everything. It was horrible, just horrible!'

'I thought it was a fascinating piece of street theatre,' Orestina comments dismissively. 'And they were very polite about it. The knife was just a prop. They left us our passports and return tickets, and one of the guys tipped me off to this great tattoo parlour by Camden Lock.'

She slips the jacket and blouse off her shoulder, revealing the full extent of the tattoo, together with a considerable amount of the surrounding flesh.

'It's disgusting!' her mother pronounces. 'Wash it off immediately. And stop exhibiting yourself like that! Have you no shame?'

'It doesn't wash off, mamma,' Orestina replies, adjusting her dress. 'That's the whole point. It's a way of reclaiming your body, personalizing it . . .'

Valeria's silence is more intimidating than any reply.

'But, mamma, I'm still the same person inside!' her daughter protests with just a hint of panic.

'You don't seem to understand, Orestina,' Valeria retorts icily. 'To me, and everyone else of my generation, you are now scum.'

'I told her not to do it!' cries Filomena, whose panic is overt and urgent. 'I begged her not to! But she never listens to me. She never did and she never will.'

'Of course I listen to your mewling,' her sister replies contemptuously. 'Why do you think we're here? Because after those guys robbed us you did your usual neurotic *prima donna* routine, sobbing and screaming about how you couldn't sleep again until you were safely back home tucked in with your teddy.'

Filomena bursts into tears and hugs her mother.

'But how on earth did you get here so quickly?' Valeria asks her. 'Why, it was only an hour ago that I spoke to you in London!'

'We were already here, mamma,' Orestina replies as though to a child. 'We flew in last night.'

'Last night?'

'That's right, *signora*,' Immacolata Higgins chips in. 'I picked them up personally and escorted them to the *Sole Mio*. Do you know it? Lovely place, very homely, spotlessly clean, never a hint of trouble.'

'Not to mention a fat finder's fee for Immacolata which turns up on the bill as "City Residence Tax",' Pasquale murmurs to no one in particular.

'Why didn't you come home?' Valeria asks Orestina. 'Not that I particularly want to be seen associating with a person looking like that, but when all's said and done you're still my daughter and I can't turn you away.'

'That's what I wanted to do!' Filomena wails. 'I just wanted to go home, but she wouldn't let me!'

All eyes turn to Orestina, who in turn looks at Gesualdo and Sabatino.

'The whole idea was to test our lovers' faithfulness, right?' she says. 'What better way to do it than by turning up completely unexpectedly?'

She smiles coolly.

'They don't seem very happy to see us, do they?'

Filomena confronts Sabatino with a pout.

'Why don't you say anything?' she demands. 'And why are you looking at me like that?'

'I expect it's just the shock,' Zen suggests in a tone of fake *bonhomie*. 'And of course your mother being here makes it all a bit awkward.'

He bends down and picks up a red patent leather shoe with a long spiked heel.

'I wonder who this belongs to.'

'It's Libera's,' Dario De Spino replies. 'Genuine Gucci, marked down as factory flawed but you'd never spot the difference. Eighty to a hundred thousand, depending on the model. Also a full range of men's sizes available.'

There is a brief silence.

'And who might Libera be?' asks Orestina.

'A friend,' Zen replies with a fatuous smile.

'Whose friend?'

'Everybody's! Libera by name and *libera* by nature.'

Orestina's smile hardens perceptibly.

'And may one meet this fascinating person?'

'Certainly!' Valeria replies with an air of triumph. 'She's in the bedroom downstairs. The one where Gesualdo and Sabatino have been spending their nights since you left town.'

'That's not true!' shouts Filomena, backing away from her mother.

Aurelio Zen shakes his head as though in embarrassment.

'It's only too true, I'm afraid. But you don't need to take my word for it. Why don't you go in and see for yourselves?'

Gesualdo steps forward, as if to intervene, but Sabatino holds him back. With a long lingering look at them, Orestina turns and marches inside the house. Filomena follows at her heels.

'That's that, then,' sighs Sabatino.

Gesualdo shakes his head vigorously.

'It won't make any difference. She knows how much I love her.'

'Yeah, right,' Sabatino replies sarcastically. 'Don't let that punk make-over fool you, Gesuà. Like she told her mother, she's still the same person inside. Face it, we're finished.'

Gesualdo looks at him in amazement.

'I wasn't talking about Orestina!'

They both turn to the doorway as the two girls reappear. Judging by their expressions, they are absolutely furious.

'How *could* you?' demands Orestina.

'What a cruel, nasty trick!' adds her sister.

'You ought to be ashamed of yourselves.'

'I could just have *died* of embarrassment! Walking in on two complete strangers in the middle of a passionate kiss!'

Zen looks at Valeria, then back at the girls.

'Eh?' he says.

Before he has a chance to express himself more coherently, two more figures appear from inside the house. One is Libera, limping in a rather fetching way because of the missing shoe. Her companion is a man of about the same age, smooth-shaven and with short dark hair, looking svelte and handsome in an old-fashioned suit cut stylishly large.

'How pleasant to know that one has been missed!' he says in a low, insinuating voice. 'Libera and I felt the need to be alone for a moment, and it never occurred to us that our absence would be remarked upon. But lo and behold, emissaries were sent to track us down and drag us back to the party of which we had presumably been the life and soul. *Most* gratifying!'

Valeria marches up to him.

'You're not a man!' she shouts. 'You're that other bitch dressed up! You just changed into some of Alfonso's clothes. You can't fool me! I'll expose you!'

The person thus addressed smiles languidly.

'That sounds rather fun. But since there are ladies present, we should perhaps be discreet. If you care to step inside with me, *signora*, I shall be pleased to offer you irrefutable proof – even tangible proof, if you so desire – that I am indeed what I appear to be.'

For just a moment Valeria hesitates. Then she squares her shoulders.

'Very well!'

The moment Signora Squillace is out of sight, Sabatino rushes up to Filomena and starts kissing and hugging her with an abandon which causes Libera to toss her head sulkily and mutter something incomprehensible. Orestina seems to be waiting for Gesualdo to do the same, but there is no response. Indeed, he hardly appears to be aware of her, or of anything else. He just stands staring at the doorway through which Valeria Squillace and the subject of the examination disappeared. Orestina starts towards him, then stops, gazing at him as though across a distance even greater than before.

When Valeria returns, all her anger and determination have dissipated. She looks old, tired and bewildered.

'He is,' she says, shaking her head. 'He really is.'

The object of this endorsement now emerges in turn, doing up his belt. But although he has proved his point, it has evidently been at some cost. His whole bearing is lumpen and lifeless, his features are drained of all expression, his air of urbane swagger has quite evaporated. His eyes dart here and there, fixing on nothing, until at length they meet those of Gesualdo. The two men stare at each other as though across a space unpeopled and silent.

In reality the place is in an uproar.

'*Ma so' femmenielli, duttò!*' exclaims Pasquale. 'You mean to say you didn't know?'

Zen gives an embarrassed shrug.

'They were out there on the street with the other whores . . .'

'And why didn't you choose those others?' Pasquale interrupts. 'Because they weren't pretty, right? They were *puttane vere*, the genuine feminine article all right, but hardly the women of your dreams. Otherwise they wouldn't be on the street. The good-looking ones are all chicks with dicks, everybody knows that!'

'I suppose I'm a bit out of touch with these things.'

Pasquale laughs.

'You're as innocent as a babe in arms, *duttò*! You should have consulted me instead of trying to do this on your own.'

'It makes no difference!' Valeria declares in a determined voice. 'If those two . . . whatever they may be . . . fooled us, they also fooled that pair of hoodlums who have the nerve to think that I'll let them marry my daughters. Now we know them for what they are! The fact that these other creatures are not what they seem doesn't change a thing.'

The vehemence of her tone shakes Gesualdo out of his reverie. He produces a laminated card which he hands to Valeria Squillace.

'They're not the only ones who aren't quite what they seem, *signora*,' he retorts with a cutting edge.

Valeria squints at the card. It is hard for her to read without her glasses these days, and even harder to admit the fact.

'What's all this?' she says, handing the card to Zen. 'Some sort of official document, it looks like . . .'

Zen stares at it for some time. Then he nods slowly.

'I see,' he says.

'Well, I don't!' said Valeria. 'What's going on? Who are these people?'

'This card identifies your elder daughter's suitor as an officer of the *Direzione Investigativa AntiMafia.*'

Gesualdo takes a second card from his wallet.

'And this one,' he continues in the same edgy tone, 'identifies your tenant as Dottor Aurelio Zen of the *Polizia Statale.*'

'Then who's Alfonso Zembla?' exclaims Valeria, completely bewildered.

Pasquale grabs Zen's identity card from Gesualdo's fingers.

'A cheap fake!' he exclaims. 'I'm surprised you were taken in for a moment.'

He palms the card and simultaneously produces another, at first sight identical, which he holds up like a priest displaying the consecrated host.

'Here is the genuine article which the *duttò* was unlucky enough to have stolen from him yesterday, and which I was able to trace thanks to my extensive network of contacts. As you see, it identifies him beyond any doubt as Dottor Alfonso Zembla.'

Valeria jerks her thumb at Gesualdo and Sabatino.

'Are you trying to tell me that these two are actually *police-men*?' she demands.

'We were,' Sabatino replies laconically.

Dario De Spino finally understands the reason for the premonitions of disaster which have been plaguing him recently. Fortunately everyone's attention is directed to his former associates, the two engaging young men he befriended and trusted and boasted to, and who now probably have enough material to send him away to Poggioreale until well into the next century. Grabbing a fistful of sandwiches and pastries for the road, Dario sidles over to the door and leaves without ceremony.

'But you told me that they have a record of associating with known criminals!' Valeria protests to Aurelio Zen. 'You said they were linked to some of the worst elements in the Camorra . . .'

'They wouldn't be much use as anti-mafia undercover agents if they didn't.'

He turns to the two young men.

'What I still don't understand is why you have chosen to reveal the truth now. For months you refused to tell anyone, even your sweethearts, yet now you have broken cover in front of people you don't know and have no reason to trust.'

'It's all thanks to you, *dottore*,' Gesualdo returns, with a bow of mock formality.

'To me? How?'

'You didn't hear what I said a moment ago,' Sabatino replies. 'We *were* with the DIA. We no longer are.'

'We resigned today, with immediate effect.'

Zen stares at them.

'But what has that got to do with me?'

Gesualdo smiles.

'Tell me, *dottore*, why do you think you're still alive, instead of having being crushed by the ram of that garbage truck?'

Zen shrugs.

'I don't really understand the details, but apparently the whole thing was part of a long-term sting operation designed to trap the terrorists. The Questore said that his men had been following me . . .'

'We know what the Questore said,' Sabatino says bitterly. 'We saw the show on TV. You gave a very good performance.'

Zen looks from one to the other.

'Are you saying it's not true?'

'You know perfectly well it isn't true!' retorts Gesualdo. 'All that stuff about you being brought down specially from Rome to infiltrate *Strade Pulite* . . .'

'That was just window-dressing to make the Questore look good,' Zen protests. 'The fact remains, if the police didn't save me last night, who did?'

'We did.'

'You? But . . .'

'We had our own reasons for being interested in you, Dottor Zen,' says Gesualdo. 'First we hear that someone of that name has tried to do a record search on our undercover aliases. Then we turn up a police identity card bearing that name but the photograph of someone we know as Alfonso Zembla, who has recently taken a personal interest in our activities. So we had a tap put on your phone, and were able to listen in to that intriguing call you received last night. As a result, we were in time to save your life.'

'Thank you,' mutters Zen.

Sabatino smiles sarcastically.

'Our real thanks has been the destruction of everything we've worked toward for months, laying our lives on the line every day, knowing that one slip or piece of bad luck and we'd end up like that poor bastard Marotta whom they tortured to death, not that he didn't have it coming.'

'I told you he was in hell!' Professor Esposito puts in. 'I was sure of it. The reception was faint, but quite clear.'

'For almost a year now, we at the DIA had been compiling a detailed study of the various factions and alliances within the Camorra clans,' Gesualdo explains in a flat tone. 'We were particularly interested in the internal fissures resulting from the massive quantities of money generated by the drug trade, and also the external pressures exerted by the political transition to the so-called New Italy.'

'But what has all this to do with those terrorists?' demands Zen.

'The terrorists never existed. The group calling itself *Strade Pulite* was simply one element in a classic power struggle between opposing wings of the Vallifuoco clan, cleverly disguised as a political movement. The young guard wanted to purge the old leadership, as well as various of their associates and clients who knew too much and could prove an embarrassment in the new judicial climate.'

'And just when we were on the point of putting together a case which might stand up in court,' Sabatino continues, 'you come along and offer yourself as living proof that this was an act of fanatical ideologues who have been thwarted by the brilliant efforts of the Naples police department! If those bastards at the Questura had done their job properly in the first place, there would have been no need to set up the DIA. So as soon as it was set up, the Questore tried to undermine its authority, and, thanks to you, he's just achieved a major victory. Well, enough is enough. What's the point in Gesualdo and me risking our lives and losing the women we love, all to no purpose? So we've requested to be transferred back to normal duties.'

He turns to Valeria.

'I also request the hand of your daughter Filomena in marriage. My character is impeccable, I have a secure job and good career prospects. I don't suppose it matters to you, but we are also madly in love.'

'*Alla follia!*' echoes Filomena.

Valeria Squillace heaves a heavy sigh.

'Clearly I have misjudged the situation. This I regret, although the fault is not mine but that of Signor Zen, or whatever his real name may be, who provided me with information which now turns out to be completely false. Needless to say, I withdraw all my former objections.'

She raises her glass.

'Here's to my daughter Filomena and Signor Nino . . .'

'Rocco, *signora*.'

'. . . and to Orestina and, er . . .'

She looks enquiringly at Gesualdo, who looks at Orestina.

'I can't. I'm sorry, but I can't.'

A smile appears and vanishes on Orestina's lips.

'That's all right.'

Valeria Squillace looks from one of them to the other.

'Would someone kindly tell me what's going on? All I want to know is who he really is.'

'I think he's only just found out himself,' her daughter replies with the same fugitive smile.

Gesualdo walks over to where the two ex-Albanians have been standing, on the fringes of these ceremonies from which they are excluded. He takes Iolanda's hand.

'You look great. There's something very sexy about a woman in male clothing.'

'But he *is* a man!' exclaims Valeria. 'I saw his . . .'

Orestina covers her face with her hands.

'For the love of God, mamma!'

'Old people are so *gross*,' comments her sister, clutching Sabatino protectively.

'Who are you calling old?' her mother shouts furiously.

Aurelio Zen holds up his hands.

'Perhaps we should try and concern ourselves less with which body parts those present may or may not possess as with what they choose to do with them.'

'That's not the point!' insists Valeria. 'Whatever those two may do – and one shudders to think – the whole thing is unnatural! It's just based on sexual thrills. It can't last . . .'

'*Aurelio!*'

'. . . like real love between men and women coming together for life . . .'

'*Aurelio!*'

'. . . to marry and have children as God intended!'

'*Aurelio!*'

The hollow wailing seems to well up from somewhere deep inside the house. Professor Esposito hurriedly crosses himself.

'The Furies!' he mutters. 'This, too, I foresaw.'

When the uninvited guests finally appear, Professor Esposito's prediction is seemingly borne out. Not only are they three females, but they are quite clearly furious.

'What do you think you're doing leaving your front door lying open like that?' screeches the central figure, who is squat and elderly. 'And in a city full of blacks! You'll be murdered in your bed!'

'Well, I see you're doing very nicely for yourself,' comments her tall companion on the left, taking in the silver salvers of

241

appetizers and the open bottles of bubbly. 'Still as irresponsible and selfish as ever, eh?'

'Your poor mother's been half out of mind with worry!' the third cuts in. 'The least you could have done was to call home once in a while, but oh, no, you're far too busy and important to bother with things like that. Just who do you think you are, anyway?'

'His name's Aurelio Zen,' a chorus of voices recites helpfully. 'He's a policeman.'

Zen turns to the assembled company with the fixed grin of someone who has just glimpsed madness, and discovered that it has its attractions.

'Allow me to introduce my mother Giustiniana, my ex-wife Luisella, and Tania Biacis, a friend from Rome.'

'You never told me you were married!' remarks Valeria.

'Signora Valeria Squillace,' Zen explains automatically to the newcomers. 'Ferrarese by birth, widow of Manlio Squillace of this city and mother of Filomena, newly betrothed to Signor Nino Rocco, and of her legitimate sister Orestina, recently unbetrothed to Tizio or Sempronio, the latter having taken up with an individual of whom the only thing we know for certain is that he or she is not Albanian.'

He turns to Gesualdo and Sabatino.

'There's still one thing I don't understand . . .'

'Only *one*?' exclaims the chorus. 'You're lucky!'

'If these Clean Streets people were just a bunch of local gangsters, why did they try and kill me?'

'You see?' barks Signora Zen, grabbing a glass of *spumante* from a passing waiter. 'I said he'd be murdered in his bed! But does he ever listen to what his mother tells him?'

'It was just the same with me,' Luisella murmurs sympathetically. 'He had to be right all the time.'

'The problem is that he's afraid to discuss his feelings,' adds Tania. 'I tried to put him in touch with his inner child, but it was no use.'

Gesualdo pushes his way through them.

'The answer to your question, *dottore*,' he tells Zen, 'is that they mistook you for someone else, a very powerful figure in the clans named Orlando Pagano who has been in hiding for some time. You look quite alike, and since you have been spending the night at the Squillace house . . .'

'Mamma!'

This from Orestina, who looks horrified.

'Don Orlando was a close associate of Manlio Squillace,' Gesualdo continues with a certain malicious pride. 'Indeed, the connection dates back even further, according to our research, to Signora Valeria's father, the founder of the Caselli textile group. Shortly after the war, Pagano put him in touch with a chain of clothing manufacturers here in Naples who . . .'

He breaks off as Signora Zen grabs his arm.

'Caselli, did you say?'

'That's right, *signora.*'

'In Ferrara?'

'Exactly.'

The old lady curls up like an autumn leaf and falls to the ground without a word. Everyone rushes around offering advice, first-aid hints and traditional herbal remedies. For the best part of a minute, Signora Zen is relentlessly slapped, pummelled and shaken. Brandy is forced between her clenched lips, while Pasquale presses the miracle-working silver casket into her bosom. Which of these ministrations proves effective is unclear, but eventually her eyes open.

'A priest! I must make confession.'

The guests look at one another in dismay.

'At this hour?'

'Not a chance.'

Professor Esposito grabs Pasquale by the arm and pulls him aside. The two confer in low tones for a moment, then disappear inside the house.

'She's not really going to die, is she?' Zen cries in a voice of panic. 'I can't manage without you, mamma. Please don't die. I need you, I love you.'

'Typical,' comments Tania caustically. 'She should stay alive because you need her. What about her? Don't you think she might want to live for herself?'

'Men are such bastards,' agrees Luisella.

243

Pasquale rushes in with an air of great importance.

'I've summoned Father . . . er, Beccavivi! He'll be here in a moment!'

Sure enough, a tall, thin figure swathed in black appears in the doorway. He hurries over to the stricken woman and kneels beside her.

'In the name of the Father, the Son and the Holy Ghost,' he intones in a nasal voice. 'Make your confession, my child.'

Signora Zen wipes her pallid lips with her tongue.

'I have many sins on my conscience,' she says, 'but the one troubling me most concerns Aurelio, my son.'

'Go on, *figlia*.'

'I had sworn never to reveal the truth, but now I feel the approach of death I feel I must. It all happened one week while my husband Angelo was away. He was an inspector for the railways, and often had to travel for days at a time. On one such occasion, may God forgive me, I went part of the way with him, taking advantage of the cheap ticket to visit my relatives in Verona.'

She gives a rattling gasp and signals for water, which is brought.

'On the way back, I was all alone. The journey seemed to take hours, and I fell to chatting with someone else in my compartment. He was a businessman, from Ferrara. I'd never met anyone like him before. Angelo was a good man, but he never took much interest in me.'

'I know the feeling,' comments Tania.

'Men are all the same,' adds Luisella.

'Not Lorenzo!' insists the penitent. 'He was different. He made me feel special and beautiful and exciting. I'm not trying to excuse myself, but . . .'

'Did you have carnal relations with this man, my child?' the priestly figure enquires.

Signora Zen smiles gently.

'Oh, yes.'

'More than once, *figlia mia*?'

'Many, many times!'

The smile fades gradually.

244

'When my son was born, I tried to pretend it was Angelo's. He never gave me any reason to suppose that he didn't believe me. To tell you the truth, he never seemed particularly interested.'

Tania and Luisella exchange a significant glance.

'And when Angelo went off to war and never came back, it was too late to tell anyone. How could I break it to my boy that his father was not a heroic victim who had fallen fighting for his country, but the owner of a textile mill who abandoned me as soon as I got pregnant even though he went on to make a fortune through a contract to supply uniforms to the local Blackshirts in return for a kickback to the local Fascist chief . . .'

'Those charges were never proved!' Valeria breaks in. 'Certainly Papa made a lot of money quite quickly, but life was a struggle for everyone back then, and . . .'

Signora Zen tugs at the black sleeve.

'Father . . .'

'Do you wish me to administer extreme unction, my child?'

The penitent shakes her head.

'Is there . . .' she breathes faintly.

'Yes?'

'Is there any more of that brandy?'

At this point a mosquito lands on Orestina's left ear, which has already been pierced twice to accommodate the silver rings which form part of the new image to which Signora Squillace took exception. Subliminally sensing this additional puncture, she swats at the aggressor. A rhinestone ring she is sporting on her marriage finger becomes entangled with the twin loops of silver, tearing the delicate flesh of the lobe and causing Orestina to utter various terms of which her mother had fondly believed her to be ignorant.

Assuming that this attractive young woman, who has so courageously asserted her independence in the face of patriarchal tyranny and gender stereotyping, has been the victim of harassment by one of the rogue males present, Tania Biacis springs to her defence, colliding with the elderly waiter who is bringing Signora Zen the beverage she requested. The bottle goes flying, and in his attempt to save it Gesualdo pushes over Immacolata Higgins, who in turn stumbles into Valeria, who tries to keep her balance by grabbing at her neighbour, Luisella Catallani *in* Zen. The resulting disturbance ripples through the gathering like a breeze through long grass, affecting each of the guests in turn, until Filomena accidentally jogs Pasquale's funny-bone, causing him to jerk his arm convulsively and thereby knock off Father Beccavivi's large, black (although on closer inspection not strictly clerical) hat, revealing the bald dome and impressive eyebrows of Professor Esposito.

Aurelio Zen clears his throat with the air of someone about to give a speech.

'A famous philosopher once remarked that everything happens twice. A later philosopher – even more famous in my youth, but now almost forgotten – commented that his predecessor should have added, "the first time as tragedy, the second as farce". I am no philosopher, and cannot say whether this is true of events in general, but my recent experiences have convinced me that it holds good for my own life. And, if I may be permitted to add my own modest footnote on the subject, better like that than the other way round.'

He looks about him at the circle of family, friends and lovers, their equilibrium now completely restored.

'But as I say, this applies only to my own life. Yours, I hope, will be free from tragedy and farce alike. Filomena and Sabatino will make a faithful and happy couple, and their children will be numerous, beautiful and charming. Gesualdo and Iolanda will be equally happy in their different but no less admirable way, while Luisella and Tania will continue to be comfortably miserable in theirs. Orestina will go back to London and Libera to the streets, each with a mingled sense of relief and excitement. Pasquale, the professor and Signora Higgins will continue to provide the range of unique and priceless services for which they are justly famous.

'My mother will make a full recovery, and never fail to give me the kindly illusion that she will be there for ever, although only when I need her. Finally there is Valeria, with whom a watchful providence appears in retrospect to have spared me from committing the only sin from which I had always believed myself to be immune. For this I am truly grateful, since it enables me to say without any fear of misunderstanding that I will always love her as the sister I never knew I had.

'Which brings me to myself, and my vision of the future I see very clearly unfolding before me. It will be . . .'

But his voice, which has been increasingly difficult to make out for some time now, is finally lost beneath the ambient harmony of car horns and birdsong, televisions and yapping dogs, children yelling and motorbikes revving, laughter and raised voices, sea-gulls and sirens, as though the whole city were joining in a final chorus expressing the conventional banalities: always look on the bright side, let reason be your guide, every cloud has a silver lining, laughter is the best medicine . . .

Only for some reason – the intoxicated dusk, the musky air, the good company, the wine – they don't seem at all banal, but resound like eternal verities, a profound reverberation of all the horrors and miseries which have taken place here, and which might yet teach us, if we cared to learn, how to live.

Author's Note

All chapter headings are taken from Da Ponte's libretto for the opera he referred to as 'The School for Lovers'. The more familiar title is never translated, a sufficient indication of the difficulty of doing so. The same holds true for many of the phrases used to name the chapters in this book. The attempt made in the Contents listing is offered only as a rough equivalent of the sense intended here, which is not always identical to that of the original. Finally, it may be worth noting that while the title of the opera is gender-specific, the masculine form *tutti* spares no one.

I would like to take this opportunity to thank various friends in Naples, particularly Michael Burgoyne and Gerardo Kaiser, for their help and hospitality.